Phelan, Tom, 1940-
The canal bridge

Also by Tom Phelan

In the Season of the Daisies
Iscariot
Derrycloney

THE CANAL BRIDGE

Tom Phelan

The Lilliput Press • Dublin

First published 2005 by
The Lilliput Press
62–63 Sitric Road, Arbour Hill
Dublin 7, Ireland
www.lilliputpress.ie

Copyright © Glanvil Enterprises, Ltd., 2005
www.tomphelan.net

ISBN   1 84351 075 8

A CIP record for this title is available
from The British Library.

10 9 8 7 6 5 4 3 2 1

Set in 11pt on 14pt Insekt
Printed by MPG Books, Bodmin, Cornwall

In loving memory of
my brother Con Phelan

To Patricia, Joseph and Michael with love
and to the men of Mountmellick
who were in uniform during World War I:

Michael Aherne
Michael Brennan
Thomas Culliton
Patrick Deegan
Christopher Dempsey
Joseph Dempsey
Michael Dempsey
Patrick Dempsey
Michael Duggan
Thomas Dunne
William Dunne
Patrick Fallon
Thomas Fallon
Seamus Farrell
George Harris
John Joseph Johnson
James Johnston
William Keegan
William Keegan Jr
Michael Kirwan
Patrick Lalor

Thomas Lalor
William Lalor
George McGee
Patrick McGee
Joe Molloy
Oliver Moran
Arthur Hill Neale
Joseph Newell
Michael O'Connell
George O'Neill
James O'Rourke
George Payne
John Phelan
Samuel Pim
Edward Reddin
'The Gong' Ryan
Christopher Shea
Victor Smith
John Staunton
and others unknown to me

Acknowledgments

Thanks are due to the following who supplied information or otherwise assisted me while I was writing *The Canal Bridge*.

In Ireland: David Coss, Dickie Fitzpatrick, Theresa Hourigan, Neville James, Bill Lawlor, Michael Phelan, Pádraig Scully, the staff of the Laois County Library, the Mountmellick Development Association, Tommy Lindsay of the War Memorial Gardens in Dublin. A big thank you to Anne-Marie Hourigan of Mountmellick.

In England: Geoffrey Charrot, the staff of the National Archives in Kew.

In France: Avril Williams of Auchonvillers.

In the United States: Marie Braccia, Joan and Séamus Clarke, Dr Jerome Ditkoff, Bob Keeler of *Newsday*, Dave Opatow and the staff of the Freeport Memorial Library, Lyn Swierski.

Special thanks to my wife, Patricia, for her help, suggestions and encouragement, and for sharing the sad trip to the Somme, Ypres, Passchendaele and many other sites where the bodies of the young soldiers of World War I are still being found.

And finally, a salute to the members of the delegation from 'the North' whom we met at the Menin Gate in Ypres in September 1999. You had come to Belgium to lay wreaths on soldiers' graves and at the monuments erected in their memory. Young men you were, former members of the security forces in

Ulster. You knew by my accent that I was from 'the South', and I told you about the men of Mountmellick. As we shook hands you told us that in the laying of wreaths you were honouring the dead, not because of where they had come from, but because of where they were.

Going Away

Missus Fitzpatrick

Matthias and Con were still in nappies. They'd be standing there staring across the Canal at each other, each with the tip of a finger against his bottom lip. Maybe they thought they were looking in a looking-glass, each seeing himself on the far bank thirty feet away, neither one saying a word. They could have been twins.

I suppose lads that young don't know what to say, don't even know yet how to call each other names.

Then one summer I was going along the bank to Missus Conway's, and I declare, three of them were out: Con and his little sister, Kitty, on the far side, and Matthias on this side, and it only eight o'clock in the morning. About a year after the girl's appearance I heard that singy-songy thing of theirs for the first time. The minute I'd step around the corner of the Canal Stores at the Harbour near the Windlass, there it would be on the water—*My side, my side*—the girl's voice as strong as the lads'. She was every bit as cheeky as the boys. When they'd see me coming in the distance, they'd stop the singing. But at that age they didn't know how voices carry on water, and I'd hear one of them saying, 'Here's Redfingers Fitz,' or 'Here's the old washerwoman,' or 'Here's the old one going to Conways'.' And the little girl imitating them, 'Here's doul wan.' 'Here's Redfingers going to wash Missus Conway's dirty drawers.'

Then, when I'd be coming home around six with Missus

Conway's shilling in my pocket and my hands red and raw, they'd still be there like they hadn't moved all day. But, surely to God, they must have gone home to get a bite during the day, a cut of bread or a potato. And I always heard them before I saw them. I'd still be at the Dakeydocks when the ghosty song would come rippling along the top of the water, all childish stuff about how the flowers and the grass on my side are better than on your side.

The little girl would still be out there instead of being at home with her mother, as country-looking as the two lads in her boots and poor excuse for a dress. But her hair was always as neat as a pin and her face shiny as an apple after a rub on the wetted corner of her mother's apron. She had the kind of eyes you'd think could see into your head; she never seemed to blink.

I'd be afraid to let a child of mine near water of any kind by himself for fear he'd fall in. One day I said as much to Missus Wrenn, may the Lord have mercy on her soul, a terrible death she had, and she said, 'Matthias knows if he gets too close the Bogeyman will stick his hand out of the water and pull him into the Canal by the shoelaces.'

Bogeyman, my foot! And me with my own two eyes after seeing the three of them children on a hot day with their shoes off and their feet dangling in the Canal, they all trying to splash the water higher than the other. The Bogeyman never frightened them lads, and nothing at all would frighten the young one. I got to thinking she was more of a boy inside those clothes than a girl.

'Hello, Missus Fitzpatrick,' they'd say when I was passing them, like they were little angels after falling out of a holy picture, and then of course, they'd start talking too soon after I was gone by.

'She's terrible fat, like an old sow,' one would say. 'Did you see the red hands of her, like carrots?' 'And the thick legs of her, like stumps?' 'Her real name is Missus Redfingers.' The sweet voices sailed along the top of the water like snowflakes blowing on ice in wintertime. Little children say terrible funny things.

The boys were born on the same day, Missus Ward running down the far bank to the Bridge to get to Missus Wrenn's house on this side just after pulling out Con Hatchel. The way Missus Ward told the story, I could nearly hear Missus Hatchel popping like a bottle after the cork comes flying out; there she was with Con in her hands and he dripping all the cleanings off him and the mother still looking like a disgrace when there was a knock at the door and a child calling her to go to Missus Wrenn's.

'Missus Wrenn wants Missus Ward quick.'

Missus Ward always put in the part about running down the far bank, like she was a hare or something, and she just about able to waddle like a too-fat duck. But the way she told it, you could see her tearing along the bank with her clothes and hair flying in the wind, her arms pumping her along, to cross at the Bridge. She made it sound like she went into a dive and skidded on her belly across the Wrenns' bedroom just in time to grab Matthias before he hit the floor after shooting out of his mother.

Then the little girl was born less than a year later—the Hatchel twins they were called, Con and Kitty, when they got to be the same size nearly. But Kitty would always say, 'We're not twins. I'm the baby,' like she was defending a title.

I saw them getting older and bigger every Monday when I was coming and going to Missus Conway's. And in all those years, I never once saw the three of them standing together. It was like they never found out why the Bridge was built. They spent days fishing, or skipping stones across to each other, or trotting along talking to the bargemen, but I never saw them on the same bank.

Then, of course, there was the dreadful fire, and Matthias was put in the Workhouse, and that was the end of them. It was like some fixture that you always thought would be there was suddenly gone, nothing but a hole left. I got crippled with rheumatism the same year as the fire, and I never walked the Canal bank again.

The washing soda Missus Conway used to buy was terrible caustic on the skin, lumpy stuff like bits of broken glass. My hands always felt as if they'd just been scalded.

Kitty Hatchel

*School of the Poor Servants of the Holy Cross, Maryborough
Entrance Examination, Part IV: English Composition*

Instructions: You must finish your composition in exactly one hour. There is a clock with a second hand over the blackboard. If you have your pen in your hand when the hour is over, you will be disqualified.

Your composition must be about your town, or part of your town, or some aspect of your town.

My name is: Katherine Ann Hatchel
The name of my town is: Ballyrannel
Today's date is: 24 March 1909

The Grand Canal at Ballyrannel

They started building the Ballyrannel branch of the Grand Canal in 1827. From where it branches from the main canal to where it ends in front of the Canal Stores in the Harbour in Ballyrannel, it is six miles long. It was ready for barges in 1831.

Each barge is sixty feet long and ten feet wide and can carry forty tons. If the load is heavier than forty tons, the bottom of the barge will get stuck on the bottom of the Canal and won't be able to go anywhere. Boats full of cargo travel at three miles an hour.

A horse, in a set of draughts and a singletree, pulls the barge with a rope so thick you can't get the fingers of your two hands to meet around it. Another word for pull is 'tow', and the horse's path beside the Canal is called the Towpath and the thick rope is called the towrope. Wherever a road crosses the Canal there is a bridge. The underside of the bridge is shaped like a half-moon made out of cut stones, and the space under the bridge is only wide enough for the barge and the Towpath. Under the bridge, the Towpath is made out of smooth stones that weigh a ton each. They are called coping stones.

The grass on the Towpath along the Canal is always half dead from the horses' feet, but in the narrow track between the worn path and the Canal, special plants grow because they need a lot of water. There's yellow iris, lilac cuckooflower, pink valerian, and meadowsweet with its beautiful smell and white silky spikes. In the shallow water near the banks, deep-green delicate mare's tails and horsetails grow. My brother Matt draws the flowers on the inside of cigarette boxes he finds on the road going to school, and my mother hangs them under the mantelpiece in the kitchen with tacks. The children pick meadowsweet and iris for the May altar with the statue of the Blessed Virgin on a white cloth.

There are eight kinds of fish in the Canal. One of them is the eel and it wiggles like a snake. It will even keep wiggling after its head is cut off. My brother Con fried and ate an eel once, and he said it was lovely, but no one else would taste it, except for Matt. The others are bream, carp, roach, rudd, pike, perch, and tench. A pike has such a big mouth and terrible teeth it could bite off your toe. Nobody likes tench because they eat dead dogs, and when a boy catches one he won't touch it. He cuts his fishing line and loses his hook. When a perch is pulled out, it raises its sail, and it could stab you if you were too near. Roach are gold and red. They are nice to look at, but my mother won't eat them because they smell too fishy, and she won't eat perch because they are full of bones as fine as the hairs on a mouse's belly.

Two kinds of birds live on the Canal and build their nests in the tall green reeds near the bank: swans and waterhens. Waterhens are black with very yellow-red legs and beaks. When there is something dark behind the waterhen, all you can see are the legs and the beak. Sometimes you would think waterhens are walking on the water like Jesus, but they are really walking on lilies and broken reeds and weeds. Swans can kill a person with their wings, and young swans are called signets and are not white. Girl swans are called pens. My father's Uncle Martin said boy swans should be called pens and girl ones inkwells.

Where the Canal is twenty-four feet wide it is four feet and nine inches deep. But then the bottom slopes up to the banks for another three feet on each side. So, the Canal is thirty feet wide altogether, except under the bridges.

The water in the Canal is dead because it does not flow anywhere, and if you drink it you will die. People throw things in the Canal to get rid of them. The worse thing is to see a drowned dog floating in the Canal. My father found a drowned man once, and he said it was not as bad as looking at a drowned dog.

One winter a man who liked to show off because he had lived in America said he could ride his bike on the Canal ice from the Harbour to the First Bridge and back in ten minutes. Some men made bets. When the man got to the Bridge the ice was not so thick because it was sheltered. Himself and the bike went down through the ice, and they kept going under the water long enough to end up under the thicker ice at the far side of the Bridge. The men left standing at the Harbour were calling him an eejit behind his back. But when they saw him disappearing they ran all the way to the Bridge. They got my father's hatchet to break the ice to make a hole to get the man, but he was dead. His neck had hit the edge of the broken ice, and his head was nearly cut off, only held on by the skin of the back. When they put him down on the bank, his head was facing one way and his body the other, and Paddy Conroy had to twist the head around the right way and rub the blood off on the seat of his own trousers. Paddy Conroy didn't sleep for a week. They never found the man's false teeth, and my father said a tench ate them.

The water in the Canal is kept at a certain level by special little rivers called supplies. The Supply that flows into the Canal beyond the Bridge, but this side of the Dakeydocks, is a good place for boys to fish for perch, because the perch are always waiting there for fat worms to come floating in from the countryside. If a boy puts a worm on his hook, a perch will swallow the hook and get caught.

The Aqueduct is where the Canal is built across the Johnnies River, but everyone calls it the Dakeydocks. Big drops are always falling from the bottom of the Aqueduct into the river. Only one girl will walk in the river under the Canal because it is so dark in there, and the boys think the Aqueduct is going to collapse any minute.

Telephone poles march like giants along the Canal bank to Dublin. The telephone lines are attached to white delph cups on crossbars on the poles. But they only look like cups turned upside down, wide at the bottom and narrow at the top. The boys and a girl use the cups as bull's-eyes, and every cup between the Harbour and the Dakeydocks is broken. When a stone smashes a cup, the people on the phone in Dublin hear a huge explosion that nearly deafens them. The thick pieces of delph fall down, and sometimes when a girl is walking in the grass in her bare feet she gets cut on the sharp edges. One girl had to get stitched and she had a limp for months and she nearly bled to death. She was white by the time she got to the doctor and her eyes were rolling around in her head like a saint's.

Boys in the summer, and some girls, put on homemade swimming togs in the bushes and jump off the coping stones under the Bridge, into the Canal. When the children were younger they wore nothing. If they were ever caught by a Canal inspector they would have to pay the judge one pound and half a crown. They make you pay the same if they catch you washing yourself in the Canal. If they catch you letting your dog swim in the Canal, or throwing him in by the scruff of the neck to drown his fleas, you have to pay the judge eleven shillings. Uncle Martin once saw a fox lowering herself, tail first, into the Canal to make all the fleas run up along her body. She had a piece of sheep's wool in her teeth, and when all the fleas ran into the wool to save themselves from drowning, the fox let the wool float away. If a farmer takes water out of the Canal for his animals when it hasn't rained for a long time, he will be put in jail. That's what the Canal rules are.

There's a Canal Song that sounds better sung at the Canal than written down on paper, because it doesn't rhyme like a normal song. When it is sung at the Canal and floats along the top of the water, it is lovely. Some of the words of the song are:

> *Come to my side, come to my side*
> *where the sun is shining,*
> *where there is no rain and there is no frost.*
> *Come to my side, come to my side*
> *where the yellow cowslips are speckled red,*
> *where the small daisies dance in the breezy grass.*

The song was made up by two boys and a girl who lived fornent each other across the Canal, and the boys were born on the same day.

When you stand on the coping stones at the Harbour, you would think a giant had made the Canal by laying down his hazel fishing rod and pressing it into the ground. The Canal as far as the Bridge is a straight line of water lying one foot below the level of the smooth green fields. In the summer there's a necklace of flowers along the banks. Some days, when there is no wind, the water is a mirror. Then the Bridge is reflected in the water, and it becomes a stone circle with the Canal flowing through it. And the necklace is reflected too, and it all looks lovely.

I love the Bridge with its smooth stones along the top of the wall, shaped like pan loaves, only much bigger. They are a lovely colour, nearly silver. Our Bridge is the same as all the other bridges on the Canal. There is a narrow ledge sticking out all around the wall on the side over the water. The ledge is about three inches wide and four feet from the top of the wall. Boys lower themselves down onto the ledge, and they hold on to the top of the wall with their hands while they edge their way all around the Bridge up in the air. One girl does that too. If they fell, they would fall into the water or onto the Towpath and get killed. Swallows build their nests in holes between the stones. Sometimes they fly out and frighten the ledge-walkers.

There is a secret loose stone in the wall around the corner from the coping stones in the Towpath. Some children keep a bar of Lifeguard soap hidden behind the stone, and on Saturday nights in the summer they take off all their clothes and wash themselves under the Bridge in the dark so an inspector won't catch them.

I love the Grand Canal at Ballyrannel. I can swim in it. Boys and girls can fish in it. I can walk beside the boats floating by on their way from Dublin and listen to the funny way the boatmen talk. They say, 'Hello Missy,' and make me laugh when they say I am as pretty as the flowers near the Towpath. I can get meadowsweet and valerian for the May altar from the Canal track. I can walk with my brothers for six miles along the bank and never have to climb over a fence. I can listen to the Canal Song all during the year. The song can be heard for miles when there is frost, and it sounds even nicer than Sheila Feeney singing *Tantum Ergo* during Benediction when the church is only half full, and Sheila Feeney won the silver medal for best singer a whole lot of times at the Feis.

Missus Hatchel

You know how it happens some-times—you're awake in the dark in the bed in the middle of the night on the flat of your back and you don't know if you've been awake for hours or if you just came to the surface.

One night I was staring into the pitch black, and my brain telling me our Kitty and Matthias were in love, that they had been swapping calf-glances, and even though I'd been seeing the behaviour, I hadn't recognized it for what it was. I knew I could be excused for not noticing, what with Matthias living with us for so long, a brother to the other two, but talk about thick!

Of course, the next day it was a glaring fact that they were behaving like sick cats when they were near each other. I had to make sure our Kitty would be all right. Here she was, a child one day and the next you're having to worry about a young lad get-ting at her. God, she was a lovely-looking girl with a smart brain. But I ask you, what girl or what young lad, no matter how smart they are in the head, has much sense when it comes to the other end of the body? At that age the urges can be strong enough to make youngsters do things without a thought for the conse-quences. We all went through that, the girls even worse than the boys, just the same as any other animal lepping all over the place and not knowing what's the matter with it. God help us, but it's terrible having to think of ourselves as animals, with all of an animal's urgings and functions. I hate to think about how much we have in common with a goat.

'I can't keep my hand over it all her life,' is what James said.

'What do you mean?' I asked.

'Isn't that what you want me to do? Keep my hand over her bird to make sure Matthias doesn't do a bit of plucking?' The way James talked at times!

'Well, you could talk to Matthias without saying all that to him,' I said.

'Couldn't you talk to Kitty? And what am I supposed to say to Matthias? If you do it to Kitty, I'll cut them off you with a beet knife and hang them out to dry on the clothes-line?'

James was very funny sometimes when he was being unreasonable, and he'd go on with this quare twaddle of his—tell you what he was going to say to someone, and he knowing and I knowing he'd never talk to anyone that way. Imagine him saying that—I'll hang them on the clothes-line to dry, just like the pig's bladder the children hung in the chimney, blew it up to make a ball—the stink of it, just like old pig-water.

'Your father didn't keep his hand over yours when I started coming around,' James said, and he laughed as he went out through the kitchen door.

'And he didn't tell you he'd cut your things off you and hang them out to dry either.'

'Begob, he didn't,' James shouted back from the middle of the yard. 'He told me he'd give me a cow and a calf if I married you right away and got you out from under his feet.'

I jumped up and ran to the kitchen door. 'My father never said any such thing to you,' I called, but I didn't know whether to believe him or not.

'When I told him we'd have to wait a year on account of Uncle Jer not dying when he was supposed to, your father offered me four cows.'

'He did not.'

'He did too,' James called as he disappeared around the corner of the cow house. I was never sure when James was codding me. He stepped back out from behind the cow house and said, 'He told me to keep *my* hand over your bird and not let you push it away, because he'd noticed you lepping all over the place like a goat not knowing what was wrong with it.'

'James!' I shouted. He went off laughing. I went in to give myself a wash and put on clean knickers because after talk like that I knew we'd be doing it that night.

Kitty was only seventeen, a child, and Matthias only a year older. If I'd been a man, I'd have told Matthias to be good to Kitty. That's all James had to say to him. Matthias would have known what he was talking about. I couldn't talk to our Kitty about anything like that beyond telling her to be a good girl. I hadn't the words to say what I knew I should say, and I was too embarrassed to use the few words I knew.

Con and Kitty and Matthias had blathered to each other across the Canal when they were still too young to talk. But once the words came, they got a sort of chant going between them, half singing and half talking, one repeating what the other said at first, and their little voices sailing along the top of the still water up to the Harbour and down under the Bridge past the Dakeydocks, the other children along the Canal hearing the chant and picking it up. There's times, still, when I go into the town for the messages on a Friday, and I hear the children singing across the street to each other what our Con and Kitty and Matthias sang across the Canal. *My side, my side. The fish bite better on my side, my side. Come to my side, my side. The roach are redder, the perch are bigger, on my side.*

Forever, it seems, they fished against each other on opposite banks, Kitty as good as the lads. When they weren't fishing, they were skipping flat stones on the water. They were always looking for the perfect stone. When they found it, they could skip it right into each other's hands as they walked along their own bank, the three of them, Kitty as good as Con and Matthias. I would see them jumping into the air and tumbling onto the grass to catch the skipped stone before it touched the ground. It was like magic, what they could do. Then, of course, the stone would get thrown wrong and sink, and the search would be on again.

The three of them took care of the waterhens' nests and the swans', kept the town lads from cutting the heads off the young swallows down at the Bridge. Something happens to young lads when they get into a herd; it's like they all lose whatever bit of sense they have and do stupid things. Cut the heads off baby swallows! Kitty used to go mad when she'd catch them, take on the toughest of the tough, and even if she lost the fight, she always won in the end because no one could make her keep her mouth shut.

Con and Matthias walked hand in hand when they went to school that first day. Kitty was left at home not knowing what to do with herself, spent the entire long day sitting up on the Bridge waiting for them to appear at the Windlass. When she saw them, she took off like a greyhound and never heard the shouts coming out of James and myself telling her to come back.

I think Con and Matthias became the best of friends because neither of them had a brother. After the fire, when we took Matthias home with us out of the Workhouse, the two of them couldn't be separated. Kitty was in the middle all the time, and there was no getting rid of her even if they'd wanted to. I don't know where she came from—not my side, for sure; maybe James had a highwayman hiding in the leaves of his family tree. On Sundays, when they got older, they were fishing all the time, or riding their bikes to football matches, or pedalling all over the country to look at castles and mountains. No place was too far for them. Con would look at a map all week and then off they'd go to Croghan Hill or Dunamase or the Windy Gap off the far side of Stradbally, even going as far as Clonmacnois once and not getting back till eleven at night, and James and myself worried to death they'd fallen into a canal and drowned. Matthias always came home with a half-drawn picture of what they'd seen, and he'd finish it off during the week at the kitchen table, the others looking in over his shoulders telling him what he'd left out.

'You've a great talent for missing what's at the tip of your nose,' is what James says to me when I fall over the dog while I'm carrying a bucket of milk or step in a cow dung on my way to Mass on Sundays. I don't know how long Matthias and Kitty were carrying on under my nose before I noticed them.

Even though I was broken-hearted at the time, I was relieved, too, when the lads joined the army; the distance might let the blood flow back into their brains. It was easy to see what was going to happen next, Kitty long-legged and as giddy as a March hare, Matthias young and healthy. The bushes at the Canal, between the Bridge and the Dakeydocks, would have been too much for them.

I don't know whose idea it was to go in the first place—Con's, I would think, because he was always reading about faraway places in Mister Hodgkins's books. And maybe Lionel Hodgkins got them worked up about seeing the world while they were still young. Young fellows are more apt to do things when they have company, like bunches of young dogs rambling the countryside killing sheep. Kitty waited at the Bridge for them for years. And I can still see her tacking Matt's drawings all over the house, reading Con's letters over and over, making a book out of the sheets of newspaper that told about Matthias's escapades.

Con and Matthias. I can still see them walking along the Canal bank that day, heading for Marbra to join up, wearing their caps to the Tipperary side, the two of them off to see the world. The night of the day they went away, Kitty never came home, and James found her at two in the morning on the Bridge wall, lying flat out on her back looking up at the moon sailing through the clouds like a ship.

Ralphie Blake

Con and Matthias left for the army on a Thursday, the day before the First Friday of August 1913, exactly one month after my mother was buried. Died roaring, as they say; may she rest in peace.

I was scooping a shovelful of dirt up into the ass's cart when I saw the two lads down at the far end of Blessed Oliver Plunkett Street, or 'Bops' as we all called it when Father Kinsella wasn't around. Everyone in Ballyrannel knew Matt and Con were going to Marbra on the train that day to sign up. That's how I knew it was them, even though I couldn't make them out—Matt tall and long-armed with a head of black hair above a well-put-together face; Con, about three inches shorter, was blond and within a hair's breadth of being too good-looking for a man.

While I leaned on the handle of my shovel I could see there was something different about them: their feet weren't touching the ground, and the piece of Bops they were in was brighter than the rest of the street, like someone was keeping the beam of a carbide lamp on them all the time. The sky was as blue as a robin's egg, not the whisper of a cloud in sight, a grand August day.

The two of them were laughing and waving and shouting back to the older women hanging on the half-doors of their kitchens. Most of the women were black-dressed grannies with few or no teeth, wrinkled faces, and grey buns on top of their heads. They had known Con and Matt since the first day they trotted along Bops on their way to school, their cloth schoolbags dancing on their backs. The hanging women had been greeting the young men six days a week for the last seven years as they walked to and from their work at Enderly.

As they came closer to my ass and cart I saw they were dressed in their new suits and caps. Of course everyone in Ballyrannel knew that Missus Hodgkins had paid Miss Bowe the Seamstress to make the lads' clothes. And now little children ran from the houses, pushed out by their grannies, to trot along with the lads for a few steps and push their faces into the new material of the trousers to get the smell.

Matthias and Con—the adventurers, as we all thought of them—each had a homemade carrying-case made from two stick handles sewn into the top of a cloth bag. As they got closer, I heard Missus Cunningham shouting over her fat arms and huge diddies, 'What do you have in the bags, lads? Your bit of dinner or what?' And Con shouted, 'Extra pair of socks, Missus Cunningham.' And Missus Cunningham cried back, 'You must have ferocious feet, Con,' and everyone who heard them laughed with them.

Along the middle of Bops they came on up into the town like Jesus going into Jerusalem with the people throwing palm leaves on the road to soften the step of his donkey, only it was the women of Ballyrannel who were laying down their gentle banter for the passing of the lads. All the women liked Matt and Con and their sister Kitty—the Hatchel triplets—and wished they were theirs. The triplets had been happy and talkative since they were young, with a certain air of innocence, as if the freshness of the countryside was always about them. Not one of them was ever cruel to animals or to other children like most youngsters are at one time or another; they had never drowned a frog or cut the heads off baby birds or robbed nests or kicked an ants' nest to bits or played football with a hedgehog. The worst thing they had ever done was put live worms onto fish hooks and thrown stones at the delph cups on the Canal's telephone poles. Of course, no one in the town would ever forget about Matt's family getting burned to death and there was still a great sadness for him even after all the years.

'You'll be the best-looking soldiers in the entire English army, lads; God bless you,' Missus Carroll called, her well-used diddies falling down and nearly hiding her arms.

'Goodbye, Missus,' Matthias called back, 'and God bless you and the children too.'

Because of the height of the half-doors and the way the women leaned on them, every woman had fat arms and huge diddies. Missus Furlong had the biggest ones in the entire length of Bops. Her diddies came up so high, she could have used either one as a pillow, and she often did too, snoring away when she dropped off for a minute on the door until her knees gave way. When Con and Matt were passing her house, she called out, 'Where's Kitty, lads? I thought she'd go as far as Marbra at least.'

'We left her at the Bridge, Missus Furlong. She's too upset,' Con told her.

'Kitty's going to miss you, lads,' Missus Furlong called back.

That bit of back and forth knocked some of the wind out of the lads' sails, and for a few steps the smiles faded and the banter quietened down.

My job as the road brusher—brusher mostly of horse and donkey and pony dung and Woodbine boxes and butts—meant that I knew most of the things that happened in Ballyrannel. I didn't want to know what people told me without even stopping as they walked by because I didn't know what I was supposed to say back to them. 'Drunk again last night,' a woman would say, meaning her husband. 'Look what he did to me,' a woman told me one time and she pulling up her sleeve to show me four purple finger marks. I didn't want to get on anyone's bad side so I just made sounds with no words that I thought they wanted to hear.

The men were as bad as the women. 'God, she was a rip last night, eating the face off me for not finding work, and I out beating the bushes all day.' Some of them would even ask me for advice and I not knowing me arse from me elbow. 'I'm thinking of joining the army, Ralph. It's the only way to get a job. What do you think?' 'Do you think we'd make it in England, myself and the wife, Ralphie?' There were so many men with no work that I sometimes felt bad about having a job, and I in full sight of every jobless man in the town.

Some people in Ballyrannel thought Con and Matthias were daft for joining the army. 'They have work for the rest of their lives up in Enderly.' But everyone in Ballyrannel knew why Con and Matt were signing up—they were off to see the world. I wished I had the balls it takes. One very holy man who went to Mass every day said, 'They wouldn't be joining only for that young Hodgkins fellow. They got too close to that Protestant, fishing and hunting with him like he was one of us.' And then there were the men who wanted to be Fenians, and a few women too: 'They're traitors to their own country, them lads. The English army is the army of our enemy.'

After passing another few houses, Con and Matthias got the jaunt back into their steps.

Missus Byrne had diddies like two prize turnips. 'I remember the first day you went to school holding hands and here you are off to see India. God bless you, lads.' Con took Matt's hand and held it up over their heads. 'We're still holding hands, Missus Byrne,' he laughed, 'and we're *hoping* we get to India.'

Missus Dempsey had a pair of diddies that would make a fellow as nervous as he'd be looking down the barrels of a loaded and cocked shotgun. 'I'll pray you get to India, lads,' she shouted. 'And you'll never be the same. When you come home you won't even remember us, you'll be so lawdie daw.'

'Oh, we'll remember you all right, Missus Dempsey,' Matthias called. 'All the times you brought us in out of the rain coming and going to school ... how could we forget you?'

'And the mugs of tea, Missus Dempsey!' Con called.

I was standing there with a big grin waiting to make my little speech that I'd been thinking up for a few days. Doctor Masters had told me five Indian words and it took me nearly a week to come up with one sentence with all the words in it: nabob, raja, jodhpurs, gymkhana and bungalow.

The lads passed Missus Dunne with diddies so big she could feed five sets of twins at the same time without running dry. 'Now lads, behave yourselves and don't be bothering them Indian nabobs,' says she, and I said, 'Feck,' to myself, and I didn't hear what the lads said back to her. Real quick in my head, I tried to change my sentence, but the lads were coming right at me and I said to myself I'd have to leave 'nabob' in there even if it sounded like I was only copying Missus Dunne. I took my chin off my hands on top of the shovel handle and took in a breath.

'Off to take the king's shilling?' someone growled from behind me, and before I turned around and saw the galoot, I knew it was Johnjoe Lacy: a tall skinny fecker who cleaned chimleys and patched roofs, never seen without his ladder on his homemade handcart full of long-handled brushes and rags as dirty as himself. His nose had the kind of shape you'd think a nose would get from always smelling something bad, a bit turned up at the tip; maybe his wife was in a constant state of wind. And he had holes in his nose big enough and hairy enough to make you think you wouldn't be surprised to see a couple of swallows flying up there into the thatch to feed their clutch of scalds.

Johnjoe Lacy was leaning on the far wingboard of my ass and cart, and he spoke again. 'You'll never get to India, you scallywags. For all you know, you could be shooting your own people here in Ireland in a few years. You're traitors to Ireland and all the men who died in Ninety-Eight and every rebellion since the English came in 1169. Bad cess to the two of you; you'd rather die for England than for Ireland, your own country.' He sent a watery spit into my cart.

Lacy was the biggest-mouthed patriot in the town, and a real pain in the arse he was about it too. No matter how many times the snot was beaten out of him for his patriotic and insulting remarks, he still mouthed on about the Cause every chance he got.

What I wanted to do right now was give Lacy a slap across the mouth two times, one for ruining my speech with the Indian words, and the other for trying to squelch the happiness and excitement out of the beginning of the lads' great adventure.

The lads came to a stop at the tailboard of my ass and cart. Con got as red as a strawberry very quick, and I could see his chest going up and down like he was ready to go on the attack. The two words that came out of him were so full of crossness they could have been made in a barbed-wire factory. But when he said, 'Mister Lacy,' Matthias touched his arm and made him stop. Con was known to be afraid of no man, priest or teacher, and was inclined to speak the raw truth without dressing it up in a bit of softness. Matthias was calmer.

'Mister Lacy,' Matt said in a voice that was all the stronger because of its quietness. 'We're not going to die for any country, England or Ireland. But if you want to die so badly for Ireland then go home and write on a piece of paper, "I died for Ireland," and then go out and find a tree and hang yourself. We'll make up a song about you and the heroic thing you did, but don't be so thick to think that Con or I want to hang with you.'

'Well—' Johnjoe started.

'Well nothing, Mister Lacy. You're nothing but a loud-mouthed gobshite. Haven't you learned anything from all the times you've had the shite kicked out of you?'

Con was looking up at Matthias like a child looking at his big hero brother.

'Listen to me, you little scallywag—' Johnjoe Lacy tried again.

'No, Mister Lacy, you listen to me,' Matt said. 'Everyone in

Ballyrannel calls you "Non-stop" behind your back because you never know when to keep your foolish mouth shut. You're nothing but a bag of wind standing over there the far side of the cart where a fellow can't get a swing at you. Now if there's anything else you want to call Con and myself besides traitors, step out here in front of me and I'll kick the shite out of you. Here, Con, hold my bag.'

'Well—' Johnjoe started again.

'Well, nothing, Mister Lacy. Just feck off to hell and leave us alone.'

Johnjoe said something under his breath as he pushed himself off with his cart.

'What's that, Mister Lacy?'

'Nothing.'

'I thought that's what you said,' Matthias said gently, like he was talking to a small boy. 'Someday soon you're going to say the wrong thing to the wrong man, and when he's finished with you that face of yours is going to look like the face of a rotten perch after a horse stepping on it on the Towpath.'

As Johnjoe Lacy went away pushing his handcart, he hesitated like he was going to have the last word. But Matt pushed him on his way with, 'If you say one more word, Mister Lacy, I'll go over there and put my fist in your gob.' If Non-stop had been a dog, his tail would have been pulled in between his legs to cover his balls.

'God, that was great, Matt,' I said, but only loud enough for the lads to hear. After all, I still had to live in Ballyrannel with Lacy, the hure.

The two lads poked each other and tittered, and laughed like hell while I was thinking to myself, 'Wait till I tell the wife.'

'Good luck, lads,' I said to them and shook their hands. 'I hope you get to India.'

'We'll make it one way or the other, Ralphie,' Matthias said. 'And we heard you have a speech in Indian for us.'

I felt shy all of a sudden. 'Ah, Matt,' I said, 'nothing I'd say could match the speech you gave to Johnjoe. Be off with your-selves and keep your eyes out for tigers.' I had to turn away because tears started scalding the backs of my eyes. I took the yard brush out of the cart and swept like hell for a few minutes. When I looked after the lads again, they were kneeling in the street, caps off, heads bent, and Father Kinsella was blessing them. The few men on the footpath had their hats off, and when the blessing was over, some people clapped and encourag-ing words were called out to the lads. Con and Matthias waved their caps to the people before putting them back on their heads.

God bless you, lads, I prayed inside my head. Please bring them back safe, Lord. They're too good for badness to happen to them. And I cried because I hate saying goodbye to someone I know I might never see again. When I looked up again, they were gone around the corner where Bops bent around to the station.

Kitty Hatchel

Matthias always put his letters in with Con's, and Con always addressed his letters to me, and Mammy and Daddy pretended not to know.

Sweet Jesus! There were times waiting for a letter I'd be as tense as the stretched-out telephone wires along the Canal with the wind whistling through them in wintertime. I'd be scrubbing the kitchen chairs in the yard on a Saturday and driving myself mad in expectation of a letter, a pain in my neck from turning to the Bridge to see if Paulie Bolger was coming on his black bike with the iron frame in front for parcels and the canvas bag. The let-down was terrible when he didn't come. Then there was the long wait till Monday. Sometimes I cried in vexation.

The March after the August when Matthias and Con took off for the army, I got a great job in Enderly. It was pure luck that I heard about the sign going up in Smith the Chemist's window.

Wanted: Girl to Work Inside at Enderly

Enderly was Buckingham Palace to Ballyrannel, and the Hodgkinses were the royal family.

When Con and Matt walked out of school for the last time at thirteen, they went straight to Enderly and got hired as apprentices because of Mammy's aunt, Poor Meg. But as well as Poor Meg in the kitchen, Daddy had ploughed in Enderly every spring and Daddy's father too, from the time he was a chap before the Famine to the year before he died. Con got the gardens, and Matthias the horses and machinery—to serve his time with Charlie Coffey. That's how they got all the books to read. Mister Hodgkins even taught Latin to Con.

It was Paulie Bolger who told Mammy about the sign that Mister Sawtel put up in the chemist's with a bit of sticking plaster at each corner. 'Not too much plaster, mind you,' Paulie Bolger said. 'That man's as mean as a priest.'

Mammy came running across the fields to where Daddy and I were sweating after getting a calf back out of Lamberts' Twenty Acres. Such running we'd done and the calf only playing with us with her tail on her back and bucking her rump up in the air. I was hoping she had a letter from Con, but I didn't want to show too much interest.

'A calf thumbs its nose by baring its backside at you,' I said.

'Or does a person bare his backside at you by thumbing his nose?' Daddy asked.

I liked working in the fields with Daddy. He was always in good humour but he seldom laughed out loud in case God would hear him and throw some badness across his path. 'Laughing out loud is dangerous,' he'd say. 'Any man who laughs too loud will pay for it in the end.'

The buds were on the bushes and Daddy was laying a whitethorn across the calf's gap when he saw Mammy coming through the field gate.

'Someone must be dead,' he said. He made another cut in the stem of the whitethorn. 'Your mother never comes to the fields, running like that.' He was always afraid that something might happen to Con and Matt in the army, and there wasn't even a war on. All I wanted was a letter, but if Mammy had one for me, she wasn't carrying it in her hand.

Daddy kept poking the bushes as Mammy came nearer. He pulled the whitethorn down and pushed it into the gap without breaking it from the stem. It was like he didn't want to be looking at Mammy when she told him the bad news. He pushed at the smaller branches with the back of the billhook, forcing them into place with his foot, making them look like a solid hedge for the calf's weak eyes.

Mammy stopped. 'Missus Hodgkins has the sign up,' she panted. She bent down and put her hands on her knees; she was never a good runner. My heart fell and my heart jumped at the same time. 'She waited four weeks, after we all saying there would be a notice before Poor Meg got cold.'

Daddy gave no indication at all that he'd been afraid bad news had been coming. He stuck the point of the billhook in the ground, put his hands on the end of the handle and rested.

'*We* said nothing of the sort,' he said without any edge in his voice. 'It was you who said Poor Meg wouldn't be long in the ground before the sign went up.' He liked teasing Mammy. She wasn't afraid to laugh out loud, especially not at the quare things other people did and said.

'I was the one who said Missus Hodgkins would wait simply because she is a Hodgkins,' Daddy said. 'And what are you waiting for, Kitty?'

'Will I put on my good dress?' I asked.

'Good dress, my elbow!' Daddy said. 'Get home as quick as you can, and go up to Enderly on Mammy's bike. Half the town's going to be looking for that job, and the early bird catches the worm. Run like a hare, and make sure to tell her Con and Matthias are your brothers and Poor Meg was your mother's aunt and that I ploughed there every spring and so did my father before me.'

'Missus Hodgkins knows all that,' Mammy said.

'It'll do no harm to remind her,' Daddy said. 'Run, Kitty. Run!'

'Don't let on you're related to your father's uncle Martin,' Mammy said. 'Remember the nuns and Uncle Martin's pens and inkwells.'

Uncle Martin had come home from the Boer War with a

few screws loose from sunstroke.

I could hear the two of them laughing as I flew down the field. I leapt over cow dungs, twisted around big thistles, flew through the gates, tore across the Pasture and Neill's Field like greyhounds with human heads were after me when I was small and Con and Matthias barked to frighten me, and without washing my face or doing my hair I got Mammy's bike out of the turf shed and belted off to Enderly along the Canal bank, over the First Bridge, out onto the road, past the Lamberts' big house, past the Harbour and the Canal Stores.

Mary Keegan was stepping it out along Harbour Lane, dressed to the nines in her mother's coat and hat. I don't know where she got the shoes because there wasn't one pair of shoes in the Keegan house, just boots. I got up speed to fly past her, but she heard me coming and looked around.

'Kitty!' she called. 'Give us a lift on your carrier up to Enderly.'

'I can't, Mary,' I shouted back at her. 'I'm in a terrible hurry, and Daddy would kill me.' I kept going.

On into Ballyrannel I went, along Blessed Oliver Plunkett Street; Bops the people called it and made Father Kinsella cross. And there was Deirdre Hogan in her father's ass and cart, standing up beating the ass with an ashplant. 'Go up, go on up,' she was shouting, like she was drowning in the Canal and shouting for help. But the ass must have been used to the ashplant on its ribs. It didn't even break into a trot.

I don't remember how Deirdre was dressed, but it couldn't have been in wonderful splendour because the Hogans hadn't much. I remember seeing wellington boots going up under the back of her dress and they were wet, like she had just washed them.

When I whizzed by I said, 'Hello, Deirdre,' and the ass jerked its head up in the air at the fright I gave it.

'Are you going up to Enderly, Kitty?' Deirdre called.

I turned around in the saddle, but kept pedalling. 'Where?' I shouted back.

'To Enderly,' Deirdre screamed.

'I can't hear you, Deirdre,' I yelled back, 'and I'm in a terrible hurry.'

Then I began to worry that all the girls in Ballyrannel were on the way to Enderly. I remembered a composition I had to write once when I was trying to get into the convent school in Marbra, how I was afraid all the other girls would get in before me and I'd be left out. Thinking about that entrance examination made my knees weak and I had to get off the saddle and pedal standing up for a while, sawing from side to side like an old farmer facing into the wind on his rusty bike.

When I shot around the corner at the far end of Bops, there was Lucy Gahan stepping along like she was trying not to run. Lucy had a good topcoat on that was twenty sizes too big; the shoulders were hanging down at her elbows. She was wearing wellington boots, and they were loose on her feet. They must have been cutting the heels off her, the way they were slipping up and down with every step taken.

I kept trying to miss the holes in the road so Lucy wouldn't hear me coming, but she heard me rattling along.

'Give us a lift out to Enderly, Kitty,' she called, and she stood out in the road like she was going to pull me off the bike. I swerved around her and kept going.

'I can't, Lucy,' I called back to her. 'I'm in a ferocious hurry.'

'You're nothing but a mean bitch, Kitty Hatchel,' she shouted after me. She must have thought I didn't hear her, because she kept calling me all kinds of bitches, even a ferret's bitch.

I suddenly had a vision of that terrible nun with her cruel rules who'd been in charge of that entrance examination in Marbra. I hoped Missus Hodgkins had no rules about asking for the job, and I thought that maybe I should have washed my face and racked my hair and washed my legs. Daddy said I failed the exam because I said the sound of the Canal Song was nicer than the sound of Sheila Feeney singing at Benediction, and the nuns thought that was blasphemy. Mammy said it was because I wrote down Uncle Martin's names for swans.

When I went out onto the Marbra Road, there wasn't a sinner in sight. I put my head down near the handlebars and pedalled like the devil was after me with a red-hot poker. Every time the back wheel went around I could feel where Daddy had tied the solid tyre to the rim with a piece of wire. *Thump, thump.* I was afraid the wire was getting loose, that the ends of the broken tyre would soon get caught in the bike frame and send me over the handlebars. And my knees went as weak as water. Off the pedals I had to get again to saw from side to side, my down leg without a bend from hip to ankle, and when I went around the last bend before the avenue to Enderly, there was big Chrissy Wallace wobbling along at full steam, all dressed up in her best coat and shoes and a scarf around her head. Everyone in Ballyrannel was afraid of Chrissy Wallace. Daddy said Chrissy Wallace was born with a stone in her shoe. She was even mean on her First Communion day, told Monica Kirwin she was nothing but a pig's fart dressed up in white because Monica had a veil made out of the kitchen curtain and Chrissy hadn't. I was always afraid to say hello to her and always afraid not to say hello. One way or the other, she could eat the face off you.

'Hello, Chrissy,' I said, as I went by on the other side of the road. She hadn't heard me coming, and she jumped with the fright I gave her.

'Where you going, Hatchel?' she shouted. 'You'd better not be going to Enderly, Hatchel. I was here first.' When someone calls you by your last name in Ballyrannel, you know they're cross with you. I didn't look back. 'I'll pull out your fecking hair for you, Hatchel, you and your oul one's bike. I hope the two wheels fall off and you go into the ditch.'

I turned off the main road onto the avenue up to Enderly,

feeling safer out of Chrissy's sight.

I knew Enderly, knew the trees along the avenue were bog deal, knew the high Famine Wall around the house and farm-yard was built to give work to poor people when times were bad. I knew the green wicket gate opened onto the pebbly driveway around the front of the house. I was familiar with the layout of Enderly because during my last year in school I used to sneak in through the farmyard entrance every day to see Con and Matthias. After all the years of being together, I needed my fill of the two lads before facing the lonely going home along the Canal bank. When I was closing the wicket gate behind me, it slipped out of my hand and slammed shut. I pursed my lips and hoped Missus Hodgkins hadn't heard it and decided I was clumsy and loud before I even knocked on her door. The noise of the golden pebbles under the wheels of the bike was enough to waken the dead. My plan was to leave the bike against the ivied wall of the house between two windows, but there was a flower bed in the way with daffodils and bluebells in it. So I just laid the bike down in the gravel and ran to the door.

Maybe it was my out-of-breathness, my hair all over the place, my dirty hands, dirty legs, bad and sockless boots, and wild eyes that impressed Missus Hodgkins. She burst out laughing and clapped her hands together when she opened the front door. She looked like she'd been making bread.

'Missus Hodgkins, can I work for you, please? And I'm sorry I didn't stop to wash and do my hair and put on my good dress because I was across the fields with Daddy galloping after a calf and Mammy came running across to tell me the sign was up and Chrissy Wallace is coming up the road after me.' I looked over my shoulder to make sure Chrissy wasn't at the wicket gate get-ting ready to pull the wings out of me like I was a fly.

'Why, Kitty Hatchel!' Missus Hodgkins said. 'Did Mister Sawtel put up the sign already?'

'I'm a great worker and I want to work in your house more

than anything in the world. I'm a good girl and my name is Kitty Hatchel.'

'Of course you're Kitty Hatchel. Aren't you the daughter of Mister Hatchel who ploughs at Enderly every spring? And his father before him too, for fifty years? Aren't you the same Kitty Hatchel who sneaked into the farmyard after school every day for a year to talk to your brothers?'

'Oh, Missus Hodgkins, I'm sorry. I didn't know you knew,' I said, and I thought I was fired before she hired me. Huge big tears filled my eyes.

'Of course I knew, Kitty. Wouldn't it be a queer state of affairs if I didn't know what was going on in my own house?'

'Will that stop me from getting the job, Missus Hodgkins? I only called in to say hello to them for a minute. I was lonely for them.' The tears fell down my face.

'What are you, Kitty? Two years younger than Con?'

'Yes, Missus. No, Missus. One year.'

'Kitty, I will hire you because I can see you do not shrink from getting yourself into your work.' The way she looked at me I thought she was seeing every speck of dirt on my hands and legs, every tear and rip in my clothes, every hair sticking out at an angle from my head. 'And, as well as that, your brothers didn't miss one day's work in seven years, and they did Lionel all the good in the world, knocked the corners off him. And Sarah was really fond of them, especially Con. And your mother's aunt, Poor Meg, God rest her, was ...' I thought Missus Hodgkins had got a lump in her throat. 'Well, Lionel and Sarah loved Poor Meg.' And after that I heard very little of what Missus Hodgkins said. She talked about Con reading the encyclopaedia and learning from Mister Hodgkins and talking about a man called Russo. But all I could think of was running home to tell Daddy and Mammy that I got the job.

'You must be here at eight o'clock in the morning, Kitty, and every morning after that. Half day on Saturday. Home at one.' Then she was telling me how Con and Matthias had never been late for work, how they were very reliable and how she'd hoped they'd stay forever, and I thought she'd never stop talking and the next second I'd hear Chrissy Wallace crunching her way across the pebbles to put her hand on my shoulder and throw me into the daffodils.

'But young men must see the world,' Missus Hodgkins said, 'and I don't know whether it was themselves or Lionel who persuaded them to take the chance.'

'I'll be here, Missus Hodgkins. I'll be here,' I said, and I going from one foot to the other like a little girl going to wet herself.

I started down the four steps before I remembered to thank her, and then I broke into a trot back to the bike, hoping I wouldn't meet Chrissy in the wicket gate.

Missus Hodgkins called after me. 'Kitty. When your father and mother ask you how much you will be earning, what will you tell them?'

'I don't know, Missus,' I said. 'Maybe what you were paying Poor Meg.' If the wicket gate banged shut behind me I didn't hear it.

Halfway down the avenue I met Chrissy Wallace in full sail. She looked like a dunghill cock the way she had her chest stuck out. She smiled and started shouting before I got near her. 'She gave you short shrift, Hatchel. Will you look at you, dirty as a pig. You should have washed your face and racked your hair. You look like a tramp, and that's what you are.' I swerved around her and passed her as quick as I could.

I was three months working in Enderly when I got a letter from Matthias telling me he and Con would be going to India. I felt like the ground had swallowed me and it wasn't until the next day I was able to finish the letter, get past the part about him sailing away to India, away from me. In the next sentence he asked me to go to Dublin before the end of June to say goodbye.

I knew Mammy and Daddy would never let me go. That's

why I asked Missus Hodgkins how could I get around them.

The first thing she said was, 'Ah, it's grand to be in love, Kitty.'

I blushed so badly I had to turn away, but she had seen my face. 'It's all right to call a thing by its name, Kitty,' she said. I blushed worse.

Missus Hodgkins was always very calm and very wise. She told me what to do. She told me the time would fly while the lads were away.

That evening when I was riding Mammy's bike home, I said to myself, I'm in love, every time I pushed down on the left pedal.

I'm in love with Matthias Wrenn, I was saying by the time I got down to the Canal.

I'm going to marry Matthias Wrenn, I was saying by the time I got off to push the bike over the Bridge because I'd been so distracted I hadn't got up enough speed to clear it.

I even forgot about India for a few minutes.

Missus Hodgkins

The sight of Kitty Hatchel on the doorstep that morning! And she trying to be formal because she had come to be interviewed for Poor Meg's job. Formal, and the boots and the nervousness of her!

The details got imprinted on my brain as sharp as the king's head on a penny: the frantic and windswept and enthusiastic straight-out-of-the-countryside appearance of the girl. And she as tall as a stork—not too big in the chest though, just the right size, no big hanging things swinging around and getting in the way. If I hadn't known the family I don't think I'd have been able to see beyond the boots, the hair, and the cow dung on her legs.

When I opened the door, I was put in mind of an exotic bird beaten to the ground in a storm, all its feathers ruffled by the fierce wind. But far from being defeated, this bird was on her feet, determined to face into the next storm, which she believed was approaching on the far side of our front door.

Weeks later I found out she had been afraid a competitor for the job, Chrissy Wallace, would suddenly touch her on the shoulder and tell her to act like a bee and buzz off. Kitty had strange figures of speech. She once told me it was raining like a cow urinating on a flat rock, and then she blushed and put her fingers to her lips. 'That's what Uncle Martin always says,' she said by way of apology. Of course, 'urinating' wasn't the word

Uncle Martin used. I have often wondered if Kitty's verbosity gave rise to Con's reticence, if he had realized very early in life that silence demanded less of an effort than did the energy to get a point across whenever his sister was around. Of course, we all used to smile at how tongue-tied and stuttery Con got in front of our Sarah too, but that was because Sarah was beautiful. Most men are intimidated by a beautiful woman even if she has the brain of a stick with the personality of a stone.

Kitty's short hair was so untidy she could have been running through furze bushes all night in the dark. Her dress was as attractive as a brown sack with armholes. Her brown cardigan was short at the wrists, and it was years past its prime, unmatching brown and blue darns all over the place. But it was her boots that took the biscuit: they had once been knee-high wellingtons made from Burmese syrup. Now they were ankle-high, and the instrument used to cut them down to size had escaped from its handler a few times, leaving behind jagged rims. There were no socks. Her shins were spattered with what could only have been blobs of animal matter, indicating that she had been running in fields spotted with fresh cattle droppings.

Our Sarah went to boarding school that same September when Kitty started slipping into the farmyard after school to get her daily dose of her brothers, Matthias with the horses or in the Machine Shed, Con in the gardens. From the first second I saw her visiting the two lads, I knew she had never been feminized, that she'd spent all her life in the company of boys. And now as I stood looking at her in the front door, I wondered if she still climbed trees and skipped stones across the Canal. A lot of country girls live like boys for as long as they, or their parents, can get away with it. It's only when Mother Nature herself forces the issue of nascent motherhood that they start learning to be girls. Some never learn and stay a bit mannish all their lives; there's nothing as pitiful to see as a spinster woman who never grew out of her tomboyishness, with hair like dried-out binder twine, hair on her chin too, skin as cracked as neglected leather, and crow-claws for hands.

But it was Kitty's enthusiasm for the job that outshone her physical presentation. She could have been one of those lovely country girls who, in a fairy tale, is swept off her feet by a prince on a white horse. But as she stood on our front steps that morning, a passing prince would only have seen a peasant girl, a milkmaid maybe. At some time in the future, like many a country girl, Kitty would probably waste her sweetness on the desert air, as Gray said in the country churchyard, but she had some sweetening-up to do before that happened. I know how a fresh coat of paint changes a room, and I knew that soap, water, hairbrush and fresh clothes would bring out the beauty of this wind-blown bird.

Little did I know that a country lad very close to home had already sniffed at this burgeoning blossom, had got a whiff as enticing as the elusive sweetness of a spring primrose shy in deep grass at the edge of a bare-branched hedge.

She didn't even ask me how much I would pay her. Standing on the step outside our door, she was oblivious to her physical presentation, and I got the feeling that her only ambition in life was to work in Enderly. But that was her gift—to sink herself into the present moment, disregard everything else. It was this intensity that allowed her to walk around the jagged rim of Knockmullen Castle halfway up in the sky; to boldly—and foolishly—walk around the parapet of the First Bridge with her eyes closed; to imitate some lunatic from the village and dive into the Canal from the parapet. And it was her ability to stick to a task that enabled her to devise a way of getting to Dublin to see Matthias Wrenn off to India—Matthias, that whiffer of shy primroses in spring grass.

Maybe it's because I'm a woman who had the same unbearable feelings not so long ago, or maybe it was because I'd spent all my life around horses, but when it came to Matthias Wrenn, it was obvious Kitty wasn't just in love; she was in heat. Of course

I never did say this to anyone, not even David. But, in my defence, it wasn't just *me* and horses; many were the nights of the days when David had bred a mare that he came to the bedroom with more than sleep on his mind. Sometimes he couldn't even wait to get to bed; he'd floor me at the top of the stairs or even in the kitchen; that was hard on the back. Fortunately, I was blessed with a vigorous willingness to perform my marital duties, and I simply weakened at the knees whenever David began pulling off my clothes before we got near a bed.

Many's the time I've leaned on the paddock railing watching the antics of mare and stallion. So often did I see them getting ready for the final lunge-and-plunge that in my dreamy eyes the mare seemed to cling to the earth by the tips of her hooves. Like a ballet dancer in Paris moving her body to the music, the mare would barely hold on, keep herself from shooting up into the sky. No mare in heat knows what to do with her body—ripping into sudden, mad, short gallops that come to stops in showers of pebbles from the tips of braking hooves—kicking out with murderous intensity, tail and mane gone from gravity's grip—not whinnying but screaming when the stallion comes at her with yellow, two-inch teeth bared to plant a bite—see-sawing in the air from front to hind legs as if she were trying to rid herself of a swarm of botflies—throwing her head and rolling her eyes like she had drunk bad liquor—snorting through flaring nostrils and sending out showers of saliva until finally firmly planting her hind legs apart and leaving herself wide open to the lustful charge of a galloping stallion.

When it came to Matthias Wrenn, Kitty was as giddy as any peaking mare, blushing and smiling when she thought I wasn't looking; starting to talk and stopping when she became aware of where she wasn't; whistling tunelessly and soft enough to put a kitten to sleep; staring out a window at a thought thousands of miles away; suddenly bursting into a fit of polishing as if remembering something she loved remembering; glancing into a passing mirror and making a face at herself as if to say, 'What does he see? I must be mad. He must be mad.'

'In love' is only a polite way of saying 'in heat', if you ask me. At that age how can anyone say what is emotion and what is bodily juices in a mad mix? When I married David, it certainly was chemistry, and when that cooled off, I began to love him; two different things altogether. When we were courting, there was something in me and him that drove me to distraction. I couldn't think of anything but David. But did I love him at that stage? I don't think I even knew what love was then. I don't think there was room for anything besides the lust.

When I'd see Kitty pressing herself low in the belly with the tips of her outstretched fingers, I'd think to myself how fortunate it was that Matthias was in Dublin, else this girl would be wearing him out in clumps of sally bushes or in tall meadow grass.

Kitty told me how her parents would never let her travel to Dublin to see Matthias before he sailed to India. The way I justified my involvement was that I believe some parents can be so obsessed with the fear of their unmarried daughter getting in the family way that they can't see with an outsider's clarity that their daughter may be more mature than they think. That's not to say that the world is not fairly well populated with foolish virgins, or that most men at a certain point of excitement will tell any lie in order to do what nature encourages them to do. There's a line in a song that I thoroughly agree with: 'Every man's a liar and every girl's a fool.' How many girls in the world have believed the lie launched off a raging male organ? *You're the most beautiful girl in the world. I think of you all the time. I love you. I'll marry you. If you don't let me, I'll get a disease. I'll take you away with me. I'll love you forever and ever.* When it comes to the urgency of sex, men can be like stallions, stallions that have been brought to such a level of excitement they would mount a blackthorn bush to get out of themselves what it is that's bothering them.

40

After three months working at Enderly, I knew Kitty was a mature, responsible girl. Although she allowed the new gardener and the farm men to flirt with her, they knew there was a line they should not cross. She was as hot-blooded as any girl her age, and more than likely, she'd already had Matthias's hands on her, had her hands on him too. But I believed that was as far as she would allow Matt to go.

Kitty's parents would be unable to allow her to see Matthias before he sailed for India, even though they would want her to go. If they told her to go, and if by chance Kitty ended up with a bun in the oven, they would blame themselves, believe they had built the bed for the performance of the deed.

Even though I trusted Kitty's good judgment, I did take into account the lack of long grass and sally bushes in Dublin before I said to her, 'Write to Con. Tell him to ask your parents to let you go to Dublin to say goodbye. That way, they will be able to tell you to go to Dublin even though they know it's Matthias you're in love with.'

Oh, the blushes of her. She turned away quickly so I wouldn't see them.

I wonder was our own Sarah showing the same symptoms when she came home for school holidays, showing them every bit as much as Kitty only I didn't notice—that mother-daughter thing. I wonder was she ever as fiercely in love, in heat, with a young man as Kitty was with Matthias. And could the young man have been named Con? Sometimes parents can't see what's going on under their noses. Sarah was always a little girl to me until that day of Cousin Andrew's wedding.

Matthias Wrenn

The smell of liver and onions frying that first night had the water slushing off our teeth before we got near the mess hall. That smell changed everything. The lads began to smile and nudge each other and wink.

Until the onion and liver smell, we had all been quiet, all sort of frightened, all a bit shy. Con and myself had stayed close together all day, talking low to keep the others from knowing we were a couple of country lads who knew nothing about anything, who'd never been so far away from home, who'd never been on a train until that very day, who'd come all the way from Marbra to Dublin, and through the windows had seen the Curragh with sheep that looked like clumps of white wool on black sticks. We were still dressed in Miss Bowe's clothes and the boots we wore from home. Most of the lads' boots were shining, but a few still had daubs of dry cow dung attached to the sides and heels.

Dublin was a terrible big place, and the trams on the tracks in the roads were like houses rolling along. A fellow could get killed if he didn't keep an eye out. And the Liffey with those granite walls instead of grassy banks. The work of it! The years some lads must have spent on it, stonemasons they had to be to get it so nice. 'If this is the Second City of the Empire,' Con said, while we were looking up at Lord Nelson on his pillar in Sackville Street, 'just imagine what London must look like.'

The best was the Guinness Brewery. After years of seeing

the gold labels on the black bottles in the shop windows, there we were looking at Arthur J. Guinness in Saint James's Gate in Dublin: the horses with the shining tacklings, and their manes in ribbons you'd see girls wearing in their hair at the Maypole; the drays and the barrels with their hoops newly painted black; the little trains disappearing through big polished oak doors; cranes twice as high as the Windlass at the Canal Stores at home—eight of them we counted. And the boats on the river were like the boats at home on the Canal, except these had a different shape and had fresh paint on them with Arthur J.'s last name all along the sides, all as clean as whistles. Down the far side of the last river bridge the big ships for bringing the porter to England were bobbing in the water like corks on a fishing line in the Canal—and they the size of churches.

'To think,' says Con, 'that we're looking at the place where all those barrels and bottles come out of, come all the way to Ballyrannel on the canal boats.'

'Mustn't Arthur J. be a ferocious rich man?' I asked. 'Himself and the missus up all night every night counting the money.'

In the barracks about a hundred of us had been slouching along like a bunch of cows stepping on each others' heels before we got the smell of the liver and onions. And that smell was quicker than any porter the way it changed everyone. The nodding and smiling and the poking there was, and the lads after trying all day not to look at each other out of shyness, or out of unease for joining the English army.

'God, there's going to be great eating in the army, lads,' a big chap beside us said. And someone else said, 'Be God, there is.' And another said, 'That's a great smell of meat. It's making my teeth run with water,' and he sent a spit shooting out of him like the tongue of a frog. Ever after, Con talked about the Liver Spit when he was hungry and smelled food. 'God, lads,' he'd say, 'I'm so hungry I could squart a Liver Spit over the mountain.'

The smell was so good that the names of places where Con

said the English sent soldiers started popping up in my head, places where the sun was shining all the time, where people on their hunkers cooked in the streets dressed in nothing but sheets—India and Kenya and Australia and Rhodesia and Jamaica and Malaya and Burma and Ceylon and Borneo too, and New Zealand. It was terrible exciting, and I knew that Lionel was right about telling us to join the army to see the world and all the great and strange things, like lads sleeping on beds of nails, or walking through fires in their bare feet, or climbing tall coconut trees with no branches, or floating in the air, or climbing up a rope that hung out of nothing and disappearing when they got to the top, or kangaroos and anacondas and camels with two humps and elephants with tusks of ivory, or tigers' eyes smouldering bright yellow in the dark forests.

The smell of frying onions and liver was a promise being made by the army that a lad could be sent to any place in the world, to any spot in the empire on which the sun never set, an empire with huge mountains and lakes with no bottoms to them; waterfalls a mile high; rivers a hundred miles across where they floated into the sea; countries so big that Ireland could fit into them a couple of hundred times over; deserts, ice fields, lakes so vast they had tides. Oh, God! The smell of that liver and onions sent my mind spinning out of my head, and I poked Con in the ribs. 'Isn't it great, Con?' I said. 'God, I'm terrible glad you and Lionel persuaded me to join up.'

And Con said, 'I never smelled anything so good in my life, Matt, not even Mammy's pancakes on Shrove Tuesday with the lemon and the caster sugar.' And he poked me back in the ribs, and I could tell he was happy to hear me say I was glad I had come. I was as excited as he was about jungles in Africa where you always had your gun ready because of wild boars, about seeing all those faraway mountains so high the snow on them never melted. Kilimanjaro. The Himalayas. The Khyber Pass. Cotopaxi. Chimborazo. Oh God!

The stronger the smell of the liver and onions, the quicker our pace got until we were a pack of dogs after getting their first whiff of something they're going to pull apart and devour in a shower of blood and pleasure. Some lads were near to dancing, and there was a good spring in the steps of the shyer lads, and I'd say every single one of us was wiping the back of his hand across his mouth and swallowing real hard.

And there were lashings of food, piles of it. The grins of the lads when the soldiers behind the counter kept shovelling the food onto our plates and telling us there was plenty. 'As many potatoes as you like,' and when we sat down at the tables, one of the new lads said in wonderment and admiration, 'Begor, lads, but the spuds look like Kerr's Pinks.' Salt, spuds, liver, onions, butter and jugs of milk—there was never the beatings of it in my life. We all took off our caps and rested them on our knees.

Soon there was nothing but the clatter of the forks and knives and the chewing. Some of the lads must have never been anywhere in their lives, the way they were chawing, food falling onto the table out of their open mouths. I whispered to Con, and when he looked at the big fellow down the table, he said, 'That lad has the teeth of a horse.' I thought to myself, I'll have to put this in my first letter to Kitty; and I did, with a drawing of a man's face with horse teeth. Kitty sent back the drawing with 'Kiss me, Buckteeth, my tonsils are itchy' written under it.

The plates were scraped clean. When the horse-toothed chap picked up his plate and licked it, so did the men beside him until everyone was pressing his plate to his face. Then we licked our knives and forks. And when there was nothing left, we all sat silent, most of us with our hands folded on our bellies. It was strange to have so many men sitting around tables and not to hear a sound. It was like there was no need for words because we were all thinking the same thing: 'I'm glad I left the place I left, and by God, I'm ready for anything the English army tells me to do. I'd march from here to Timbuktu on a feed of onions and liver and spuds.'

The laughing we did that night! When there was little light left in the windows and all the lads settled down for a great night's sleep, everything got quiet. Then someone let rip with an explosion, the likes of which I had never imagined possible to come out of a man. It started off low and quickly rose in pitch, and then there was a blast like you'd hear in the distance when lads are using dynamite in a quarry. Before anyone could laugh, the whole place erupted in one big blow-up as we all let fly at the same time. When the rest of us ran out of ammunition, two lads, one at each end of the hut, started shooting against each other with farts, and we laughed them on until they ran out of air, and we all laughed and laughed and laughed ourselves to sleep in a few minutes.

And we all slept, until the next thing we knew someone was standing in the doorway bellowing like it was the end of the world, roaring at us to stand at our beds with no humps on our backs. I never thought anyone could shout so loud.

In nothing but our long-tailed shirts, we all stood to attention. Some legs were so hairy they were nearly black.

The early morning sun was in the windows.

Matthias Wrenn

The likes of the lights in Dublin that Christmas in 1913 had never before been seen by any of us in the barracks. When the streets were wet, every light was doubled. The colours of them! Red lights like the redness of strawberries, and the green lights as green as the weed stems in the Canal in late August, and white lights the colour of a harvest moon rising.

With humps on our backs, hands buried in deep pockets, we stood on the Ha'penny Bridge for hours, nine of us, looking at the lights in the Liffey water. We were on our way home from Clancy's Public House, feeling warm on the inside. Between us we had scraped together the price of two pints of Guinness each. On the Ha'penny Bridge a shout went up, like when someone catches a big perch in the Canal. And one of the lads was pointing to the water: 'Look lads, there's a line of soldiers marching. Look, quick, look.' Of course, none of us could get to his place on the bridge to see his vision before it rippled away like bits of glass falling out of a church window.

'Look! A crowd of women dancing with those big dresses on them. Hoops.'

'Look, lads, a crowd of horses with their arses in the air.'

'Are they farting, Mick?'

'Will you look at that! Just look at it—a hen with a clutch of chickens and them as yellow as anything.'

'Look, lads! A flock of green geese rising into the pink dawn.'

'Green geese?'

'A huge big red flag and a thin giant carrying it.'

The wind coming off the sea up along the river would cut a fellow in two, but we had our big coats on us, caps pulled down over ears. No one even complained of cold feet. We had great boots on and warm socks. Nothing but the best for the men in the army. The vapours of Arthur J.'s brew were in our brains, our bellies were full, and a full belly in the body is like a good fire in the kitchen, as Uncle Martin would say.

I started to think about Kitty again, how she would love to see the lights at Christmas time in Dublin. When the army wasn't taking all my attention, I seemed to think of nothing but Kitty. When I'd be going to sleep, I'd waken myself up again remembering the times we used to be together in Ali Baba's Cave between the Supply and the Dakeydocks.

That first time she led me there! And I not suspecting a thing, even though she was doing the thing I'd often dreamed of doing myself, but was too afraid to do. I had been living with the Hatchels so long that everyone saw Kitty and me as brother and sister. I used to think that way too, until I was about sixteen. And then one day, Kitty and I saw each other differently.

When we came to the narrow gap in the whitethorns where I'd seen big people disappearing all my life, we loudly cleared our throats by way of knocking on the door that wasn't there. There were no warning shouts from the far side, no cross man shouting at us to feck off. Inside the Cave was a small grassy patch as big as the gravedigger's shed in the cemetery.

When we were small we had often been here, looking around and wondering what the big people did when they came to the Cave. Once, we found four pennies in the grass, and Con said we were in Ali Baba's treasure cave. Sometimes when we saw a man and a woman going through the gap after clearing their throats, we'd wait for a while before we threw handfuls of loose clay onto the roof of the Cave from the field behind the hedge. The clay would fall through the bushes like raindrops shaken from a tree by a stray breeze long after it has stopped raining. Most times, the man and woman in the Cave said nothing. But sometimes the man shouted words we'd never heard before.

And now here I was, a big person, in Ali Baba's Cave with a woman, and my heart was racing at the thought of what might happen. When Kitty pulled a couple of sacks out of a hole in the bushes, I nearly passed out with the feeling that scraped its way across the inside of my chest. I was nervous.

I asked her about the sacks. Where had she got them? How did she get them out of the house without anyone seeing? How did she get them all the way along the Canal bank without meeting anyone?

Kitty came over and put her finger to my lips. 'Help me to spread them,' she said, meaning the sacks. I could hardly stand with the excitement.

At first it was all very awkward when we lay down. I was on my back looking at the remains of a bird's nest in the bushy branches above us. Afraid I'd touch Kitty by accident, I kept my arms at my sides. Now, when I look back at those first few minutes I feel like a jackass, and that's what she must have thought I was too, a real jackass, and a dead one at that.

Until a year before the visit to the bushes, I had never even thought of Kitty as a girl. Since she was born, she did everything Con and I did, and some things a lot better. That time at Knockmullen Castle—I get weak in the knees when I think of it. Knockmullen is nothing but four high walls and a circular stairs attached to one corner of the old tower. The castle was one of a line of towers across the country hundreds of years ago. Fires were lit on top to warn everyone that invaders were coming.

When we were twelve, Kitty decided to walk around on the top of the walls—eighty-seven feet up in the air. We measured it afterwards with a million pieces of twine knotted together and a stone tied to one end. She was already gone a few steps when she told us what she was going to do. Con and myself were too terrified to speak to her, to tell her to come back. Along the broken walls she went, her arms held out for balance while she stepped over wide holes and clumps of ivy and old nests of crows.

I think Con and I stopped breathing and stayed stopped until she finished the journey, but when she skipped down onto the little landing beside us, we shouted at her until she cried; she thought we should have been cheering for her. We did applaud when we'd calmed down, maybe two years later.

When she was five and we were six, she persuaded us to take off our clothes and cover each other with sand in the Lamberts' sandpit: it was on a hot day and the fine sand was cool. She was the first of us to walk across the walls of the Bridge and the only one to do it blindfolded, Con and myself dying with the terrors on the Towpath. She was the only one who climbed to the top of Joe Mack's tree, so tall that it was a landmark when we were struggling home on our bikes after a long Sunday ride. The sight of the tree always gave us new encouragement, like a mare smelling her foal after a long absence and suddenly getting a pain in the elder.

In Ali Baba's Cave, Kitty got up on her elbow and looked down at me. 'Are you a corpse or what?' she giggled. 'Are you afraid I'm going to do something terrible?' Then she bent over me and put her lips on mine.

They were softer than moss.

I lay there while she moved her lips across mine and back again. Then she slowly touched her lips to my forehead and down along the side of my face and across my lips again and up the other side of my face and onto my eyes. She came back to my mouth, and her lips were wet. She moved them back and forth across where my lips met.

My body felt like it was bottling up a storm.

She brought her lips to my ear and when she whispered, I

could feel the heat of her breath. 'Now, Matt, it's your turn.' She lay down on her back on her sack, arms at her side.

When I propped myself up and looked down into her face, she was smiling, but her eyes were closed. I leaned down and tried to do what she had done.

'Again, Matt, only this time go twenty times slower. You have the softest lips,' she said.

When I finished the circle of her face and wet my lips for the second run across her mouth, she slowly brought up one of her knees as if she couldn't help it, like a dog thwacking the ground with its back paw when its ear is scratched.

'You have the softest lips, Matt. Put your arms around me.'

I never thought two people could have so many elbows between them. We gasped and giggled our way into each other's arms, facing each other and with nothing for a pillow. I would have been more comfortable lying on a clothes-line.

'Wait,' I said, and I felt useful because I had something to offer. I took off my short coat and rolled it up, and Kitty raised her head as if we had done this a hundred times before.

The pillow was very short, and when we put our arms around each other again our faces were inches apart and our noses, like our elbows, were in the way. I could feel her breath on my face. Kitty closed her eyes and pulled my head into the side of her neck. From chests to feet our bodies closed in on each other. Half up on my elbow, to take the weight of my head off Kitty, I pulled her into myself, and along my body I could feel her chest, her belly, her thighs. At first I was afraid she might feel something poking her, but I relaxed and found the terrible comfort of holding Kitty's body to mine, feeling her holding my body to hers.

I could have stayed in the bushes on the Canal bank till the end of the world. The comfort of it. The completeness of it. But my elbow and shoulder were killing me. We moved, but held onto each other. Then our mouths were together, and her lips were wet. I wet mine too, opened my lips to do it, but it was Kitty's tongue that did the job, the tip of her tongue running slowly back and forth across the width of my mouth.

The softness of her. I just could not believe how soft her lips and face were.

She brought my hand to her cheek, urged me to move it around, and I explored every nook and cranny of her face. For sixteen years I had been in the presence of that face, and I had never thought of touching it. Oh, the excitement of touching her, the excitement of being invited to touch her. We felt the insides of each others' lips with our tongue-tips, while my fingers felt the shape of her ear.

Then she took my hand and brought it down to her chest, and when I touched her there she groaned and her thighs moved in against me.

And the softness of her. Like her lips, every bit as soft, and she squirming against me the more I moved my hand around, and she groaned too, like a cow softly saying hello to its calf. I circled and circled and felt the hard knot where her chest came to a point. When Kitty opened the top buttons of her dress, I saw her and my mouth went to that hard knot without my brain even telling it what to do.

Lying there on the sack in the bushes with my arms around Kitty, with my lips stuck to her and she lying there stroking the back of my head, I felt like we were floating in the sky at night with a billion bright stars floating with us; like we were rolling slowly through grass in a sunny field glowing with a billion yellow dandelions; like we were rolling slowly, with our arms and legs around each other in the deepest sanctifying grace of the Canal, without making a stir on the surface, the roach and the perch sliding around us, looking. In Kitty's arms, I discovered a feeling that I hadn't known existed.

Slowly, I let my hand slide down the outside of Kitty's dress, down between her opening thighs, and as if she had been waiting for me to make that move, she slipped her hand down the inside of my trousers.

As the lights were turned off in the Liffey, the wind got colder, and in small groups we drifted back to the barracks in silence. I imagine most of the lads were thinking about Christmas time at home. If they were lucky like me, they had memories of a girl holding them, of a girl leading them into spaces where only a girl could bring a man.

I sent Kitty a drawing of the outside of Ali Baba's Cave with snow on the ground and two pairs of footprints disappearing into the opening.

Con Hatchel

The delight we took in our bod-
ies those first months in the army! We were young stallions
driven out from the winter stables for the first day of spring
ploughing. We were young bulls charging down sun-filled, buttercupped fields of fresh grass after a long, dark winter in a hungry shed, young rude bulls with their tails curled over their backs
exposing their parts to anyone who wanted to look and admire.

Bulging with energy in every muscle, we were brimming
with life, young as the sun, invincible, indestructible, immortal.

We were willing and able to show the Imperial British
Army that we could do much more than was demanded of us.
We threw back our heads and threw out our chests and threw up
our knees and did things they didn't ask us to do. We stepped
higher, we pushed harder, we shouted louder. At the end of long
marches we were still kicking up our heels, still laughing out
loud when the sun was setting.

And the pure joy of it all—of being young, of being together,
of trying to outdo each other. We were adventurers-in-the-mak-
ing with nothing in our future but foreign lands where we would
trek across mountains so high that their tops were above the
clouds. We would march across deserts to palm-treed oases. We
would take long journeys across wide seas.

There would be hurricanes, blizzards, glaciers, waterspouts,
sandstorms, typhoons, monsoons, icebergs, monstrous rivers, water-

falls and desert windstorms, and we would be able for them all.

'If only the English owned Alaska we could live in igloos for a while, learn all the different names for snow,' I said to Matt, 'and we could translate them to fit all the different kinds of rain in Ireland.'

There would be black people who lived in reed huts and carried spears; Indian people burning corpses beside holy rivers; Australian farms so big that two Irish counties could get lost in them; flocks of sheep so vast you couldn't see across them. There would be trees in deep forests with rubber dripping out of them into buckets; trees alive with oranges and dates and olives and lemons and pears and bananas; trees we had no names for dripping with sweet fruit that became juice in the mouth and made a man's insides joyful.

And the names! Madagascar, Bangalore, Darling. Music, music, music. I had always loved living in our school atlas. I loved poems about places far away. *In Xanadu did Kubla Khan A stately pleasure-dome decree: Where Alph, the sacred river, ran Through caverns measureless to man Down to a sunless sea.* I loved the sound of the sounds. *In Xanadu did Kubla Khan.* I could taste the words. Xanadu.

There would be crushing snakes and diseased flies and biting spiders and poisonous frogs, birds eating rotten meat in the sun, laughing dogs, bats hanging upside down in caves, birds that flew the oceans for months without going home, animals of shapes and sizes we couldn't imagine. Anaconda, hyena, tsetse, albatross, platypus, komodo dragon, alpaca.

I told the lads about llamas when we were sitting on the crest of a Wicklow mountain. 'They spit like horses kick, or bulls puck when they're cross or frightened; spit right in your face.' And we all laughed and spat over the side of the mountain into the wind, and the wind blew our spit back onto us.

With the good and regular food, and with the non-stop training, our bodies began to do things we ourselves never knew they could do. And when we would land in those foreign places our bodies would become tougher still; our skin would cook brown, our eyes get bluer, our hair turn yellow. The army was doing for us what nature does for caterpillars. We were country bumpkins changing into golden-skinned warriors; peasants turning into knights who could look any man anywhere in the eye; paupers we had been, but now we were men with a jingle in our pockets. We had new boots, we were wearing uniforms, we were walking straight-backed, and we had the confidence of soldiers who could shout 'Sir' into the face of the fiercest sergeant.

And the laughing we did at the names the sergeant called us when he didn't mean to be funny, at the lads who fell at the worst times, at one of the lads from King's County who fell on purpose at all the wrong times. The laughs he gave us! Losing his balance when saluting and ending up at the sergeant's feet, the purple face of the sergeant shouting at him, 'Get up, you fucking bogman'; falling in the mess hall with a tray full of food and not spilling a thing with the sergeant shouting, 'Get up you awkward shite'; falling in the washroom when he was naked, ending up with his hole pointing at the sergeant. 'Get that arse out of my face, you ugly fucker!'

Food, exercise, and sleep. And how we slept! When our heads touched the pillows we were still as railway sleepers until the sergeant bellowed in the doorway before the sun came back. There wasn't a morning when I didn't jump out of bed wanting to dive into the day ahead.

In the morning mess hall we were hungry bullocks in wintertime, all jaws and drool, as we shovelled the food into mouths that were flaming doors in a ship's furnace. Mugs of steaming sweet tea, cuts of bread an inch thick and butter as yellow as beastings. And then the sprint to the Twenty-Seater where we sat side by side and grunted and groaned with our trousers at our ankles.

A few months earlier we were cupping our mickeys in our hands when we made our water, afraid someone would see. And here we were sitting together in the Twenty-Seater, firing away.

'A fellow can get used to anything, if he wants to or not,' Matt said.

'There's nothing to beat a bit of soft grass for your arse,' one of the lads said when he found out what he was supposed to do with the paper. The stink in the Twenty-Seater was terrible, and the jokes were always funnier in there than anywhere else.

'Did you hear about the fellow shovelling out the five-seater in the Square in Marbra, and he afraid someone would come in and plop a shite down on top of him? He got one of them balloon things full of gas and floated it up tied to a piece of twine through the hole where he was working below. A woman came in and sat down, and the balloon came up beside her and she started screaming, thought it was the head of the headless horseman. Yer man stuck his head up through another hole and said, "Will you whist, woman? It's only a fart with a skin on it."'

The first time in the washroom in the barracks was very tough for everyone, all of us shy about taking off our clothes. Even when the sergeant's shouting got louder, no one moved any quicker. Then we were all standing naked with our fallen trousers at our ankles, trying to kick them away so we wouldn't have to bend down. Everyone's hands were casually dangling at their crotches—as if hands could casually dangle there. We didn't know where to look.

The sergeant brought us to attention. We stood there with our arses as tight as two potatoes squashed together, wondering what our arses looked like with nothing on them, and all we had to do to find out was to look at the arse in front of us.

The sergeant shouted, 'At ease'; then he made the two lines face each other. He ordered us to put our hands over our heads, to spread our legs, to move our hips so that our mickeys swung back between our legs and then slapped up against our bellies. Then he shouted at us to look at the swinging mickey in front of us. The laughing started, and that was the end of being shy. I was going to write all this to Kitty to make her laugh, but in the end I didn't.

On a long march one day with full gear I realized how proud I was of myself for deciding to join the army, even if it was Lionel's talk that gave us the idea first. But it was me, me myself, who had taken charge: for the first time I had stopped letting other people and events decide the twists and turns of my life. I had joined up because I wanted to go to places where the sun was shining, where there weren't thirty-six different kinds of rain, where there wasn't mud and muck for most of the year. I had made the decision, and as I trooped across the fields and hedges and hills of Wicklow in my strong boots and my new body, I felt like a man for the first time, an adult in charge of myself.

To the people in Ballyrannel who told me not to join the English army, to the ones who told me I was a fool to leave my job at Enderly, to Johnjoe Lacy who had shouted Irish patriotism at us the day we left, to all those people who would have held me back, I wanted to shout out, 'Stop hanging onto me while I'm climbing the ladder out of the place you want me to live in. You had your chance to make the most of your lives, now let me have a shot at it. I'm stepping away from the place where I landed when I was born, and I'm going to look around the world. Stop telling me to do what *you* think I should do.'

They had not heard the names of distant lands calling them since the first time they opened a thirdhand, tattered school atlas. But even though I had heard the names singing to me, beckoning, I had never believed I would one day be standing on the threshold of the world, ready to step forward.

But here I was. If only Sarah could see me now.

Con Hatchel

As we sailed out of Dublin everyone pushed for a place at the railings. Lads laughed goodbye to Ireland, cheered when we steamed out between the stony arms of Kingstown, cheered louder when the first waves of the Irish Sea sent the nose of the ship diving. After that it was all groans and green faces when the ship rose and fell for the next nine hours. It was only when we sailed back out of Portsmouth into the English Channel with Cherbourg on our left that we began to recover.

Cherbourg! We could see France. Less than a year ago we were all boggers, and here we were, sailing south in a ship as big as one of Arthur J.'s sheds in Saint James's Gate, Cherbourg within sight, the wind in our hair, the sun on our faces.

'Cherbourg!' Matthias said, standing beside me. 'Doesn't it sound terrible foreign, not a bit like Ballyrannel or Ballyhuppahawn or Ballynafunshin? You have to be superior to say it—Cherbourg—like something is wrong with your nose. Can you believe it, Con? France on our left, and soon it'll be Spain and Portugal. I just can't believe it.'

And we sailed down into the Bay of Biscay. Sweet Jesus tonight, as Mammy used to say. The Bay of Biscay! Until now it had only been a blue place shaped like a backward C in the atlas, and here I was leaning over the rail looking at the front of the ship slicing through the smooth water like the sharp coulter of a plough pulled through a field of lea by three strong horses.

The Bay of Biscay, I repeated to myself, trying to engrave on my brain what I was seeing so that, at a later time, I could lie on my back under a leafy tree and remember every detail about the journey. Pirates had sailed here in galleons out onto the Spanish Main to rob the golden ships coming back from the Americas—doubloons and black beards and patched eyes and mouths full of evil teeth; gleaming swords shaped almost like sickles; slaughter and screams and murder; red blood and gold coins mixing together under the frantic feet of fighting men. Once upon a time, those were only imaginings in a young boy's head, and here I was where it happened. I could almost hear the screams, see the sun reflected off the terrible swords, the thousand ropes of a sailing ship bending in the breeze, the sails bellying out in the wind.

Matthias stamped his foot on the iron floor of the ship, pounding into his head that what he was seeing was real. 'Spain. The Spaniards. Spanish. *And Spanish ale shall give me hope, my dark Rosaleen, my own Rosaleen.*'

We stood up straight, held onto the railing and faced onward toward the setting sun. India, here we come. India, 4500 miles away, here we are in the Bay of Biscay sailing straight at your Bay of Bengal. Jesus! I tried to convince myself that everything was working out as we had daydreamed it would.

The power of the monstrous ship throbbed through us. The vibrations of the engines went into our bones and livers and kidneys and testicles, and we became part of something that was far bigger than we could ever be. We were inside the pumping heart of the British empire.

And all the lads, all twelve hundred of us, even the English ones who'd joined us in Portsmouth, gawked and walked the decks, pointed and asked questions that showed how much we didn't know.

'Will there be whales?'

'What happens when the tide comes in?'

'How quick are we going?'

'Did you think the water would be this level after the Irish Sea?'

'Are we nearly there yet?'

'What's them yokes for?'

The sailors were dressed in the same outfits that we'd seen all our lives on the John Player cigarette boxes—*Navy Cut.* In their strange hats and wide collars, they were costumed actors on a stage. Everything they did was performed as if it had been rehearsed a thousand times. All tasks were quickly done with such precision that it was obvious there was only one way to do every little job. They all walked at the same speed, coiled ropes in exactly the same way, climbed ladders with the same steady deliberation, returned everything to the place it had been taken from. If another crew suddenly appeared on the ship to relieve the present one, not even a tiny shiver of hesitation in the ship's onward determination would have been noticed. If the ship ploughed through an invisible wall into a stormy sea with waves as high as churches, the sailors would surely carry on just as calmly as they did on a sea of glass.

'What's the Pillars of Hercules?'

'Who's Hercules?'

'How far apart are the pillars?'

'Pilar is a girl's name in Spain.'

'Spain's over there to the left.'

'We had a neighbour called Mick Spain, but he wasn't from Spain.'

'Where was he from?'

'Who? Mick Spain?'

'No, Hercules.'

'I'll tell you one thing—he wasn't from Ballyhuppahawn.'

The loudspeaker instructed us to move away from the back end of the ship. Six sailors appeared like trained ponies trotting into the circus ring when a whistle is blown. The three biggest worked a small crane. The shorter ones worked the hooks and ropes, and within minutes the ship had sprouted four thirty-foot wings, two out of each side. They hung high above the water, white and rushing from the passing of the ship. The six sailors disappeared.

'They're for fishing from.'

'They're for drying the wash.'

'They keep the ship balanced in a big wind.'

'There's fifteen holes in each wing.'

'Four times fifteen's sixty.'

'Sixty holes.'

'They remind me of the Twenty-Seater in the barracks.'

The loudspeaker said, 'Now hear this. Now hear this. The heads on this ship are for the officers and sailors. All others will use the flying shite-holes mounted off the stern. The flying shite-holes are only for shitting and pissing. They are not to be used for the enjoyment of the scenery. Any man spending fifty seconds on a shite hole will be denied arse paper for his next shite. Two sheets of arse paper are available to each man. The sailor on arse-paper duty in the kiosk in the stern will dole out the arse paper. That is all.'

Twelve hundred soldiers stood on the decks in silence. Everyone was looking at the flying shite-holes, and everyone was wondering the same thing: would it be better to sit in the back row and have to look at the fellow in front of you, or to sit in the front row and have the lad behind look at you? Out loud, someone said, 'I'd hate to get a faceful of shite-and-piss from the chap in front of me.' And there was a stampede to the arse-paper kiosk.

The front rows of flying shite-holes trembled as men clutching their paper ran out to claim a hole. Groups of hesitant men gathered at the entrances to the second rows, and the loudspeaker said, 'Now hear this. Now hear this. You men with your supply of arse paper, take your places on the second rows. On the double. That is all.'

The instant the holes on the second rows were filled the ship's hooter exploded into a scream of steam. We could feel the sound in the iron of the ship, like the ship was a huge tuning fork after getting smacked on the edge of the teacher's desk. Then the sound was manipulated down until all the sea around us trembled under the vibrations of a gigantic farting noise. Everyone cheered and clapped and laughed, and the lads on the flying shite-holes did their business. There wasn't a sailor in sight, but they were someplace, watching and laughing. That night in the dark in our bunks, a voice said, 'Imagine you're a fish and you're looking up out of one of your beady eyes and you see sixty bare arses and sixty mickeys and a shower of shite and yellow water coming at you.'

There was a big map hanging on the wall outside the mess hall. Four times a day, a sailor moved a red arrow to the position of the ship along the blue of the sea. On the second day out from Portsmouth we noticed the sun swinging slowly off to our right, and that evening the arrow was facing into the gap between Gibraltar and Cueta. We would be in the Mediterranean Sea in the morning.

'Now hear this. Now hear this. Every man will wear his tropicals in the morning. That is all.'

Tropicals! Tropicals for a tropical climate. Ireland, with its temperate climate, wasn't temperate with its rain and clouds. Just the word 'tropics' was enough to excite any Irish person and fill them with longing.

Tropicals! Good God! In no time at all we'd be on the coast of Malabar, a few hundred miles north of the equator, all the lads wearing their whites, showing off their knobbedy knees.

Con Hatchel

Even though all traces of modesty had been squelched out of us by a long line of barking and snapping and spittling and gnashing sergeants, we were all self-conscious that first morning in our tropicals. The bottoms of the short trousers and the tops of the high stockings framed the knees and gave them a prominence they wouldn't have had if everyone was naked.

'It's like going around with your balls hanging out of a hole in your crotch.'

'If a man wore short trousers in Ballyhuppahawn he'd be burned at the stake.'

'That's a great pair of knobs you have.'

'With knees like that, you'd have no trouble with a woman.'

'That's what I call them, leg forcers.'

And then one fellow showed how the loose flesh on a straight knee could be squeezed into the shape of a crease. 'What's that, lads?' he asked, and the knowing ones laughed too loudly and poked each other with their elbows. Then the ones who didn't know what the crease meant were made to feel like little boys. 'You'll be finding out soon enough in one of them harems in India,' they were told.

In a matter of minutes, hundreds of soldiers were bent at their waists creasing their knee flesh.

'Begob, Murt, you could hire that out for half a crown a go.'

'Does it go up and down or crossways?'

'Will you stop showing off how thick you are!'

'Did you ever see any animal with one that goes crossways?'

'I did. It's called the cross-arse.'

The talk veered into the topic of willing Indian women, who were once more put on public display, disrobed, and made to behave in imaginative ways. As the conversation expanded to include many naked women doing many things to one naked man, many of the men drifted off into a trance, their mouths open and the fronts of their new shorts distorted.

'Now hear this. Now hear this. Roll call will be at six hundred in your designated area. That is all.'

Of course there was more than roll call. The images of willing Indian women faded quickly as energy was diverted into other muscles by the energetic calisthenics and drilling. There was parading in confined quarters, running in tight circles. Even though it was early morning, the iron deck was already warm to our hands. In the hot sun, sweat trickled, shirts were soaked, eyes were blinded by the flowing salty water.

Instructions were issued before dismissal. 'You don't know it now, but you are all getting burned. A burned soldier is no good. The kilted Scots found that out in South Africa after being pinned down all day in the sun; they couldn't walk for a month with the burns on the backs of their knees. You will change out of your tropicals every morning after mess.'

We had sailed into the Mediterranean through the Straits of Gibraltar during the night. Morocco was off to the right. Europe was up there, and Africa down there. I knew exactly where I was, but I had to keep telling myself that we were in the Mediterranean Sea, the Mediterranean where Italy and Spain and France and Greece and Turkey were. Turkey, for God's sake!

Bulgaria was Hungary, took a piece of Turkey, dipped it in Greece and fried it in Japan.

Jeez! Only a few years ago I was in Mister Bennett's class

gaping at the two big circles on the wall map and daydreaming; the western and eastern hemispheres, the seas of blue, and red the colour of the British empire. And here I was sailing across the round surface of the earth from the western hemisphere into the eastern hemisphere. And the sun and the heat! 'If we only had a few days of this sun at hay time,' we said to each other.

'We missed your man's gateposts—Samson's.'

'The Pillars of Hercules, you culchee.'

'Timbuktu's in Africa.'

'The Africans are very quare; they walk around naked and carry big spears.'

'If I had to walk around naked, I'd be up on a woman every second minute.'

'Them knees would come in handy then.'

On the second day after roll call we were instructed about Moslems and Hindus. 'They look like each other. The Hindus don't eat beef, and the Moslems don't eat pork. In Hindu parts, cows are sacred animals. Don't touch the cows. In some places, monkeys are sacred animals. Don't shoot at the monkeys even if they throw their shite at you.'

We passed Algeria and Tunisia and swung a bit to the right to go below Sicily and above Malta. With everyone on the decks at the same time looking at the sun setting it seemed there were thousands of us.

'You'd swear it was going to start the sea boiling any minute.'

'What does monkey shite smell like?'

'Do they have a good aim?'

'Just imagine getting a pawful of monkey shite in the face.'

'I'd blow the balls off the monkey that got me in the face with his shite.'

'The Hindus would slice your balls off for shooting the balls off their sacred monkey.'

'Jesus! That would hurt.'

''Twouldn't hurt a bit—they'd have sliced your head off first.'

'Oh! Don't say that.'

It took all of the third day to pass Libya but we couldn't see it.

'The Sahara's in most of Libya.'

'There's camels in Libya, and they have camel races.'

'What? With jockeys and everything?'

'They have kangaroo races in Australia.'

'Kangaroo races, my arse.'

'My mother's brother was a kangaroo jockey till he fell off going over a jump and broke his back.'

'Don't be daft. People can't ride kangaroos.'

'Jesus, but you're thick. Of course people can ride kangaroos. The country children ride kangaroos to school, put their school bags in the kangaroos' pouches.'

We were told about the poor people who lived on the streets in the cities of India. 'Don't give them anything. Shout at the beggars before they get near you. Shout like you'd shout at a dog that's going to bite you. If you give to one you'll be mobbed and they'll take the clothes off your back, take the boots off your feet, take your socks. They dress in rags and piss and shite in the street. Don't stare at them. If you see a dead body in the street, just keep going. They have lads to take dead people away.'

Before we passed Tripoli, the sky began to get cloudy. The sergeant was drilling us when the front of the ship suddenly fell into a hole in the sea. Everyone stopped and looked at each other, everyone wide-eyed, everyone weak-kneed. After a very long time the front came back up, and creaking sounds we had not heard before ran the length of the ship. The nose went down again.

'Holy Mother of God, we're fucked, and I can't swim.'

Some men staggered and went down on their hands and knees. A sudden wind whipped through the railing and whistled in the wires.

'Now hear this. Now hear this. Vomit over the side of the ship. Do not vomit into the wind. Below deck, vomit into the vomit bags supplied by the vomit master. Do not vomit into the sinks. Do not vomit when using the flying shite-holes. Do not slip in the vomit. That is all.'

Suddenly, at regular intervals along the deck, individual sailors took shape out of the background of grey metal pipes and ladders, looked as if they had been there all the time with brass-tipped fire hoses in their hands, only we hadn't seen them till now.

The nose of the ship fell into the sea hole again and, no sooner was the first spout of vomit spewed than a forceful stream of water came bouncing across the deck like a greyhound with the smell of a rabbit in its nose.

The sailors with the hoses gave no quarter to the slow movers. The liquid brooms gathered up the vomit and carried it over the side in clouds of mist. There was a stampede for the deck's railing, and the sounds the men made were full of *gaghs* and *ahs*.

In half an hour all the bunks below deck were filled with men moaning, some mentioning their mothers, others offering their souls in exchange for deliverance. Some sat motionless on their bunks' edges, eyes unfocused, faces the same greenish hue as a five-day corpse, all sitting as if afraid any movement would make them die. I lay with my mouth open for hours, my eyes fixed on the head of a painted rivet. I had not known it was possible to be so sick and still be alive. No one moved when mess was announced at midday and again at evening. Just before lights-out the box squawked.

'Now hear this. Now hear this. There will be roll call at twenty-two-hundred. Do not think you cannot walk. After roll call every man will go to the mess and drink four pints of water. That is all.'

When we got between Crete and the edge of Egypt during the night, the wind went away, and on our fourth morning in the Mediterranean men rose from their beds announcing they could eat a horse. Some said they could eat a bullock, horns and all. One lad said he would eat a monkey, even if it meant having a dozen Hindus in sheets after him with spears. And the British empire heard the cries of her hungry soldiers. Vats of creamy and sugary porridge, miles of sausages, eggs by the gross, tons of bread, tubs of butter, gallons of sweet and milky tea were served at breakfast, and when we left the mess every plate and mug was empty, the knives and forks licked clean.

'I told you before not to lick the fucking forks and knives. Are you fucking savages or what?'

Foul digestive airs belched and farted unabated for two hours at roll call and drill.

At the end of the afternoon drilling and marching, we were told we were not going to India for our holidays. As the lieutenant reminded us of our duties to the Imperial Army and our responsibilities to His Majesty the King, I thought that no matter what was expected of us I was already on holidays, and that I'd be on holidays all the time I was in India. It was being on this ship, it was this journey through the Mediterranean, it was all the strangeness, the difference and the newness that I was seeing with every new minute that were the very makings of a holiday. Even the sight and sound of a thousand men vomiting in unison were parts of the holiday.

India was going to be a great adventure, where I would see the places I'd read about and the millions of things I still knew nothing about. And I didn't just want to see these places—I wanted to soak them up and bring them home with me to enjoy for the rest of my life; I wanted to think to myself in years to come, 'When I was in India.' Oh, God. I was like a young boy going on his first visit to Dublin after hearing about Dublin all his life; it was like I was on the train with my head sticking out the window and the smell of the coal smoke wrapping me up in its clouds of strangeness and difference and newness.

And then a rumour went around that we would be so close to the shores of Egypt we'd see the pyramids.

'Egypt is where Moses was found in the bulrushes.'

'Where was Moses when the lights went out?'

'In Egypt.'

'No. In the dark.'

'We'll see the pyramids.'

'What's a pyramid?'

I had to keep reminding myself that in the army rumours sprung up like mushrooms on a hot night in August. One fellow could be told there's pyramids in Egypt; the next minute the rumour was that we'd see the pyramids.

While we sailed closer to the Suez Canal a rumour came to our card game that Moslems caught stealing in India had their right hands cut off, that the robber would have to use the same hand to wash his arse and put food in his mouth.

'Imagine that! Having your hand cut off.'

'How do they do it?'

'A hatchet and a block of wood, the same as cutting sticks for the fire.'

'No!'

'Yes. The Handcutter is a tradesman in India. He's at it all day. "Next," he shouts, and down goes the hand, up goes hatchet and off comes the hand.'

'No!'

'Yes.'

'Jesus! Are they savages or what?'

Another rumour doing the rounds was that Germany and France were going to have a war with each other.

'When them lads aren't fighting each other, they're talking about fighting each other.'

'Last time, the Germans grabbed a bit of France where there's coal and iron. Maybe the French are going to take it back. Who's deal is it?'

'As long as there's no war in India, I don't give a shite.'

'Will you put your money in, Ryan, you hure. Why do you always have to be reminded?'

'When a man dies in India the body is burned on a pile of sticks and his wife has to jump into the fire and get dead too, because there's no one left to take care of her.'

'The shite that flies around the army is enough to cover the Curragh six inches deep once a week.'

'Ryan and his money are hard to part, that's why he's always trying not to pay up, you hure, Ryan.'

'It costs money to play cards, Ryan. Will you put your money in without having to be told every time, or else don't play, you hure.'

'Every Ryan I ever knew was as tight as a goat's arse in January.'

Matthias Wrenn

It wasn't until we were packed into close quarters on the ship that it became apparent how little many of the men knew. Most were country lads who were very much in tune with the seasonal workings of the countryside. Their experiences were as limited as Con's and mine, but most had never read a book or a newspaper, had never heard of Mercator's projection nor seen a globe. Some had never heard about north, south, east and west. Many seemed to have stopped learning once they knew a few hundred words along with 'feck' and 'fuck'.

That's why many of the lads needed convincing Egypt was no longer on the right side of the ship on the morning of our fifth day in the Mediterranean.

'What difference does it make what side Egypt's on?'

'How do you know where Egypt is if you can't even see it?'

'Who gives a shite where Egypt is?'

If the relaxed atmosphere on the ship for the past week could be described as a sagging string between two posts, then the changing mood on the morning of our fifth day could be compared to the string of a fiddle being stretched beyond tuning. In the mess at breakfast, loud voices proclaimed ignorance about the directions of the rising and the setting sun. Louder, more impatient and more anxious voices tried to explain.

'But why are you so fucking cross about it?'

'Because we're not going to India anymore. We're on our way back to the war that's starting between France and Germany.'

'But we're in the fucking English army, you thick. We're neither French nor German.'

All the men in the mess looked at the two shouters, all eyes as unblinking as those of a mouse in the instant of knowing it has sprung the trap that is going to kill it.

'There's an agreement. England *has* to fight for France.'

'Oh, good fuck!' Only one man said the words but everyone breathed them.

In that huge mess hall not one stirring spoon whacked the side of a single mug; no fork or knife was moved. Through their open mouths the men breathed in what they had heard, their eyes as lifeless as puddles on a country lane on an overcast day. If they had been told we were sinking, they would have sat there in those same moments of stupefaction before jumping up and charging for the side of the ship.

And when the realization sank through their staring eyes and gaping mouths that their lives had changed radically, the mess hall exploded. Questions were thrown into the air, questions that the askers knew the answers to before they asked them.

'But what about India?'

'Will there be bayonets?'

And then hopes and wishes were shouted.

'It'll be over before we get there.'

'I hope it's quick—a bullet in the head.'

One lad said, 'We're all going to get killed.' And others voiced variations of the same theme. 'A bayonet in the guts is the worst.'

'I hope I get shot. Get shot in the head and not in the guts.'

And a louder voice said, 'Will you shut the fuck up and stop talking like that. No one's going to die.'

Silence began to take over, and when it was complete, the men stared at the tabletops. When the signal was given, we traipsed out of the mess in our embarrassing tropicals to our designated areas. Before we were put through our paces the officers told us what we had already figured out. The only new thing was that we'd be going back to England first to be outfitted for war in France. And in the meantime, for the next four days, there would be long hours of bayonet practice. Open palms were lifted to stomachs as if the soft bellies had cried out for protection.

Even though the sun was shining hotly on the backs of our legs and necks, we could feel the return of the chilly winds and rains of England. A dark cloud of disappointment descended on the ship and it did not stir for two days as we all tried to get used to two new terrible ideas: we were not going to India and we were going to war. It was like we'd had a double-barrelled, rotten trick played on us.

Con was so angry, so distraught, that he went into some dark space in his head. When spoken to, he responded in grunts that could have meant anything. 'Fucking France!' were two of his muttered words that I understood in the time it took us to get back to Portsmouth. 'No fucking India.' He was a caged wild animal suffering from complete loss of control over his life. 'Fucking German fuckers.' During free time, he leaned over the railing, even during thunderstorms, staring at the water sliding past, staring at the front of the ship ploughing its way back to England. One time, when I went to stand beside him, he was crying. I leaned on the railing and didn't say anything because there was nothing to say. Maybe half an hour later, Con said through clenched teeth, 'I'm so fucking fucking mad, so fucking fucking cross. I'm going stupid with crossness. It's not the War; it's the not getting to India.' I stayed there until he went away.

Then I cried in bitterness and anger by myself because I knew that all the little bits of extraordinary luck that had coalesced to put us on the journey to India had finally flown apart. We knew that India was gone forever. We knew it in our bones. We had been walking on a tightrope that had suddenly snapped.

We had got no further than the beginning of the great adventure and all the mysterious places were gone forever. The magic of the possibilities had turned out to be an illusion after all.

When I went down below to bed, Con had his blanket over his head. Something in him began to fade the moment he realized the grand plan had fallen apart, from the moment he knew India had slipped out of his grasp. The fading never stopped till he slipped out of the cellar in Ocean Villas nearly four years later.

I got under my own blanket and while I was remembering lying beside Kitty in the bushes beside the Canal, my hand on her breast, I realized everything had changed for her too.

The War

Dennis Hayes

It had taken us four days and five changes of horse to get to Ballyrannel with a load of potash and phosphates in sacks because the hures in Dublin gave us too big a load. As well as that, one of the horses went lame after stepping on a piece of a ceramic cup that some fecker of a country fecker broke off a telegraph pole with a stone.

The three of us—Paddy Finn, Jack Gleeson and myself—had to stay to the back of the boat trying to keep the nose from scraping the bottom. We couldn't even get to the kitchen to make a pot of tea without stopping the horse. By the time we were halfway to Ballyrannel, we knew we'd arrive on Saturday night, wouldn't get unloaded till Monday and wouldn't get filled up again with Arthur J.'s gold till Tuesday.

'If that place is so dead during the week, it must disappear entirely into the ground on Sundays,' Gleeson said.

A little while after we floated out from under the Bridge, we could see people on the coping stones at the Harbour. The Canal is as straight as a die for that one mile between the Bridge and the Harbour. My father used to say that when you're looking over water you can see clearer. We could easily see the people moving around on the quays where the wooden Windlass stands in the shape of a couple of black triangles that have their sides all entangled in each other. It must have taken a genius to figure out the workings of a windlass—had to be an Englishman.

'Begob, they must be having a cock fight in Ballyrannel,' Paddy Finn said.

A young buck-toothed lad was fishing off the bank near the burnt house. We had seen this youngster a hundred times before and he always asked us the same thing. The horse was on top of him before he pulled his line out of the water, one sock at his ankle, the other halfway up the calf, one leg of his short trousers higher than the other, the shirt neither on him nor off him, his hair like the flower of a Scottish thistle after an ass has been at it with its thick lips. He squinted at us and pulled his top lip further up his teeth. He was the ugliest child in God's creation; only his own mother could see anything to look at in him, and that only if she was nearly blind.

'Hey Chappie,' I called, 'what's happening down at the quays?'

'Feis tomorrow. Getting ready. Can I get onto the ship?'

'Will you stop asking that, you little scut?' Jack Gleeson growled. 'You know we can't take you on, so stop asking us every time we pass by. And it's not a ship, it's a boat. How many times do I have to tell you?'

'What's going on at the Feis?' Finn called.

'The Feis is.'

'He's so thick he doesn't know he's alive,' Gleeson said under his breath.

The boy threw his line back into the water when we had passed. 'Can I get on the ship the next time?' he called after us while he pulled at himself between the legs.

'Will you feck off!' Finn shouted.

Sitting beside each other on the wooden seat at the tiller, we watched the Harbour getting closer over the hump of the oil-cloths covering the load of fertilizer. Except for the creaking of the horse's collar, there wasn't a sound in the world. I couldn't even hear his hooves on the soft Towpath. A high, wide, disorganized flight of crows silently sailed toward the rookery on the far side of Ballyrannel, the birds drifting around in the sky as if already half asleep after their day's work of cleaning up the world. A huge evening cloud was poking its forehead over the entire ridge of the mountain and it was hard to tell the deep blue of the mountain from the deep blue of the cloud. There could be rain for the Feis, I thought to myself. Then, about a hundred yards away, a girl came walking along the path coming out of the clump of sallies growing around Three Chimneys. We had our own names for houses and places along the Canal.

'Here comes your sweetheart, Dinny,' Finn said, and he poked me in the ribs with the sharpest elbow in Ireland. I hate getting poked in the ribs.

Kitty Hatchel came up onto the Canal bank. She was carrying a folded barley sack in her hand.

I knew Kitty when she was a babby, and God, she had grown up into a smashing young woman—the lovely face of her, the long legs of her. Missus Hodgkins had made her shine. She was the same age as my youngest girl. Somewhere in a little pigeonhole in my brain, I always thought of Kitty and her brothers as my children away from home.

Walking off Three Chimney's path onto the Canal bank, Kitty had her head bent as if trying to figure out something, or else making sure she didn't step in animal dung.

For the last couple of years, whenever I was told to bring a barge to Ballyrannel, the first thing I'd think of was Kitty; would I see her and get the chance to freshen up her picture in my head? I'd think too of the Canal Song slipping along the polished surface of the water to meet us before we even got near the Supply beyant the Bridge. How many times had I heard it and snatches of it?

Come to my side, come to my side. My side where daisy petals have red rims. On my side the skylark has a nest of speckled eggs. My side. On my side the water hens polish the water with their yellow toes, on my side. My side.

Of course I hadn't heard the three of them singing that

song in years. The two lads had joined up to see the world and Kitty was the only one left. Since the boys had gone away she hadn't been herself. Since the War started she seemed to be walking around in a dream.

When we floated within Kitty's ears I stood up and called, 'Hello Missy.' I always said the same thing to her, had been saying it for years now. 'You're as pretty as the Towpath flowers.'

'Mister Hayes!' she said, as if she hadn't noticed that a barge, a horse and three men were within fifty feet of her. Normally, she had a great smile, fresh and open like she was inviting you to play with her. But she didn't smile at my compliment as she always did.

'Any word from the lads?' I asked.

Kitty stopped walking, waited for the horse to pull the barge level with herself. 'Last week,' she said, 'near a river in France called the Somme waiting for something to happen.'

'Song? I never heard of that one.'

'Somme, Mister Hayes. S-o-m-m-e.' Kitty turned and started walking along the Canal bank with us.

'They have quare names for places in France,' I said. 'How's Missus Hodgkins doing?'

'She's not doing bad, considering,' Kitty said. She could have been reciting the times table like a dreamy child in school. She spotted the two lads sitting on the seat at the tiller and, for a moment, she livened up. 'Mister Gleeson! Mister Finn! Are you hiding back there or what?'

Gleeson spoke up. 'Ah, Kitty. Dinny here won't let us do anything. He's so good to us he hasn't let us off this seat since we left Dublin three days ago.'

'That means they overloaded you again,' Kitty said. She hadn't been living on the edge of the Canal all these years for nothing. 'Have things quieted down in Dublin?'

Paddy Finn liked having Kitty's attention too. 'A lot quieter than at Easter,' he said with his terrible flat King's County accent. 'At least the big guns are gone. Now and then there's rifle shots. If the English hadn't shot the feckers the whole thing would have ended in a week. The leader was cross-eyed. Always beware the cross-eyed man, my mother said.'

'Which of the lads wrote last week?' I asked.

'Con. He's still talking about missing India by a few days. And he said: "Tell Mister Hayes I said parley voo and stop scraping the bottom."'

Oh boy, oh boy, but I can't tell you how good that felt, being remembered by the boys like that, and they off in France. 'Anything new about the Scarlet Pimpernel in the paper lately?' I asked.

'Not for a month now. I just wish they were home.'

Paddy Finn could see that the conversation needed to be turned again. 'What'll be happening at the Feis tomorrow?' he asked.

Kitty dragged her mind home from France. 'Oh, the usual. Dancing and singing competitions. A fiddler or two and then, of course, the tug-o-war to let the men show off how tough they are, and stupid. I have to get on home, Mister Hayes.' Kitty stopped walking and we slowly floated past her. 'I was bringing a clocking hen to the Hippwells and I told my mother I wouldn't be long.' She raised the hand with the sack like she was explaining something.

'That's one of Arthur J.'s sacks,' Finn called, pretending to accuse her of robbery. 'I can see the red letters on it.'

'It's the same one you gave me four years ago, Mister Finn,' Kitty called back, smiling at last.

'Are you going to the Feis?' I shouted to her.

'I don't know yet. Maybe,' she called, and she turned toward home.

I sat back down on the bench beside Finn and Gleeson. It was like Kitty's mood had settled on us, had sent the three of us to trenches full of men waiting to go over the top into a storm of bullets.

Finally Finn said, 'I tried to learn the fiddle once. My father could play and my sisters. My mother and myself had tin ears, is what my father used to say. Tin ears. I always thought that was funny—going round with a pair of tin ears sticking out of your head.'

'I love hearing a good fiddler,' Jack Gleeson said. 'Maybe tomorrow won't be as bad as we thought.'

Father Kinsella

I didn't like it when there was a boat in the Harbour when we had the Feis. Because they were from Dublin the boatmen thought we were all bumpkins—you could see the superior sneers. And I thought we were lucky that year until about six o'clock on Saturday evening, when I was looking over the site with the committee. I looked up and there was a boat floating out from under the Bridge. There's some things you can't control.

Only for the organizing committee going over to the soldiers in Marbra with cap in hand every April we'd never have had the Feis. I wasn't expecting we'd get permission in 1916 after what went on in Dublin that Easter—that cross-eyed Pearse and his crowd; so badly he wanted to be a mythical or mystical hero he just couldn't wait to get himself killed. He read too much poetry, that fellow, including the rubbish he wrote himself—moved to heroism by his own words. Him and his crowd just couldn't wait for the War to be over. There was no need for anyone to be a martyr for Ireland, unless they wanted to occupy a niche in the national pantheon of mindless zealots, have bad songs written about them to be sung in drunken and tuneless voices forever. Home Rule was on the books in London, and not even Lloyd George could wiggle out of it. Idiots, the whole lot of them. Dead idiots. Mindless zealots. Blind idealists. Pearse makes me very cross whenever I think of him—so vain he

85

wouldn't let himself be pictured head-on.

All the other villages in the county had lost the Feis permission for allowing unpatriotic shouts about the king. But I had such a grip on Ballyrannel that the people knew if one of them sneezed the wrong way at the Feis, he'd have to deal with me. Someone had to be tough. The soldiers would have banned the Feis if the wrong song was sung, if there was too much green in sight, even if the fiddler sounded defiant. Of course the Redcoats knew I was connected with the Feis, but I kept out of sight, used Herby Kelly as organizer—scraping the barrel bottom there, I was. The English have been suspicious of priests since 1789 when all those French clerics came here with their continental notions.

My reason for having the Feis at all was the dying culture—the language and the dancing and the singing and the fiddle-playing. We would have Home Rule the minute the War was over and we had to be up and running to restore our lost culture the minute the country was ours again.

It was the dancing and music and singing and the sports that brought the people to the Feis. But every child in the school had to compete in the Gaelic-speaking contest, as well as all the adults in my Irish class. I made sure the best prizes went to the winners of the language competitions—silver medals bought out of parish funds with inscriptions in Gaelic, with harps and wolfhounds and round towers on the skyline, and not one shamrock in sight—lovely medals, heavy. I hate shamrock; it's nothing but a bloody weed.

Every year I was exasperated by the people's lack of interest in the Irish-speaking competitions. But it was the very nature of the dancing and the music and the singing and the sports that attracted the people. Listening to someone going mad on the fiddle or looking at a group of children dancing like hares on the borrowed farmyard doors was far more exciting than standing around listening to one of the town teachers asking a child questions in Irish. But there were always the few thick boggers who not only cared less about the language but who would snigger at the ones doing their best to improve themselves. 'Who does that one think she is?' are the discouraging words thrown into the hearing of anyone who's trying to advance themselves in this country.

There's times when I think the Irish begrudge and belittle each other more than the English humiliate us. If they can't do something themselves, they'll keep everyone else from doing it with their belittling. I don't know how the people in the singing competitions mustered the courage to face that rude and scoffing multitude, especially Sheila Feeney, who was always winning. She'd be about to reach for the highest note in *Fáinne Geal an Lae*, a fiddle humming along with her, when someone in the crowd would ambush her with loud fart sounds. Of course, Sheila Feeney made the rest of us feel excluded from the heights of Olympus, except for all the young lads who wanted to get at her in the bushes. It was Jimmy Nannery who got her in the end, but I think she never sang the same once she had sexual intercourse.

It was the sports that would make a cat laugh. Nobody would have practised for anything, and suddenly you'd have all these young men competing against each other—the high jump, the long jump, the tug-o-war, the big-stone throw, the long-distance puck with a hurley, and the ball a thing of rags sewn into a lump with twine. They used to have the hop-step-and-jump until one year Paddy Conroy, at full speed, forgot what came after the hop and ended up with a broken arm when he crashed into the ground after a short flight.

The lads were all so serious and ungraceful, there were times I laughed into my handkerchief. They thought they were showing off how strong or quick they were, but they only emphasized what big ungainly galoots they were—young long-legged bulls not yet used to the weight of their own heads.

The sports became part of the Feis more by accident in 1908 when a few of the lads started running to the far hedge and back again. And there you are—we had sports in the Feis. Then one year someone on the committee asked Kevin Walsh to bring his ass's reins for a tug-o-war, and that's how that started. I was nervous about the tug-o-war from the beginning because all the cheering might draw the attention of the Redcoats to the Feis. But it was all over in a couple of minutes with nothing only cut hands and dirty clothes to show for the monumental efforts.

Let them get their steam off, I said to myself, let them pull their rope and shout and fight. The tug-o-war is only an extension of the vying, the striving, the competing that goes on the whole year round between them. They try to out-scythe each other in August fields—out there in the golden straw in their collarless shirts with sleeves rolled up on white arms, shouting loud-mouthed, good-natured insults at each other across the hedges. On the bog in June, there's the racing against each other in the cutting of the turf; in March they're out-ploughing each other; on summer Sundays out-swimming each other when they race from the Bridge to the Harbour and back again, out-diving each other when they do their suicide jumps off the Bridge into the four-and-a-half feet of water below.

As long as there's young lads there will be outdoing to be done. I wonder is that what keeps all the lads in Flanders and France at it—is the War just another version of a scything race, a ploughing race, a tug-o-war? Get a crowd of young men together and they turn into a pack, a herd, a flight of starlings that twists and turns like a solid cloud in the sky at the mercy of the will of the group. They drive each other to deeds of wonderful stupidity they would never even dream of doing if they were alone and unobserved.

In the name of outdoing each other, the tug-o-war warriors will ruin their Sunday boots and pull their only set of decent clothes apart at the seams. If they would rather pull on a rope than exercise their brains, then let them pull and be damned. As well as that it will cool their ardour, put a wrinkle in their determination, keep their foreskins from stretching.

I wonder how Con and Matt are doing.

Matthias Wrenn

The Canal. The Canal. A million miles away. A million miles.

Millions of miles away, so far away I think I'll never ... And then I imagine I'm on my way and it's only two more miles. Cork Corcoran's house is in sight on the bog road. I have walked a million miles—walked and marched and run and crawled and clawed and crept and cried. Con with me everywhere. Con.

My side, my side. The plover ... It's going to save me again, the Canal, like it saved me the night of the fire.

There's no water in the Canal, only warm sanctifying grace, grace so clear you can see the little weeds on the bottom, green completely, like they'd been dipped in green paint the colour of springtime's hazel leaves. Every little branch of the taller weeds green too, like the greenness of new-grown moss, where the perch and the roach hide in the shade on summer days, not bothering with the bait even when it touches their lips. Fish lips. Fish eyes never close.

'My daddy thinks they won't bite when they're too hot,' Con said when we were eight, me with my hazel fishing rod that Daddy made, the fishing line brown so the fish wouldn't see it, small staples for eyelets, a short bit of stick like a knife's hilt to wind the line around.

He was on the far bank—Con—sitting there with his bare feet in the water on the hot August day, Kitty beside him like she was sewed to him. Everything happened in August, no matter what year it was. We even signed up in August, the year before the real August happened in 1914.

I made the bait Daddy's way at the kitchen table: in a saucer, one small handful of flour, a few strands of the wool from the sheepskin Mammy won in the Christmas draw for the nuns, a couple of drops of water, and then mix. It was always sticky and cloying until the water and the flour evened out.

The wool kept the bait from falling off the hook. But that day in August, when I silently slipped the dough down in front of the fat fish in the weeds, the roach just hung there in the sanctifying grace looking like panting dogs in the sun, mouths wide open making a different whistling sound when the air was going in and coming out.

Heen, hout. Heen, hout.

Heen, hout. The soldier had no face at all above the mouth. There was no nose or eyes, no forehead. It looked like someone had swung down on him with a beet knife, caught about an inch of his forehead and gone down behind his eyes and nose till it stopped above his top lip; then the beet knife was pulled out and slammed, blade first, into his face just below the nose. It was all so neat. No jaggedy edges at all, no flowing blood as if everything had been cauterized by the heat of whatever had hit him.

His grey brain was in what was left of his eyeholes. Sometimes shells did the quarest things.

Face wounds were the worst. I never got used to them, and the air making a whistling sound through those lips—the lips the only things left of his face. There was something obscene about it, the way any part of the body isolated looks strange. I hated seeing heads in the muck, or legs or arms.

Heen, hout. And the noise was the sound of the terrible effort to get that air in and out.

Knifey slipped into my hand by herself. Out of the scabbard she was as sharp as a January wind for cutting away dangling legs and arms; so sharp, she'd bite if you touched her without thinking, but at the same time, she'd kiss all the pain away if that's what was wanted.

Heen, hout. When I ran her up between the flaps of his topcoat, all the tense buttons popped away from their buttonholes. The same with the tunic and then the braces, the tension going out of the elastic the second Knifey touched them. Along with his gansey, I pulled his shirt out of his trousers. No matter who it was—English, Irish, French, German, Indian, Senegalese—I'd sing all the time like I'd sing to a dog when I'd be taking a thorn out of his paw, telling him not to twist around and bite. I sang quietly when I was using Knifey, not much above the hum of a bee, an inch from the ear, if there was one. I wanted him to think he was on his mother's lap before bedtime, the two of them in the red-warm glow of the kitchen fire.

Knifey slipped in over his fourth rib while I hummed. Knifey stole straight into the heart, like a mother's kiss to the top of her baby's head, and me leaning down nicely on him like I was a body he was used to snuggling with. Then I waited so he wouldn't feel Knifey going away, and I'd sing my mother's lap song again while I waited for him to slip off into death.

An English doctor showed me how to do it between the ribs. 'Don't bring them back, Pat, if what's left wouldn't want to be kept alive if he was you.'

'But how'll I know?' I asked him.

'You'll know,' he said, and he was right.

Con was kneeling with me in the muck the first time I used Knifey to save a man. While I cleaned Knifey on the dead soldier's coat, Con said, 'Would you save me like that, Matt, if I was bad enough?'

'I would, Con,' I said, 'and you'll do it for me too, won't you?'

Beneath his toughness, Con had great regard for people and animals, and it was the tender side that got him in the end. As tough as nails he could be, like when he was at home killing pigs or castrating calves with a straight-edged razor; or playing hurling and taking on the toughest lads on the other team, stopping them dead in their running; 'as unforgiving as an elm fence post' is what someone said about him. But in France, sometimes it got to where he couldn't hide his tears, jumping with fright all the time, like a boy soldier on his first day at the front. Near the end, whether it was over a horse with its arse and back legs missing or the head of a German lying there in the muck still wearing his helmet with the spike on top, Con cried a lot.

And it was near the end too, while the lines of young lads got ready to jump up into a hail of machine gun bullets, that he begged the ones nearest him to stop. He shouted at them, then screamed and called them names. He was threatened by sergeants who were trying to keep the lads' spirits up.

'What's wrong with you?' Con would shout. 'Why are you killing yourselves?'

Why?

Ah, Con. I don't know either.

The sun was shining at seven o'clock that first day of July in 1916 when the whistles started blowing. The lads from Ulster got farther than anyone else. They all did it because it was expected of them, climbed out of holes and faced into a slanting storm of terrible bullets—twenty-seven thousand of them dead or wounded between seven and eleven in one morning, and a mother and father to cry for each one of them. Twenty-seven thousand young lads! If you squeezed all that sadness into a bomb you could destroy half the world with one explosion.

Do you remember, Con? We were waiting with our stretchers for permission from the Germans to carry back the wounded. Twenty-seven thousand down in four hours, and we saying that the people in Dublin thought they had something to cry about with the twelve lads shot in Kilmainham that same Easter. Twenty-seven thousand lying in the muck in front of us, many of them from Ireland, but all that Ireland could think of was twelve bastards who stabbed in the back every Irishman fighting against the Germans. Couldn't they have waited? Did they need to be heroes that badly?

Con Hatchel

A lad from Carlow carried with us for two months in France. His name was Martin. One morning he became part of a cloud of dirt sent spewing by a Jack Johnson. Puff, and he was gone as if he had never been; nothing at all left of him, not even his hat, not even a sigh. The remembrance he left of himself was very dim. Martin, in life, had been a body more than a person. It was only after he died that I learned Martin was his last name, Mick his first.

Mick Martin hadn't the faculty to imagine any more than a blind man has the faculty to see. He revealed himself one day when Matthias and myself and a lad named Bart from Brixton were lying on our backs looking at a meandering line of crows heading to a rookery after a day of pecking. The big guns had been silent for a month, and the birds were back as if nothing had happened, although their pickings must have been richer with all the meat in the muck.

We were imagining what it was like to be free like a crow.

'They own nothing.'

'No socks.'

'Nor a cap.'

'Never have to hold it. Squart it out the second they get the urge.'

'No kettle to boil in the morning.'

'No coat to put on when it's cold.'

'Not even a scarf.'

'No hot-water bottle when the winter's cutting the feet off them.'

'Just imagine owning nothing.'

'No boots.'

'When they fly off in the morning they haven't a thing to leave behind and nothing to bring. Doesn't matter a damn if they ever see that roost again.'

Then Martin said, 'You're all daft. How could a crow wear a cap?'

'With the strap tied under its chin,' Matt said.

In the few sentences that followed, it became clear that in Martin's brain crows did not, could not wear boots and scarves; the idea of a crow carrying a suitcase full of socks dangling in its claws was ridiculous. He couldn't see that a cloud in the sky was a snorting horse. A cloud in the sky was a cloud in the sky and nothing else. A horse was a horse. How could a cloud snort? It was amazing, unbelievable at first, this lack of imagination. I had thought everyone had the same imagination. I could imagine Sarah as easily as I could open my eyes, see her that day floating toward me in the garden in Enderly, her sky-blue dress snug above the waist, the bottom half flared and all movement. In her pale blue eyes was diamond dust, a touch of brown in her pure skin and auburn in her hair. She had come to show herself to me, as she had promised, before she went to her cousin's wedding. If she had only known that inside my head I was drowning in my drool she would have understood why I stammered like a blathering fool. Sarah the Beautiful. Only Matthias knew about Sarah the Beautiful living in a hidden corner of my mind.

Whenever someone I knew got killed, I felt myself hammered down another notch into the bottomless hopelessness of the ruination around us. But when Mick Martin became part of that sky-bound spurt I didn't miss him at all—he'd had less personality than a hated mule, or maybe, finally, inurement was creeping in without me noticing.

One night, in the stable where we were billeted, I tried to imagine having no imagination. What I imagined was so unsettling that I stopped and never ventured into that area again; too much dazzling darkness and murky brightness and high circular windowless brick walls enclosing me. Martin must have spent his life plodding his way from happening to happening in a stark world in which what he could see with his eyes was all there was. He had been a yoked ox walking in a tight circle turning a wheel that turned a wheel that turned a wheel, never knowing what the last wheel turned, never knowing what it was doing besides walking.

But there were times when I thought Mick Martin was blessed and I was cursed.

In my first few days of the War it was my imagination that kept the terrible things away. Through my hooded eyes, bloated horse-bodies floating in dark shell holes were hippopotamuses in pictures in Mister Hodgkins's books; the muck was ploughed fields in Ireland on a tired Sunday evening after hunting rabbits on a miserable wet day; bodies and pieces of bodies emerging from the muck were the white trunks and boughs of bog deal uncovered at turf time; heads of horses, screaming, wild-eyed and wild-maned when death fixated them, were the heads of the charioted horses in the line drawings in Mister Hodgkins's *Ben Hur*; bits of heads and faces of men were sculptures that hadn't yet fully emerged from the block of marble; complete heads were what was left of a noble city's statuary after the Vandals had passed through; the screaming men we rolled onto our stretchers were the pigs in Enderly dragged out to be slaughtered; the men going over the top by the thousands were little boys playing King of the Hill; the acres of dead bodies under a low-slung black sky, with lightning flashes on the horizon, were sheaves of barley before stooking.

But like a cottage-sized boulder thundering down a moun-tainside, reality smashed my defences as if they were eggs in a plover's nest. And not only did reality force itself on me, it took my imagination and worked it against me. Suddenly, there was nothing more nightmarish than the dead heads of screaming horses. Not hindered by expectations of any kind, the horses had made no effort to hide their anger and pain and total terror. As death ripped their bodies apart with the tearing teeth of red-hot shells, everything they were feeling was registered on the heads and faces of the dead animals: fierce eyes on the verge of popping out of sockets; grimacing lips as taut as the rope of the Canal Windlass lifting a ton; long yellow teeth bared savagely, seeking to chop through the very bones of their tormentors; flar-ing manes held in horrific outlines by the ubiquitous muck; and hides of twisted necks pushed into ripples by the underlying muscles as the dying horses sought out their mortal enemy.

I never saw terror on a man's dead face to match the terror on the face of a dead horse. Poor dumb beasts. And because they were poor dumb beasts my imagination gave them personalities as tender and as vulnerable as those of children. And then in my imagination, the men in shell holes, the men in the muck beside the duckboards, the men we stepped on in the trenches, became poor dumb beasts too. Dumb, dumb, dumb. Dumber than the squealing pigs of Enderly. At least when the level of violence and cruelty against them had risen to unbearable, the pigs had fought to escape. The soldiers didn't fight to escape, to live. They lived to fight, lived to jump out of a hole into a bar-rage of bullets as destructive as the whirring steel teeth of a pulper against the soft flesh of a turnip. The soldiers knew what was up there, knew what they were climbing into. And they dumbly climbed up believing it would be the lad beside them who got the blast of blunt bullets that would shred him in a bit of a second. Dumb. Dumb. Dumb lads at the mercy of the men who led them from behind.

What my imagination had protected me against for a few days was ratcheting me downward. Instead of hearing delighted children playing King of the Hill, I heard hard-charging soldiers calling to their mothers as they ran against moulded chunks of metal shrieking toward them to whip out their guts, rip off their legs and arms, smash their hard skulls into smithereens, explode their brains into grey puffs, rip out their balls and send them flying in so many tiny fragments, in so many directions in so many pieces that not even God himself could find the pieces, never mind put them back together again.

Humpty-Dumpty God.

But of course there is no God in a battlefield or anywhere else, unless he is a lousy, sadistic fucker of a hure's melt. Whatever God I had imagined once upon a time died very suddenly in France. God became nothing but a package of mental shite handed down from one generation to another, like bad health or bad teeth. The package got bigger and more destructive as it travelled down from ancestor to grandfather to father to son. There are no atheists in shell holes, some self-righteous preacher said. But in shell holes and trenches I have heard God cursed back across the ages into the nonexistence from which he emerged in answer to the question 'What happens to us when we die?'

On the first day of July in 1916 I knew my mind had taken a beating under the deadening drumbeat of horror and terror and stupidity and wanton death. And Wipers was still a year away; Wipers, where, most days, it took eight men to carry out one wounded soldier; where seventy thousand men became so minced up with the mud that no trace was ever found of them.

Say that one slowly, my friends. Say it very slowly—seventy thousand men became muck in the fields around Wipers. Seventy thousand—the population of one hundred and forty Ballyrannels.

They got ploughed under like dung in a spring field in Enderly to make the potatoes grow.

Whose God oversaw Wipers?

Will there be bountiful crops of spuds in Wipers for a thousand years?

Will the crows of Passchendaele and Messines and Wipers ever be thin again?

Matthias Wrenn

For five weeks we lived in a straw shed in a place called Collins Camp not far from Ocean Villas. We got the straw shed because we were among the first to arrive. It was one of the few times we were lucky. Within a few weeks there were so many men in the place that we stopped asking if there was going to be a big push. If the rumours were to be believed, it was now only a matter of when.

There were so few of us at Collins Camp on that first day that we washed for hours, scrubbed until our skin was as wrinkled as an old potato that has escaped the pot for two winters. We soaked our clothes and tried to murder the lice in the seams with hazel sticks. Then with our uniforms drying on the bushes we lay naked in the hazy sun; hundreds of white bodies with their white exclamation marks hanging down off the bottoms of the black crotches on the cool grass of France.

'Don't get burned or you won't be worth a damn!'

'If I get killed in a trench would that be better?'

'We could use your corpse to stand on in the trench, but back here you're not worth a shite dead.'

The luxury of it—of being out of our lice-filled clothes; of rubbing our bodies on the grass like horses fresh out of sweaty tacklings after a day's ploughing. To be free of lice was every man's most wished-for wish. And it was probably because of the heavenly enjoyment of those few lice-free minutes that a new rumour took hold and brought the men to the edge of mass hysteria.

By some wonderful and miraculous misplanning by the army, a Foden Disinfector had arrived at Collins Camp. As the rumour sped across the pasture, the men leapt to their feet and ran to the hedges to collect their clothes. Like an ants' nest disturbed by a child with a stick, Collins Camp was suddenly overrun by hundreds of men clutching their bundled-up clothes to their bellies. Hither and thither they ran like huge white insects carrying their eggs to safety. Then suddenly, as if someone had shouted out a silent signal, all the men veered in the same direction and a river of white arses flowed through a gate into a barbed-wired area where heaps of supplies as big as small houses were hidden under canvases. Some of the men were already peeling off one of the covers. The rest of us stood around cheering the naked unveilers, waiting to get at the machine that would fumigate our clothes and rid us of the purgatorial lice for the first time in two years. Even Con was grinning at the rude comments about the arse sizes and other exposed body parts of the men on top of the canvas piles. Con had not smiled for a long time. It seemed that every new horror he saw fed his anger at the generals who gave the orders and at the men who followed the orders.

But of course what was uncovered by the naked men was not a Foden Disinfector at all. It was nothing but a huge water tank. And the next canvas-covered heap was a tank and every one after that too.

A crowd of military police appeared out of nowhere. Shots were fired in the air to get our attention and we were so urgently ordered to rewrap the tanks that they might as well have been secret weapons. More shots were fired and we were warned to stay away from the barbed-wire enclosure. Disappointed and grumbling at the ill humour of the police, we went back to the bushes and spread out our damp clothes. When we put our uniforms on at the end of the day the scratching began again.

It was during our stay in Collins Camp we felt for the first time the effects of what the lads in Dublin had done a few months earlier. Up to June of 1916, I had heard no words of awkwardness expressed between Irish and English soldiers; we were all young lads in this dung heap together and it didn't matter to anyone where anyone else came from, except as a matter of curiosity. But after Pearse played out his fantasies in Dublin at Easter, everything changed. Suddenly, we Irish were suspect and the Germans made things worse by putting up signs in their trenches inviting the Irish to come over to their side, promising to treat us better than the English had treated the Easter rebels.

In Collins Camp the Irish lads and the English lads started keeping to themselves. 'Which side are you blokes on?' is how the English taunted us, while we cursed the stupidity of Pearse who'd been so taken up with being a martyr for Ireland that he couldn't hold on to a job for long. He had lived with his mother and sister to save himself from dying of hunger while he scrawled poetry in his garret. A few hours in a trench in France on a wet day would have knocked the illusions out of that lad.

The rumours continued to run through the swelling camp. Because the ordinary soldier didn't know what the next day would bring, nor the next minute, nor the next second, rumours gave our unstable lives a few minutes of stability— until the next rumour broke out. The prevailing rumour was that the day of the big battle was coming soon, that this new push would be the one to break the Germans' backs, that Haig's cavalry would break through the lines and be halfway to Berlin before the Germans knew what had hit them. We'd be home for Christmas.

And some of the rumours were confirmed when the big guns started up near the end of June: the flashes in the dark for miles: the noise. It was like living in an enormous building the shape of the First Bridge except the arch was made of noise instead of stone—screeching, howling, roaring, piercing, bone-shaking, head-splitting, explosive, brain-numbing, non-stop non-stop non-stop non-stop.

The new rumours had to be shouted into ears by up-close lips. And the rumours were still encouraging. The big guns, with their undercarriages almost touching each other, were stretched along the front for miles; two million shells would be fired; the shells were shredding the German barbed wire and destroying their trenches; our soldiers, when the push began, would climb out of their trenches with their seventy-pound packs, would walk across no-man's-land and take over the German trenches; the cavalry would charge through and that would be the beginning of the end of the War.

On the fifth day of the shelling, our platoon of stretcher-bearers was ordered forward, and we joined the long lines of men marching to the front with hope and gladness in their hearts, their huge backpacks turning them into strange two-legged creatures. There was the singing of the usual songs, the monotonous 'Tipperary' as worn out as an oversung Christmas carol. And as we marched along a tree-lined lane leading out of Collins Camp, we saw soldiers stripped to their waists and digging in the field not twenty feet from where we were, digging deep and wide holes and using wheelbarrows to move the soil to the edges. The singing stopped, and in their forward movement, the lines seemed to stagger.

'What are they doing?' a collective voice seemed to ask.

'Digging mass graves,' Con said.

'Graves for who?' and I could hear in the collective voice that the collective voice already knew the answer to the question.

'For us stupid fuckers!' Con roared. Suddenly he was Jeremiah, tall in the crowd and looked up to by a flock of dumb sheep. His rolled-up stretcher was a shepherd's crook in his hand. 'They're for us. Those are our graves. We're not going to Berlin. We're going to our deaths. We'll be piled on top of each other in those holes like sticks.'

'But I thought ...'

'Oh, sweet Jesus.'

Ralphie Blake

My insides always warned me to keep away from Johnjoe Lacy the way they told me to keep away from a dog with the mange having a fit. Even as I was saying yes to him, I was telling myself I was going to be sorry for saying it. And the first time I was sorry was in October of 1916 when I saw him attacking Kitty Hatchel. He must have thought Kitty, being so young and a woman, would be an easy mark. I never heard of him attacking any of the other women in the town with men in the war.

Two weeks after them lads in Dublin were shot for shooting at the English soldiers through the windows of the Post Office at Easter, Johnjoe leaned on the wingboard of my ass and cart. It wasn't easy to look at Johnjoe since he'd called Dan Griffin an Englishman in front of everyone at a Fair Day just over a year ago. His nose was in the wrong place, and his jaw was out of line with the rest of his face. I hated when he leaned on my wingboard because I knew I was in for half an hour of his patriotic shite.

As well as that, I had to keep telling him to stand back every time I moved the ass and cart to the next pile of dirt I'd swept up. Mind your feet there, Johnjoe, I'd say, and at the same time I'd be wanting to say, Will you get the feck off the wingboard and go and sweep your chimleys?

'Ireland is on the lookout for a few good men, Ralphie,'

Johnjoe said after glancing up and down the road to make sure no one was listening.

I didn't ask him what he was talking about because I knew I would hear the History of Ireland from the coming of the Fir Bolg in their magic whirlwinds to the killing of Pearse and his crowd in Dublin. 'Aye begob, Johnjoe,' I said, 'the farmers are complaining about the scarcity of labour since the War began.' Wrong turn you took there, you eejit, I said to myself the minute I mentioned the War.

'Feck the farmers; they're always complaining.' Johnjoe didn't talk to you as much as preach like a priest, like he was the last word on everything. He had the makings of a great bishop in him. 'It's not farm labourers I'm talking about, Ralphie. It's patriots, strong men to step forward now that it's our chance to fight the English while their backs are turned.'

Stories had been going around about Johnjoe since Easter-time in Dublin, that he'd been involved in derailing the train on the main line near Marbra to slow down the English soldiers going to Dublin when the shooting started at the Post Office. Stories were going around too about how he was getting together some of the locals in case they were needed if the English started getting tough. I didn't want to get mixed up in any of that stuff, get caught by the English and have my head covered with pitch and hung from the nearest tree till my guts fell out, or get sent off to Van Diemen's land forever. So, when Johnjoe said it was now our turn to fight the English, I wanted to take a shite. And while I was trying not to make a show of myself in public, Johnjoe asked, 'Are you an Irishman or what?' so loud that it sounded like he wanted other ears to hear his question or his accusation.

'Will you whist, for Christ's sake,' I hissed at him, and I looked up and down the road for perked ears. 'Do you want to get a fellow hanged?' There was always someone ready to run over to the Redcoats in Marbra to report whisperings of rebellion.

'Someone's always going to get hanged, Ralphie, and it's now our—'

'Johnjoe!' I went around to his side of the cart pressing my arse cheeks together and dragging the clattering head of the shovel behind me over the hard road. I was very close to his ear when I whispered, 'Johnjoe, I don't want to be hung. For God's sake, don't talk so loud.'

But Johnjoe was like a tick that's buried up to its arse in your skin. He wouldn't talk quiet. He wouldn't go away. He told me he wouldn't leave me alone until I 'made a commitment', tormenting the life out of me by raising his voice on purpose. In the end I was so afraid that I gave in and made a half-hearted promise just to keep informers from hearing him talking rebellion to me. I could be counted on to help out when 'the lads' needed me if they had to make a strike to defend Ireland. The hure. The bastard. The stupid fucker.

And as Johnjoe walked away pushing his barrow with its ladder and rope and rags, I thought to myself that someday I was going to be sorry I'd given in. No matter how weak the promise was that I'd made, it was still a promise.

I didn't sleep for a week.

It was on account of this promise that I did not, to my shagging shame, take Kitty Hatchel's part later in the year when Johnjoe attacked her. Even though Kitty did not need me or anyone else to take her side against Johnjoe, I still felt terrible bad standing there as he tried to beat her down. It was like I stood by and did nothing while a rancid old bollicks raised the front of a young girl's dress with the tip of his walking stick.

Since that day Johnjoe 'recruited' me, as he liked to call it, anti-English activity was heating up around the country. It's strange how things can change so quick: at first the Easter Post Office lads were being shouted at and spitted on because of all the hardship they'd caused in Dublin. People couldn't get to work, and a man with hungry children is more interested in getting paid at the end of the day than in the higher things like poetry and patriotism. If the English had only given them all a good kick in the arse and sent them home to their mothers the whole thing would have been over and done with in a matter of days. But when Pearse and his gang were shot in Kilmainham, everything changed. It all happened as quick as Christ's turn-around with the resurrection. Christ was an eejit when he was a corpse and a hero when he came back alive, while the lads in Dublin were eejits when they were alive but heroes when they became corpses. The magic was done by the English with their firing squad.

Kitty chirped and fluttered a wing at me like she always did when she went by that morning in the Enderly pony and trap. As she was tying the reins around the pole outside Ward the Harness Man's shop, Johnjoe Lacy ambushed her.

'Still working for them Protestant hures, Hatchel?' he asked loudly.

God! I wanted the ground to open up under me. I let on I hadn't heard Lacy. I kept sweeping and looked out through my eyelashes. Kitty tried to pretend too that she hadn't heard anything. When she finished with the reins, she turned around to go into Mister Ward's shop and pretended to almost fall into Johnjoe's barrow. She put her hands on the edge like she was saving herself from falling.

'Youps!' she said. 'I nearly went into your barrow, Mister Lacy.' She blew soot off her fingers.

'Did them brothers of yours get killed fighting for the English yet, Hatchel?' Lacy asked so loudly that Kitty couldn't pretend any longer.

'I hear Mister Griffin broke your nose and jaw last year and left you lying in the cow dung, Mister Lacy,' Kitty said. 'When Con and Matthias come home from the War I'll ask one of them to break your nose again so you can move it back into the middle of your face.'

By God, Kitty! I thought to myself.

'They won't be coming home, Hatchel. They're as good as dead. Every Irishman who abandoned Ireland to join the English army deserves to die and good riddance to them is what I say.'

'You say an awful lot, Mister Lacy, and from what I hear most of it is all blather, like the things you said to Matthias and Con when they were going off to see the world. But when Matthias stood up to you, you soon took off with your tail between your legs. And what are you doing now, Mister Lacy? Attacking the woman when the man is away? You're a tough one, Mister Lacy. I'm shaking in my boots.' Kitty was nice to look at when she was being normal, but when her fights were up she looked like a woman warrior. And from where I was standing it looked like the ambusher had been ambushed himself, as my father once said after kicking a cat in the arse just before it pounced on a thrush.

'Some women need to be attacked, Hatchel, or do you call yourself Hodgkins?' Johnjoe didn't know what to do with Kitty's counter-attack and his nose was moving all over his face. 'You work in a Protestant house. Your brother is off fighting for the Protestant English. And so is the orphan, Wrenn; the army is a great place for orphans.' Lacy made 'orphan' sound like 'bastard'. Kitty had crossed the footpath and was standing in the doorway of Mister Ward's shop.

'Before the War, them lads were Sunday beaters for the Hodgkins chap when he was home from his posh school, beating the bushes for the gentleman with his shotgun and his hunting clothes, and bringing him into your own house for tea and sweet cake when the poor lad was in danger of fainting from too much walking; bringing the murderer in for tea, I ask you!'

In Mister Ward's doorway Kitty looked like a painting in a big picture frame, blue dress the colour of a September sky in the morning, cheeks red from raised blood, eyes blazing. 'Lionel Hodgkins never murdered anyone, Mister Lacy. Why don't you stop making up stuff? I hear you turned over a train on the far side of Marbra all by yourself last Easter, put your back to the engine and threw it off the tracks. You're such a tough man, Mister Lacy, that you frighten the life out of me. Look at me shaking.' Kitty shook herself like a dog spraying water into the sunshine after climbing out of the Canal.

'Neither your brother nor the orphan will come home from the War, Hodgkins … I mean, Hatchel. They should have been fighting in Dublin at Easter instead of fighting for the wrong side in—'

Kitty would not let him finish. 'Why are you picking on me, Mister Lacy? Are you practising at being an eejit or what?'

'Let me finish what I'm trying to tell you, you little brat—'

'Why aren't you picking on all the other women in Ballyrannel? Everyone in this town has a relative in the army, and nearly every house in this town gets a cheque from the English government every month. And where was yourself at Easter, Mister Lacy? I didn't see you running up to Dublin to fight. More likely you were under your bed making up a story about lifting a railway engine off the tracks by yourself. You don't need any more practice at being an eejit, Mister Lacy, because you're perfect as you are.'

Mister Ward the Harness Man came into the door frame beside Kitty, a crooked leather-cutting knife in his right hand, an apron older than himself hanging from his neck on a piece of twine. Two women in headscarves, carrying homemade baskets in the crooks of their elbows, stopped to listen. Johnjoe suddenly had more people to hear him and he loved that.

'You're going to talk yourself into an awful lot of trouble, Hodgkins. If you keep on praising the English, some people might start thinking about tar and feathers.'

Kitty took one step back out onto the footpath. 'Oh, aren't you the clever one, Mister Lacy, to start talking about tar and feathers. That's always the answer of the brave Irishman when he's ashamed of his own cowardice and stupidity and jealousy—get attention away from himself by tarring and feathering a woman and cutting her hair off and getting a free feel while he's at it.'

By God, Kitty. Give it to the old bugger, I thought from the handle of my shovel. It was great to see Lacy getting it back quicker than he could give it, especially from a woman.

'We might be tarring and feathering your brother and the orphan too, if they ever come home.' Lacy never knew when he'd lost, like the time he wouldn't stay down after Dan Griffin punched the shite out of him at the Fair Day; he just kept getting up for more, like his show of bravery would make the onlookers forget the stupid words that got him into the fix he was in.

'Con and Matthias will come home, all right,' and I heard a tiny crack in Kitty's voice. 'If you're going to tar and feather men who joined the army, why haven't you done it to Ownie Egan and Mick Nolan—one shell-shocked and the other with a wooden leg? Why don't you go right now and pull them out of their houses and tar and feather them, Mister Lacy?' Kitty wouldn't let Lacy interrupt her. 'Because you know right well that Ownie Egan and Mick Nolan didn't join the army to fight for the English. They joined up because it was the only job they could get to support their families, the same way my brother and Matthias Wrenn only joined so they could see the world.'

'They're fighting for the English ar—'

'They're not fighting for the English. They're fighting to save Belgium. They're fighting against the Germans for all of us.'

Lacy opened his mouth, but he was cut off by Mister Ward in the doorway, his white wild mane all over his face and ears. 'Why don't you take yourself off, Lacy, and take a good shite down someone's chimley? It'll do your brain all the good in the world.'

The two women with their baskets snorted. Lacy tried to get his bluster back, but Mister Ward pushed him away with a wave of his crooked knife. 'Be off with you,' he said, and then he turned to Kitty. 'I just this minute finished the collar. Come on in and don't be letting that windy old bollicks upset you.'

'Be janey,' one of the basket women, Missus Ryan—Liam's wife—said, 'you met your match there, Mister Lacy, and she nothing but a slip of a girl. We'll have to tell everyone.' Missus Ryan gave the other woman a poke in the ribs and the two of them sauntered away.

I began brushing like hell and kept my head down in case Johnjoe started sharpening his teeth on me.

The second time I was sorry I'd agreed to help Johnjoe was when I went with him and his lads to burn down the Lamberts' house.

Matthias Wrenn

The roach were silvery-red, sitting there in the still water, so still they were almost invisible. Like playing crows sitting up there facing into the breeze and not moving a feather, the roach kept themselves in position by whirring little silver feathers near their gills. The perch were wrapped in swatches of almost-black and almost-green, a spined sail on their backs that went up when there was danger or when you pulled one out of the water with your fishing rod.

'Fishes have no eyelids,' Con said one day, across the Canal. 'They sleep with their eyes open.'

'You can't sleep with your eyes open,' I said.

'Fish can,' Kitty said.

The first time we saw a dead man in the muck with his eyes open, I said to Con, 'He's sleeping like a fish.'

After that we always call dead men Fishes, except the ones floating in the shell holes after days dead. Those ones, with bellies so big you'd wonder how they kept from bursting, look like the bloated, floating bodies of the dogs people drowned in the Canal.

A pointed hazel stick is what I used to make the dogs sink. I'd wade out in the shallow water near the bank and poke the stick through the skin to let the stinking air out. The dog would shrivel up like a pig's bladder with a puncture and drift slowly to the bottom, the hair floating upright off the body and then

waving like ripe barley in a breeze before lying down flat against
the dead skin. Everything would be gone in a few weeks, because
the tench would eat the body and scatter the bones around in the
weeds. Whenever I caught a tench, I'd chop it in pieces on the
Canal bank with Daddy's spade.

Daddy saw me sinking a dog one day and he got very cross.
He told me people could get diseases from the stuff that comes
out of dead animals. He told me I couldn't fish anymore unless
I promised never to do it again.

The night of the fire, I was in the Canal in the dark, sinking a dog, after pretending I was going over the Bridge to Con's
for his atlas. I ran up the bank to the drowned dog and got the
hazel stick I had ready. When I stuck the dog there was this loud
swoosh sound, but it was from our house that the sound came,
not from the dog.

When I looked back, our house was lit up on the inside
with a bright red light. And that's what it was, the constable said.
He said Daddy had been filling the lamp and that the flame
must have got into the can of paraffin oil. The constable said
people should not fill their lamps while keeping them lit to see
what they're doing.

I seldom hear the star shells exploding, just see their light
spreading silently across the heavens, lighting up the clouds and
the earth. Every time a star shell lights up the sky, I see the
flames roaring in our thatch.

By the time I ran back, the smoke was coming out through
the roof. When I put my thumb on the latch there was a huge
gust of wind, and the door was whipped out of my hand and the
wind went past me screeching.

Mister Hatchel came running from the far side of the
Canal, Con and Kitty behind him panting, and then Missus
Hatchel. I was sitting with my back against the elm, looking at
the dying fire. The roof had fallen in, and the two blackened
gables were standing there like two bad teeth screeching with

pain. I knew the cooking smell mixed in with the stink of the burning thatch was Mammy and Daddy and the girls roasting in the fire. But when Mister Hatchel asked me where Daddy and Mammy and the girls were, I didn't answer him. I didn't want to make it real.

Con Hatchel

There was this soldier sitting in the trench. The trench was a scar across the muddy countryside made by a giant with his giant plough. It was eight feet deep in the middle.

As far as I could see, the landscape was as torn up as the ground around a summer watering hole where the thirsty, fly-stung, too-hot cattle have ploughed up the earth with their sharp hooves, sinking deep into the black soil softened with streams of piss and heaps of loose shite.

But at the Somme, the earth had been torn up by ferocious shells and it was made liquid by the blood and guts of boy soldiers. Deep, water-filled holes bigger than front gardens had been made by repeated explosions that blew the blood and guts and bone and piss and shite and terror high into the sky in sudden plumes. The water in the holes had bits and pieces of men and horses floating on the surface along with bits and pieces of shattered timber that had once been wagons and gun carriages. Bits and pieces of horses and men were half-buried in the muck of the ruined farmland. Whole bodies lay on the surface too, their arms still in sleeves, fingers curled purplish in death; bits of heads covered with matted hair stirring in the moving air; lower jaws of men and horses, all teeth; bits of horses' legs with iron shoes still nailed onto the hooves; big balls of guts and strings of guts; bits of rifles; sitting on a tiny muck-hill, a pipe

with a curled shank, its bowl full of unlit tobacco; Tommy helmets battered and crushed and twisted, and others in perfect
shape with their chin straps clean; a soldier's decomposing face
staring at the blue of the summer sky with empty eye sockets, a
rat feasting on his lips; broken horse collars with the once-cush-
ioning golden straw spilling out through rips in the fabric;
chains that had once been draughts of wagons; pieces of shafts
with grease glistening on the iron fittings; ropes and ruined tacklings hopelessly entangled with pieces of men and horses; purple, bare buttocks with no legs, ribbons of grey tattered guts stuck
flatly to the rotting flesh like a bunch of forgotten and dead
flowers collapsed over the rim of a vase. There were a million
hoof-holes and the million hoof-holes were brimful of rainwa-
ter, and a million small lakes winked in the sloping sun.

The stink. The stink, especially when I stepped into a hidden carcass and punctured it; the horror of my foot sinking
through the rotting muck-camouflaged ribcage of man or animal; my terrible sleep haunted by graves through which I suddenly sank into the rotting corpses below. I knew that if I lived
to go home to Ballyrannel, if I lived to be a hundred, my body
and mind would never be free again. My memory was being
scarred forever and I knew it.

We saw this one live soldier in the trench, Matt and myself.
His arse was on a narrow ledge of earth about one foot above the
slushy muck in the bottom. All around him filthy corpses lay
across each other, on top of each other or by themselves, some
with their faces buried so deep in the muck they might have
been headless. Arms and legs were bent at such unnatural angles
that, had these young lads been alive, the pain would have
pushed them into insanity. It was only by their boots we could
tell German corpses from English ones, bundles of them so
entangled they could have been dolls thrown into an old box by
an uncaring nursery maid.

For twenty yards each way from where we were standing on

the edge of the trench, the bodies lay motionless, no breeze in the bottom of the trench to stir hair that had once been carefully combed to impress imagined girls. And all along the trenches, the noses of fat rats were twitching in gluttonous anticipation.

In the middle of all the corpses we saw this one soldier alive. He was bareheaded. The liquid muck of the trench came up to his knees, or else his legs had been shot off. He was so thickly covered in muck he could have been English or German or one of the black African soldiers. The whites of his eyes were very white and his lips were like two thin, dead worms. It was only the wet of his staring eyes that gave the soldier life, and it was only his sitting up that had drawn our attention to him in the first place. Not even the layer of drying muck could hide the horror-knotted flesh of his face.

Our boots were ankle deep in the wet earth on the edge of the trench. We were wet and mucky and cold in the crotch, and the skin was chafed at the tops of our thighs. Our uniforms and faces were blotched with patches and swipes of mud in varying stages of drying out. Matthias had the rolled-up stretcher on his right shoulder, his muck-caked right hand holding it in place. All across the landscape, pairs of stretcher-bearers like us were looking for live ones who had some chance of being put back together. They were all seeing what we were seeing, a countryside without trees or markers or grass, strewn thickly with the rotting bits of men and horses, like so much scattered animal dung coating the surface of a spring field in readiness for ploughing.

Standing in solitary clarity across the trench from us was a big-spoked and red-painted wheel, the iron rim and wooden felloes gone, leaving the spokes arrayed like the rays of a rising sun drawn by a small child. Beyond the wheel was the silhouette of an enormous gun still on its carriage, but with the barrel tilted down, the mouth buried in the muck, the whole thing looking like an enormous snipe with its beak sunk into the ground, sucking nourishment out of the fecund, black, shite-strewn, and hoof-churned earth surrounding a watering hole for large animals.

The sitting soldier in the trench was holding his hands out in front as if keeping a threatening dog at bay. We had been looking at him for several minutes when Matthias said, 'How can he keep his hands held out that way without them shaking? It's like he's carved, except for the eyes.'

The soldier did not look up when Matthias spoke, nor did his eyes move from whatever they were staring at.

After trudging and wading our way across this half-mile of deathland, of making the effort to hold on to our sanity in the face of the mishmash of guts and hardware and barbed wire and timbers and remains of animals and men, this one living soldier in the bottom of the trench gave us purpose. If we could save this one poor bastard, we would achieve something, pull something live out of all the rottenness.

Then Matthias said, 'He's mad. He doesn't even know he's alive.'

I lowered myself backwards down into the trench with each of us holding an end of the stretcher and Matt acting as anchor. Some rats scampered, but they were too inured to the presence of men to go very far, too fat to keep going.

I let go of the stretcher and leaped across the soup in the bottom of the trench. My feet landed on the mucky ledge beside the arse of the sitting soldier and I grasped his shoulder for balance. He was so still, he might as well have been a piece of wood.

Matthias said, 'Feel to see if his legs are gone.'

I knelt down, put one hand on the soldier's thigh, and felt with the other in the liquid at the bottom of the trench. 'He has them,' I said, and I shook the stuff off my hand, went through the motions of cleaning it by rubbing it on the back of the man's mucky coat.

'What do you think?' Matthias asked.

I moved my hand in front of the soldier's face. He didn't blink.

'He's gone in the head,' I said. With the edge of my knife, I scraped the muck off his front and looked for stains of blood. He may have had many more, but when I stopped counting, I had found thirteen bloody slits where bayonets had stuck him.

'Will he live?' Matt asked.

'He's lived this long,' I said. 'They must have missed the important stuff.'

For a long time Matthias stood on the edge of the trench looking down at the soldier trapped insanely in a horrific present from which he was unlikely ever to escape, for all eternity staving off thrusting bayonets aimed at his guts. 'I'd use Knifey, but it looks like he's all we've got,' Matt said. 'Maybe it's better to bring in one mad one than nothing at all.'

It took us a long time to get the frozen soldier out. In the end, we tied a rope around his chest and pulled him on his back across the trench bottom. When he landed dripping on the bank, he lay there for a moment before he toppled over, his arms still outstretched, his knees still bent. When we were tying him onto the stretcher we saw the deep cuts in his palms and fingers, so deep the bones were visible.

For a flying second, I remembered an incident on the Canal bank when we were small, the three of us hysterically excited as we got in each other's way trying to pull out a big pike that had taken the bait on one of our night lines. The bait had been a large frog we'd found beheaded by the mowing bar in one of the Lamberts' summer meadows.

When we went to our ends of the stretcher, Matt said, 'I'm only bringing him to make myself feel good. What do you think, Con?'

I looked at the poor bugger for a long time, tried to imagine what the rest of his life would be like. 'I'll do it, Matt,' I said, and I held out my hand for Knifey.

Matthias Wrenn

After slogging across the fields of Fucking Belgium for hours, the tiredness reminded me of the tiredness of walking with the big people when we were small, their steps three times longer than ours.

The first hour of those Sunday morning jaunts were full of activity—Con and Kitty and myself trotting on ahead like ten-week-old pups, sticking our noses into everything that was new; smelling flowers and weeds and brushing up against stinging nettles; climbing gates to imitate the sounds of goats or a thick-headed bull with a brass ring in his nose; following old tracks in the long grass, afraid we might come upon a sleeping rabbit; climbing down the steep sides of ditches and disappearing into the culverts under the road—shouting to make echoes; hunting for dock leaves among the tall field daisies and cow parsnips to rub on the scalding white nettle blisters.

Always running, always on the move, we tired ourselves out long before the men had reached their halfway point. And then like whining, tired pups we badgered the men to carry us, and cried when they wouldn't. We hung out of the corners of their coats and knew that home was moving farther away with every hopeless step taken.

Unless it was pouring, Daddy and Mister Hatchel never missed a Sunday walk. That was in the years before the fire in our house when I was sinking a dog.

Two by two, twenty of us had been slogging across Belgian fields since four o'clock. It had been dark when the sergeant wakened us. He was a small man off a farm near Scunthorpe. 'Call me Wilkie, lads. I'm no better at milking a cow than the rest of you,' he told us one time. Half an hour later we were on the move, the sun below the horizon shining pink on the undersides of the high clouds that could have been skeins of wool rolled up by a crowd of old women during the night and laid out snugly against each other across the sky.

'A red sky in the morn ...' someone muttered, and let the rest of us finish it in our own heads.

Our path through the fields ran more or less parallel to a road. The land was better than the fields around Ballyrannel, with none of the symptoms of the bad soil we had at home— daisies, nettles, thistles, rushes, docks, buttercups, ragwort. But an hour after sunrise there was some talk, complaining mainly, about the conditions underfoot. Because of all the war traffic and the recent rain it was as hard to walk across these Belgian fields as it was to walk across freshly ploughed Irish fields after a night's rain. With every step forward we slipped back. With every step taken we lifted our mud-caked, waterlogged boots out of three inches of muck, and the muck—the sticky Belgian muck—had worked its way up along the inside of our boots and leggings. It had crept along the cloth of our uniforms until we could hear and feel the wetness between our legs. Once, for a few minutes, the under-footing lost its looseness, its wetness, and when we looked up we found ourselves on a village street. But the village was only scattered stones now, pieces of roofs and windows the only things to show that houses had once been here. No people at all, no chickens, not even a sniffing dog.

Three or four or five or six times before we stopped to eat, it had rained, as the red sky had warned us. Mindlessly we slogged on, the early morning talk long gone into silence, only the sergeant speaking every half hour, telling those of us with the rolled-up stretchers it was time to pass them over to our part-ners. It would have been less painful if we hadn't moved the stretchers at all, left the wooden handles sitting in the fleshy groove on our shoulders.

We were bareheaded, our tin hats strapped on to our packs. It was July 1917.

Out of step, slightly bent forward to ease our loaded backs, we slogged on with eyes bent to the lifting heels of the man in front. The rest of the world had gone away.

In that peculiar hypnotized state that exists between wake-fulness and sleep we moved ever closer to Wipers. For a while, I had kept bits and pieces of Ballyrannel and the Canal in my mind, but they too flickered out. The red fire that burned Daddy and Mammy and the babies had flared for a moment before I got rid of it. I had never gone beyond the redness of the fire to what was happening to the four of them inside the heat of the fire. Hours ago I had brought Kitty into my mind, but even she could not keep me company. I lay down beside her in Ali Baba's Cave on the Canal bank, put my hand on her chest, then lay on top of her, her legs around me, our mouths joined, but I could not hold on to her.

The tiredness wasn't just in our bodies, it had seeped into our heads, and my brain was satisfied with the boots of the walking man ahead of me. If I raised my head and looked to the left or right, I knew I would have seen a moving landscape of brown uniforms split in the middle by a dark line of wagons and guns and horses; tens of thousands of men walking to Wipers, thousands of horses pulling thousands of wheeled wag-ons and guns and kitchens and hospitals along the road to Wipers; in the carts were boxes of bullets, cases of shells, bags of bandages, gallons of morphine, stacks of surgical saws, bundles of grave-digging shovels.

When we'd stopped to eat and rest hours ago, Con had looked at the moving landscape and said, 'The migration of the animals across the Serengeti plain must look like this.' More than anyone else in our platoon of stretcher-bearers, Con was the one who'd read enough to be able to compare one thing with another. The one and only consolation we had since our ship to India turned around at the far end of the Mediterranean was that Con and I had managed to stay together. The Irish Twins we were called in this particular group of stretcher-bearers. Wilkie, our sergeant, was called Milky when he wasn't being our officer.

When Con, in his offhand way, mentioned something exotic, one of the lads would say, 'Come on, Twinny, tell us about it!' And that's how it happened that on the way to Wipers, Con told us about Tanganyika and Kilimanjaro, and the lakes nearly as big as Ireland. And he told us about the herds of animals moving to 'fresh fields and pastures new'; the great migration of elephants, buffaloes, giraffes, antelopes, wildebeests; the tigers and lions and jackals and hyenas and leopards that kept pace with the herds; the vultures that soared so high a person mightn't see them; the blazing sun every day of the year except when rains as heavy as the ones at Noah's deluge came—and we all sitting on our wet, cold arses in a circle in a field of last year's unharvested turnips in Fucking Belgium.

'And here we are,' Con ended up, 'all moving north to Wipers like the animals migrating from the Serengeti, all looking for new food.'

'I wish we could find some new food besides this shite,' one of the lads said, and he spooned another spoonful of the shite into his mouth.

'There's turnips buried in these fields from all the lads walking them down into the muck,' the sergeant said.

'Turnips are for cows.'

'Turnips are sweet and juicy,' the sergeant said, 'especially if they've had a touch of frost like these from being out all winter.' He pulled a bayonet out of one of the lads' gear and poked around until he felt a sunken turnip. He used the toe of his boot to pry out the prize. It was black, covered in muck. Milky stuck the bay-onet into the ground beside the turnip, opened the buttons in the front of his trousers, and fished out his watering pipe. He sprayed the turnip, moved it around with the tip of his boot until the maroon and pale yellow skin was washed clean. There was steam. After stuffing his pipe back into his trousers, the sergeant–farmer dried the turnip by swiping at it with the flap of his coat. Then he hacked at the outer skin with the bayonet until he was left with a cube of yellow turnip with a few smears of mud on it.

'Peggy's Leg, lads,' he said, in his peculiar accent, as he cut the turnip into slices and then into thick strips. When he walked around distributing the pieces he reminded me of the old, demented nun in the convent playground who distributed tiny squares of jammed bread off a white enamel tray to young children with watering mouths. The crunchy, juicy turnip was so good that, before we moved off, each of us had a turnip in his pack. Some of us had two. All the turnips had been washed.

'We'll be mooing before we get to Wipers,' one of the lads said, as we set off again, and we lowed like cows.

Very soon, we were back into our mindless trudging, depend-ing on Wilkie to keep us in our place in the great migration. For hours, the only voice was the one telling us to hand over the stretchers.

And then we heard a bell ringing.

After all the slurping and sucking sounds of the day, the peal of the bell was the song of a blackbird in an apple tree in October. We all stopped walking at once, all looked up, and there, not a quarter of a mile away, was a village still standing, the spire of a church pointing up into the sky, a desire in stone to be united with a divinity.

The bell sang out a loud and joyous bong-bong, bong-bong, the kind of bell you'd imagine ringing for a wedding.

'Maybe they're glad to see us.'

'Maybe they're glad we're all moving through, not stopping

to eat them out of house and home and shite in their ditches.'

'Maybe they think we're on our way to kick the shite out of Gerry.'

'Maybe we'd better get a move on,' Wilkie said, 'before the lads in front get away and the ones behind run over us.'

But the bell had raised our spirits.

We pounded the muck off our feet when we stepped onto the hard village road. We fell in step without being told, straightened up and ran our fingers through our hair. Half-smoked Woodbines were nicked between thumb and forefinger and slipped into breast pockets. We were about to go on parade. We would march through that village with our heads in the air, have the local people cheer us on—we who had come from the ends of the earth to save them.

We passed through the gable ends of two houses and were suddenly in a small square. The group of soldiers ahead of us had stopped on the street that led out of the square on the far side. They were looking back, their faces as grim as if they were looking into the coffin of a dead brother.

A tall man was pushing a wheelbarrow around the square followed by a scraggly line of noisy children. People on the footpaths pointed at the wheelbarrow and laughed, but it was mirthless laughter, forced laughter, like the squawking of chickens after a feed of dry barley.

A German soldier was sitting in the wheelbarrow. He was fat under his great coat; a spiked helmet was on his head and both arms were up in the air as if he were leading a crowd in a roar of victory. His jaw was hanging open.

Little children ran up and poked the soldier in the belly, shrieked, and fled. It was only when a little girl with a long pigtail ran up and slashed the soldier across the face with a stick that we realized the German was dead. The nose was beginning to disintegrate and lose its place on the face.

We stood still and stared. The tall man jerked the handles

of his wheelbarrow until the head of the dead body nodded and the propped arms moved up and down. The adults on the footpaths cackled their soulless laugh, pointed and shouted sounds that were the sounds of hate in any language. Like hungry chickens dashing in to steal flecks of food from starving dogs, the children scurried up to the barrow and desecrated the corpse with their sticks. The church bell had lost its joyful tones.

Suddenly there was a scream in my ear like the scream of a horse in flames, and Sergeant Wilkie grabbed my stretcher and ran across the square. Before he reached the wheelbarrow, the folded stretcher was already swinging through a wide arc like a heavy and ancient battle sword, and at precisely the right moment, the other end of the oak handles crashed into the chest of the man pushing the wheelbarrow. The pusher fell on his back and as the legs of the barrow touched the ground, the sergeant grabbed the handles and saved its occupant from tumbling out.

As he stepped away from the barrow, Milky stumbled over the fallen barrow-pusher. When he recovered, we were not looking at a Yorkshire farm boy anymore. He whirled around in a circle, taking in all the people in the square and, when he spoke to them, he was screaming.

'You fucking savages! You demented fucking savages! You stupid, stupid people. Look at your children, for Christ's sake.' And tears sprung out of Milky's face like drops of hard rain. He blew his nose into his hand and wiped it on the back of his trousers.

When Wilkie had run across the square, the rest of us had followed. We now stood close beside him as he shouted, 'Someone here speaks English?' When there was no answer he roared, 'Who speaks English? Who's the schoolmaster?'

A woman wearing a white kerchief pointed to the tall man lying at the sergeant's feet. 'The master,' she said.

Milky, who had been wrestling farm animals to the ground since he was a child, pulled the master to his feet, reached up, and slapped him viciously. 'You stupid fucker,' he screamed into the man's face. He shook the tall teacher back and forth—Milky the terrier, schoolmaster the rat. 'You tell these fucking ghouls they're to bring this soldier to your parish graveyard and dig a grave for him.'

The master was too stunned to do or say anything. Milky pulled the man's face down to the level of his own face and screamed the spitty words at him, 'Tell them to do it now!' Milky pushed the master away and pulled out his revolver. He shot a bullet into the stone wall above the heads of the people. A twitch ran through the crowd.

The schoolmaster spoke to the villagers. When he was finished, the sergeant spoke to him again. 'Tell them our platoon will oversee the burial, and tell them whoever doesn't attend the funeral will be shot.'

While the man spoke, the sergeant undid Con's great coat from his pack and covered the corpse in the wheelbarrow. With the schoolmaster and the wheelbarrow leading the way, our platoon of stretcher-bearers funnelled the people into a procession. As we made our way over to the graveyard surrounding the church, the only sound was the scraping of feet on the cobbled square. The bell started ringing again, and now it had the plaintive tones of the dead bell in Ballyrannel telling the countryside that someone has died.

Before the wheelbarrow passed through the rusting wrought-iron churchyard gate, the people of the village had begun to clutch at their forgotten humanity, had cast quick glances around as if they were all suddenly naked and ashamed. By the time Sergeant Wilkie had picked out a spot for the grave, sobbing could be heard, sounds like the after-bursts that shake a child's body at the end of a long, sad cry.

Sergeant Wilkie's temper had changed too. He pulled his entrencher out of his pack and marked out the edge of the grave in the grass. Then he began to dig, but he had only dug a few sods when one of the village men touched him on the shoulder. Then more men came over to us and borrowed our short-handled, narrow-headed shovels. The fresh earth began to pile up quickly near the wheelbarrow. When the hole was five feet deep, the villagers moved forward and surrounded the deepening grave. Some of the women near the front knelt and men nearby leaned on each other and went down on one knee, just like the ones at the back of the church on Sunday mornings in Ballyrannell.

When the last digger was pulled out of the grave, the schoolmaster uncovered the dead German. More men stepped forward, two overcoats were produced, and the corpse was laid on them. With two men on each side holding a sleeve, the body was manoeuvred over the grave. As they lowered the dead man, the pallbearers sank down with their burden, sank down until their bellies were on the grass, their holding hands stretched down into the grave as far as they could go. The corpse came to a gentle rest on the bottom of the grave. Two more overcoats were passed forward and spread over the body to protect it from the first shovels of cold earth.

The grave was filled in and when the mound had been patted into shape, two of the entrenching tools were placed across each other on top of the mound, just like they were in Ballyrannel at the end of a funeral. But in Ballyrannel the crossed shovel-handles were a sign for the priest to begin the prayers for the dead. Maybe there was no priest in the cemetery that day, or maybe he was too ashamed to step forward.

After a few minutes, Sergeant Wilkie realized that the villagers were looking at him, waiting for him to say something. He stood there blushing and rubbing his hand across his mouth. Our sergeant's outrage had run its course, and the Wilkie we knew was back. But he took a small step closer to the grave.

'May God have mercy on the soul of this man,' he said. With hands folded and head bent, Milky stood there in the silence that had replaced the tolls of the dead bell. Finally, he stirred himself, looked at the village people, and gently said, 'There's times in life when we all need someone to tell us we have gone mad. Everything's all right now,' he said. He looked at the schoolmaster, and the schoolmaster looked at Milky, as if waiting for him to say more.

'That's all,' Milky said. The schoolmaster spoke the sentence to the people in their language, and then, to the sergeant's surprise and embarrassment, the teacher leaned over and kissed him on both cheeks.

We were on our way trudging across wet fields again, maybe a mile or two beyond the village, when Con asked, 'Sergeant, who's going to tell us when we've gone mad?'

'I know I'm insane already,' Milky said. He brought us to a halt when he himself stopped. 'Who in his right mind would do what we're doing, walking to Wipers in Fucking Belgium where fifty thousand men have already disappeared into the muck there. Fifty thousand men gone without a trace, part of the muck, and here we are making our way there to take their places in another big push. I don't know about you, lads, but I know I'm so far removed from the Wilkie who lived in Scunthorpe that I'm not normal anymore.'

Four weeks later, between Wipers and Passchendaele, Milky was pointing Con and myself to a shell hole where he'd seen a wounded man. I heard a shell coming, but terror turned me into a stick. Like many shells, this one didn't explode, but it struck Sergeant Wilkie, and before he fell, I saw the ground behind him through the hole in his chest.

Missus Hodgkins

From the day Lionel and Sarah landed in France, I listened for Paulie Bolger in the pebbles when he stepped through the wicket gate with the letters in his hand.

The longer Sarah and Lionel survived in the War, the more nervous I became. I worried that the longer they survived the more likely they were to get killed. Kitty saw things the other way around—the longer Con and Matthias stayed alive, the better was their chance of coming home. Neither line of reasoning made much sense, except that mine made me fearful and Kitty's made her hopeful. My beloved husband, David, went around like a man holding his breath but pretending not to. The tension of having two children in a war was visibly wearing him down, was wearing me down too.

We didn't speak about our fear but each of us read it in the behaviour of the other: David would disappear for hours across the fields on his horse; he knew I no longer waited for Paulie Bolger's steps in the stones, that instead I had taken to waiting outside the wicket gate or even walking in the rain bareheaded and without a coat, along the avenue to meet him.

On the morning of the third Monday in September in 1916, I opened the door and I didn't even see Paulie Bolger in the pebbles—I only saw the letter in his hand. And then, as if the lights had gone out for a moment, Paulie was on the top step holding the letter out to me. I swatted at it the way I'd swat at an attacking wasp. A feeling of weakness gushed over me: sweat itched its way out all over my body and I thought I would vomit. I swayed over against the door jamb and heard Paulie calling Kitty's name, and I wondered why he was doing that, calling Kitty. Then my eyes and my mind took in the letter again, and I leaned over to vomit, but nothing came, just a jagged pain in my diaphragm and a cavernous-sounding belch. Paulie touched my arm and at the same moment I felt Kitty's hands on me.

My brain was overloaded with the knowledge that one of my children was dead and I was in the position of having to choose which one it was. Who did I hope was not in the envelope? I wanted to bang my head against the stone wall, wanted to bang myself into unconsciousness before I could begin to make a choice. And that's what I started to do, bang my head against the door jamb until Kitty wrestled me out onto the steps outside the door. She pushed me against the wrought-iron railing at the side of the steps and snatched the letter out of Paulie's hand. As she ripped open the envelope, I vomited down into the flower bed.

'Sarah's in a hospital,' Kitty said quickly. 'She's expected to survive.'

With a firm grip on the top rail, I lowered myself down because I knew my knees were about to give out. I ended up kneeling and even though prayer was very far from my mind, my mouth said, 'Thank God. Thank God she's alive. Thank God.' Water was running down my face but I wasn't crying; my body was simply releasing built-up terror, was letting it escape any way it could. I wet myself.

Kitty was kneeling in front of me on the top step, holding my shoulders. My water was spreading across the concrete toward her knees. She told Paulie to go to the farmyard to look for David, and the moment the postman was gone, she said, 'Quick, Missus Hodgkins, before the men get back, get into the kitchen and sit on a chair so they won't see your dress.'

The small things that concern us when we're in the middle of a crisis.

Paulie and David came rushing through the back door. Kitty and I were at the kitchen table, Kitty with her arm around my shoulders. She gave the letter to David, and the way he read it he was like a turkey gobbling down food, totally self-absorbed. David collapsed onto a chair and Kitty led the postman out through the back door. 'I didn't want him to see the wet step and talk about it,' she told me later.

'Oh, David,' I said, 'I thought I was going to die. I wanted to die. I wanted to be dead before I knew who it was. Before Kitty opened the letter I was still trying to choose between them, who I wanted it to be, who I didn't want it to be. Wasn't that terrible? Oh, David. Oh, God. I hate myself for having thought that way. How I hate God sometimes, the trials he throws at us!'

'There is no God,' David said. He moved the hand that was still holding the letter. 'How could there be a God this stupid?' He put his forehead on his arms on the table and wept for Sarah or for himself or for me or for Lionel or whoever it is we weep for when we are knocked off our feet by a wave of the world's sadness. Eventually he came around the table and knelt on the floor beside me, put his arms around me.

'I wet myself,' I said, but he didn't hear me.

'At least she's alive,' he said. 'We'll have to find out where she is as quick as we can.'

Trying to get information from an army in the middle of a war is difficult, and only for Uncle David's connections from the Boer War we would have waited a long time to find out that Sarah was in a hospital called Pine Haven near Edinburgh. Pine Haven had only recently become a hospital when the army requisitioned the large building for the treatment of shell-shocked soldiers. In plain English, Pine Haven was an asylum for people who'd gone mad in the War.

If Enderly ever had a stiff upper lip, it collapsed with the madness of Sarah.

Every day I wrote to Sarah begging her to respond to my letters. Every day I waited for an answer; every day I trembled in fear that another letter would come to tell us Lionel had been killed.

Sometimes it takes an outsider to take you by the hand and point you in the right direction. It was Kitty who told us what to do. She would move into Enderly, take care of the place and the men, while David and I went to Scotland to see Sarah.

'But what will happen if a letter comes about Lionel while we're away?' I asked.

'At this very minute,' Kitty said, 'Lionel is all right. Sarah isn't. You can't sit around not taking care of Sarah because you're afraid something might happen to Lionel. As well as that, the two of you will be taking care of yourselves by taking care of Sarah.'

Kitty the wise! It was only three years since she landed on our top step, cow dung on her shins, her head like a burr that's scraped against the fur of a mangy dog.

Kitty brought us to Ballyrannel's station in the pony and trap. Then it was Marbra, Dublin, Belfast, Clydebank and Edinburgh. I held on to David's arm all the way, hugged it to myself. Yet it was a lonely journey for the two of us, the first time in our marriage that David and I were unable to support each other with words. There was no talk between us at all, no pointing out of curiosities, no comments about fellow passengers. There was only the blind staring at the speeding countryside and the listening to the unending clacking of the wheels that unconsciously sneaked into the brain and became unwanted words: *Sarah mad Sarah mad Sarah mad. Lionel lost Lionel lost Lionel lost.* There was nothing I could think of to say to David, not one thing. It was as if language had become nothing but noise.

A horse-taxi took us to the hotel in Edinburgh at midnight. As I drifted off to sleep with my front to David's back and my arm around him, I imagined our Sarah close by, five miles away, in a mental hospital. Our beautiful Sarah was mad. I cried silently.

As we neared Pine Haven the next morning, I felt the same as I would have felt if I'd been approaching a morgue to identify the body of my dead child. My desire to get to the hospital to see Sarah was opposed by my dread of what I would find. And when the hospital loomed into sight a fist of cold steel squeezed my insides. The dreary, three-storied building might have been beautiful once in its newness, but after years of sooty wind and rain it was now an ugly wart. Its pillars, and the balustrades of its stone balconies, were like the short legs of fat women. Bay windows, piled three high on top of each other, were divided into angular pieces by the stained, cut stone. A forest of sooted chimneys sprouted like black weeds from the grey roof slates. Maybe my impression of the place was coloured by my frame of mind, but this was the least mind-lifting, least encouraging place in the world.

The welcome we received matched the coldness of the building. From the moment Nurse McMurray opened the front door, it was obvious that we were interfering, that we were gravel in the gears of the hospital. We argued our way into a parlour. On straight-backed, hard chairs we waited for hours until David sallied forth and fought his way into a doctor's office.

Interference from families set the patients back, Dr Robertson told us. Their progress was halted rather than helped by visits from the outside.

'But our Sarah,' I asked, 'how is she? How bad is she?'

'Miss Hodgkins, at the moment, refuses to sit down with a staff member,' the doctor said. 'She does not speak to anyone.'

'What happened to her?' David asked quietly.

'She was in a fire. She saw some people being burned to death.'

'Can we see her?'

'I already told—' Dr Robertson's lined face was the face of a man who was overworked, who needed a good night's sleep.

'I mean can we see her, look at her from a distance?'

'It would be too risky. If she knew you were looking at her, it would upset her too much.'

'For Christ's sake, man,' David blurted out and I put my hand on his leg. 'Let the woman see her own daughter, even from a distance. Just let the mother see the child. Surely that much can be arranged. We've come a long way—'

'You should have written first and saved yourself the—'

'You're a heartless man,' David said in a strong voice. 'You made the rules here. Surely you can bend them and let a woman look on her own child.'

He let us see Sarah. For three hours we sat concealed behind some aucuba bushes on the far side of the driveway. The front door opened and closed many times before I buried my fingers in David's arm. There she was, dressed as they told us she would be. The most obvious thing about her was the veil, and the veil was no more revealing than the chador of a Moslem woman. It could have been anyone, even a nurse sent out to satisfy us and get us off the grounds. But it was Sarah's walk; it was her body. Her hands showed no signs of burns or injury. Her legs below her calf-length skirt were not marked. And oh, God, I wanted so badly to run to her.

David stood up as if to move out of the bushes, but at that same moment a large man walked into the driveway with his arms folded across his chest. He was a figure of threat. When I stood, David turned and buried his face in my shoulder. He shuddered like a horse with the flu. He sobbed.

Slowly, Sarah walked the length of Pine Haven hospital twice, and then she went in. With hands as fluttery as the tail of a courting wagtail, she must have touched her veil a hundred times.

Con Hatchel

The Machine Shed at Enderly was Charlie Coffey's kingdom. All the hand tools of farming hung on the walls, everything in a state of readiness, no tool put away until it was cleaned, tightened, sharpened, and rubbed with an oily rag that had its own hanging nail. The machines of farming had their own special space on the floor, all accessible from narrow walkways between them, all as ready as the hand tools.

On wet days during the winter, while overseeing the repairing and making of lesser equipment, Charlie Coffey worked on the McCormick reaper with Matt as his apprentice. They took the machine apart one small section at a time. Charlie knew every cotter pin and cogwheel, knew the smoothness of every canvas rivet. He showed Matt the path of the binding twine through all its loops and holes and eyes. He examined each link of the heavy driving chain. He cleaned and greased and oiled.

Charlie was one of those lads who could have taken a rifle apart in the rainy dark in a mucky trench, cleaned it, and put it back together again. So fast could he disassemble and reassemble the three mechanisms that wrapped and knotted and cut the twine that bound the sheaves, that not three minutes were lost in a summer of scarce sunshine.

Every year, when Arthur J.'s Gold hung heavy in the barley ears, the Cyrus McCormick was wheeled out of the Machine Shed like a purebred stallion, brought prancing out for inspection by top-hatted punters. Two of Charlie's men pulled at the end of the beam, and two pushed from behind. Mister and Missus Hodgkins always attended this opening of the harvest season.

Charlie's pride in the machine showed in the creases in his face, in the sparkle of his eyes. It was easy to see, too, that the Hodgkins were proud of their ownership of this most up-to-date piece of agricultural machinery. And it was plain that all Charlie's men, by the way they neatened themselves up for the occasion, were privileged to be associated with such a modern farm.

There was an air of expectation in the yard when the reaper made its appearance, a feeling that all the planning and toiling and weather-watching since springtime were about to richly yield up the rewards. The knowledge of the upstanding, wind-swayed twenty-five acres of golden barley had everyone in smiles.

The eight wooden beaters, hanging above the front of the reaper like the sails of a windmill, glowed in their fresh coat of red paint. Every metal part had been burnished with the oil cloth and the canvases were stretched taut. The thirty-two triangular blades of the knife shone sharply in their toothed metal sheath, honed to mow through ripe straw with the ease of a hot knife slipping through butter.

Like a priest chanting in a cloud of incense smoke, Mister Hodgkins spoke in the wafting aroma of new paint, fresh oil and new goose grease. 'God bless the harvest,' he said, and Charlie Coffey and his men answered, 'Aye, Mister Hodgkins. God bless the harvest.'

'And God keep the reapers safe,' Missus Hodgkins added.

'And you too, Missus,' the men muttered, and they meant it.

'And God bless Matthias and Con on their upcoming adventure,' Mister Hodgkins said.

The blessing of men and machine was a pleasant little ceremony that had developed over the years in the shadow of the Machine Shed, Catholics and Protestants praying together in a farmyard when they weren't allowed to pray together in a church, the unspoken defiance uniting the participants.

It was our last year at Enderly, and Poor Meg played her part in the little drama by bringing out a plate of hot scones soaked in melted butter and strewn with strawberry jam. She was sick then, limping from the pain, dying already I suppose. Missus Hodgkins, to spare Poor Meg the extra walking, sent Matthias and myself into the kitchen for the jug of sweet tea and the mugs. Missus Hodgkins was good like that, taking care of the people who worked for Enderly. 'And make sure you bring a mug for Meg, Con. Nine altogether.'

It was early August of 1913. The old people said they had never seen such wonderful crops. All year the weather had magically struck a balance between light rain and hot sunshine. The black, fertile earth of Enderly had responded with the fecundity of a magician's well-stocked hat.

'It's not magic,' Missus Hodgkins said to me one day down in the gardens. 'It's a mistake, Con, when the weather is this good. Irish weather is always bad because we wrongly think it should be better. The weather is normal in this country when it's bad at all the wrong times. This amount of sun is unnatural. People will get sick.'

The people in Spain and Arizona don't get sick from the sun, I thought, but I would never have contradicted Missus Hodgkins. All the people in Ireland, who knew about the sun in Spain and Arizona, were always thinking of those faraway lands when it was raining in Ireland, trying to imagine the unimaginable.

On the day after the rolling out of the reaper in 1913, I was harvesting the peas in the vegetable garden, dropping the fat pods into the basket that Danny Gowan had woven from sally scollops during the winter. Since early morning, the pleasant, droning clatter of the reaper had been part of the live murmur of that high summer's day. The hum of the insects and the music of the birds folded over the silence whenever the distant reaper was stopped for the changing of knives or horses or men or the replacing of the roll of twine. And except for those brief stoppages, the reaper was kept moving all day. The harvesting of the ten barley acres in the High Field would be finished in twelve hours if God was willing and if everything went right. And although God didn't give a damn one way or the other, the reaper did not break down because Charlie Coffey had made sure it wouldn't.

In the afternoon, it was Frank Shanahan who was driving the three horses, hupping and tongue-clicking, and wrist-flicking the encouraging reins onto the flanks of the outside animals. In the high seat of the reaper, he sat across from the spinning beaters that pushed the cut barley onto the first canvas. Mile after mile, Charlie Coffey walked behind the reaper, his eyes and ears on the bits and pieces of spinning and shuttling and clacking metal involved in the tracking, the packing, the making, the tying and the kicking out of the sheaves. He also gave unnecessary instructions to Frank Shanahan on the shifting of the various levers and, like any man receiving directions he had neither asked for nor needed, Frank Shanahan was annoyed at Charlie's omniscient interferences.

Since Shanahan had taken over the reins, Mike Gallinagh had been busy in the shade of the elm near the gate, bent over a portable metal bench, hand-sharpening the blades of the spare knives with a red-handled whetstone. Nothing would slow down the cutting of the barley, neither tired horses, tired men, nor blunt blades.

'Keep the blades sharp, lads,' was one of Charlie Coffey's unnecessary cants, and he applied it to many things besides the reaper's knives. His uncombed and unwashed and pelt-clad ancestor of five thousand years ago probably canted the same thing to his men before they ran against the invaders: 'Keep the blades sharp, lads.'

Poor Meg gave Matt and me the legs of a rabbit for supper that first evening of the reaping, told us there was only enough meat for two people, and that we wouldn't be having it only the other men were still in the fields. But we knew Poor Meg was only using words to keep away her sadness for me and Matt leaving for the army in a few days. She knew and we knew that Poor Meg would be long dead before we would get home again. So I tried to distract her by asking her to tell the Enderly stories that she had seen unfolding since she was fourteen. She remembered and talked but the sadness did not go away, stayed there looking in over our shoulders. And when she finished, we told her what a good cook she was, how her new spuds, her boiled cabbage chopped fine and fried in butter, her rabbit and gravy was a feast fit for a king.

When we stood to leave, Poor Meg painfully pushed herself up. She supported herself against the back of the chair and she could no longer keep the pain of our separation at bay. 'Sure, lads,' she said, 'why do you have to leave us at all?' and she could barely finish the sentence. She was crying but trying to control the tears at the same time by compressing her lips.

Like two awkward bullocks, we stood there gawking across the table, knowing what to do but too shy to do it. It was Matt who finally stepped around to her side to comfort her, to put his arm around her shoulder and, in the end, to pull her into himself to let her cry on his chest. I stood there looking, pushing down my own sadness and tears until they became an aching pain in the back of my throat. It was Missus Hodgkins passing through the kitchen who freed the three of us from the paralysing emotion. She took charge of Poor Meg and, using her eyebrows, sent the two of us on our way.

Matt took off at a near gallop because he had to be near Kitty. I had been keeping out of their way for several months now, so I took the long way home. I passed the fifteen-acred Back Batens where Jim Hanley and Danny Gowan had spent their third day cutting the headland with scythes, clearing a track for the first passage of the horses and the reaper in the morning.

The two men were sharpening their scythes. They spotted me looking in over the hedge and acknowledged me with uplifted whetstones. Then, with the precision of two altar boys reciting the Latin responses at Mass, they called, 'Night, Shakespeare,' because everyone on the farm knew Mister Hodgkins was teaching me from books—continuing my education, as Missus Hodgkins said.

If the weather had been threatening at all, Danny and Jim and Matthias and myself and anyone else from the town who could have been hired, even Mister Hodgkins, would have spent the day stooking the sheaves as they were kicked out of the reaper in the High Field. But in the firm belief that the summer weather was going to last, the sheaves were left where they fell, would be taken care of when all the headlands were cut.

Half a mile farther along the dusty lane I stopped at the gate of the High Field. The last few feet of the final swath of barley were disappearing between the two rolling canvases that fed the straw to the rear of the reaper. Charlie Coffey stuck his hand into the guts of the reaper and sprung the binding mechanism because the last sheaf was too light to do it on its own. The half-sheaf fell at Charlie's feet, and from where I was standing, I thought I heard the men and the horses and the machine and the field itself sighing. Frank Shanahan disengaged all the gears and there was silence except for the whoosh of the wide, metal driving wheel through the stiff straw stubbles.

With my chin on my arms on the top bar of the wooden gate, I watched as the reaper was driven between the rows of fallen sheaves to the place where everything had begun that morning. The silent men, following a system developed over long years of working together, helped each other with the fitting of the transporting wheels, the winding up of the driving wheel, the lowering of the beaters, the shifting of the beam and horses to the new pulling position, the folding of the iron legs of the portable sharpening bench and the loading of the extra mowing knives in their long, thin wooden sheaths.

When they were ready to leave, I swung the field gate open. The tired horses had slowed after the sustained effort. Stained with sweat, they plodded home to the farmyard, Charlie Coffey walking beside the sagging heads, his hand in the ring of the winkers of the horse beside him. A few dangling straws hung upside-down from the back of the reaper. Too weary to talk, Frank Shanahan and Mike Gallinagh plodded along the dusty lane behind the clanking, miraculous collection of interconnected parts.

In no hurry to get home, I went out into the High Field and closed the gate behind me. Matthias and Kitty would soon be setting out for Ali Baba's Cave down at the Canal. For weeks now, I had been wondering how long it would be before Mammy realized what was happening, what she would say when she did realize. Even though I sometimes found myself wondering how far they were going with each other, my imagination didn't allow me to dwell on the matter because one of them was my sister and the other might as well have been my brother.

I strolled through the stubbles, listening to that peculiar sound of stiff straw against leather boots. At the huge elm, where Mike Gallinagh had been working in the shade, I stepped up onto the bank and sat down at the butt of the tree, sat in the same indent in the grass that Mike's arse had made when he was eating his lunch. I started to reach for *Twelfth Night* in my coat pocket, but when my eyes swept down across the ten acres of reaped barley, my mind slipped off the question of music being the food of love.

The thousands of sheaves scattered evenly over the ten acres of the High Field had an effect on me that I can only describe as sphincter-tightening. There were so many sheaves, as if the earth had been ridiculously wasteful in her generosity. In close lines they lay on the ground as far as I could see, the tight twine around the middles giving them the strange appearance of sleeping men who have cinched their belts too tightly. In the terrible silence that had taken over from the reaper and the birds and the insects, the sheaves lay there in the stubbles.

The same terrible silence descended on the Somme battlefield four years later. I was afraid to poke my head up. After a week of non-stop heavy guns, of screaming, screeching shells, I could see the silence in the bright sky like huge spinning Catherine wheels, their irregular speeding tails colliding against each other. Even the German machine guns had stopped their deathly twicking, and everyone in the stretcher corps waiting in the trenches knew something terrible had happened. Thousands of men had been going over the top since seven o'clock, and now at eleven, into the dreadful spinning Catherine wheels I poked my head above the rim of the trench.

It was the first day of July in 1916, and the soldiers lay there as far as I could see, most of them motionless. Of course, there were thousands more than I had seen in the High Field, and they were not as neatly laid out in straight lines. These sheaves near the banks of the Somme were carelessly scattered and there were no stubbles. The earth beneath these sheaves was torn up, as if a herd of giant, truffle-hunting pigs, ten million strong, had nosed its way across the landscape. Soldiers were hanging on the barbed wire barriers like bedsheets tangled on a clothes-line after a storm, and there were piles of bodies where once there had been gaps in the mare's nest of wire. The advancing English soldiers had tried to pass through those openings. The German soldiers had kept the same passageways in the sights of their machine guns, guns that could shoot out six hundred bullets every minute. Do your sums, my children.

'What's wrong, Canalman?' a voice whispered from the floor of the trench. But I couldn't answer. I climbed farther up the ladder and stepped out onto the rim of the trench.

'Get down, you fool.'

But there was no way I could get down, because what I was

seeing was pulling me up. I stepped away from the rim of our trench and stood there in the sights of every sniper and machine gunner in the German trenches. I wasn't afraid. It wouldn't have mattered if I'd been torn apart by a shower of bullets. At that moment, my own life was nothing; I was valueless.

After the terrible noise of the last seven days of non-stop shelling from the thousands of big guns, followed by four hours of the shouting and whistle-blowing and machine-gun-twickings and rifle fire, I stood looking across this field of death shimmering beneath the spinning wheels of white silence in the sky. And as I stood there, two hundred yards away a German soldier climbed out of his trench. He stood on the parapet and took off his helmet like a man takes off his hat when he's faced with a terrible sight, who takes off his hat because he has to do something in the face of the terrible thing he is seeing.

'What's happening, Canalman?' someone whispered from below.

'Come up and see,' I said, without turning around. More German soldiers came up their trench ladders and stepped out onto the edge of no-man's-land. None of them had guns. Some of our lads came up and stood beside me, and I knew they were standing there with their mouths open, that the warm air was drying up the insides of their mouths and their throats just like it was doing to mine. And more Germans came up out of their trenches, and every one of them removed his helmet and stood there with it hanging in his hand at his side. And more of our lads came up and gaped. And whether or not it was because the Germans were doing it, we took off our tin hats too, stood bareheaded there with humps on our backs gaping at the thousands of dead men lying like sheaves after the passage of a Cyrus McCormick reaper.

Without their helmets on, the soldiers across the way looked just like us, same height, same coloured skin, same coloured hair, same age, every bit as dirty. They could have been a crowd of lads from the next village you'd see on a Sunday at a football match. And to them we must have looked like a crowd of chaps from their own towns and villages.

Then we were all surprised by a loud voice rising out of the line of German soldiers: 'The stupid bastards!' a man shouted in English.

The words grated like a desecration. 'The stupid bastards! Why did they keep coming? Why did they keep coming?' The voice rose up into hysteria, and a German soldier ran out into no-man's-land. He began kicking a body. 'Why did you keep coming, why did you keep coming?' He ran from body to body, kicking as he went, screaming until he was just a ranting lunatic. Eventually he became entangled in strands of barbed wire, and hysterically, he began to smack at the clinging wire the way a man would hopelessly smack at a swarm of attacking yellow jackets. Two soldiers went after him and pulled him back to the trench. We could hear the sobbing, slobbering cries of the disturbed man as his friends dragged him down onto the ground and held him.

Some of the German soldiers swiped at their noses with their sleeves as if they were being pulled into the vortex that had swallowed up their comrade. But a sharp voice was raised. The men put on their helmets, and following the shouted orders, they disappeared one by one back into the trench. There was only one German left standing looking across at us. I supposed he was the one who had shouted out the orders.

Carrying his helmet in his left hand, he zigzagged slowly through the dead and the dying, stepped around the horrid clumps of wire. He was older, thirty-five perhaps. His uniform was very dirty, and he hadn't shaved for a long time. His bloodshot eyes were the eyes of an animal who has been waiting every second of every minute of seven days for death to dart in and snatch him.

When he was twenty feet away from us, he stopped. Then,

in accented words, he said, 'They walked at us like little children going to kindergarten with their schoolbags on their backs.' Then he turned and for a long time stood there as if he were just looking. Slowly, he walked back to his trench, careful of his steps, and disappeared into the ground without looking back once.

We stayed staring at the field of sheaves for minutes or hours or days or years until someone broke the spell.

'I wonder will Haig come to see this.'

'Haig's in bed thirty miles away, resting after all the months of planning he put into this.'

Fifty thousand casualties were counted. Fifty thousand young lads dead or near death in the same field; fifty thousand sheaves to be picked up and stooked; fifty thousand doors to be knocked on; fifty thousand 'We regret' letters to be handed into trembling hands; fifty thousand mothers and fifty thousand fathers to take the shocks like punches to the chest that would keep them reeling for the rest of their lives.

Matthias Wrenn

In the black water of the shell hole we all came to the surface at the same time, the five of us spluttering and flailing, someone screaming like a wounded horse. I lunged for the side of the hole and dug my fingers into the soft earth, clung there to keep myself from sinking back down into the vile vomit of the gods of war. It was me who was screaming like a wounded horse. Even if I could not see what was in the hole with us, I knew what was there, knew some of it had got past my lips, up my nose. And then I added my own vomit to the swill. Everyone vomited. We wiped our compressed lips with our filthy hands and spat at the same time as we tried to keep anything from getting into us.

Like black and crenulated midnight slugs we stuck to the wall, heads bent back to widen windpipes to drag air into frantic lungs. When the sounds of spitting and coughing and choking and panic died down, the dull booms of the faraway guns re-established themselves.

'There's only five of us. Who's not here?' Professor asked.

'Trossachs got it,' Dave said, with the sounds of breakdown in his voice. 'He stepped into wire and they got him.'

'We won't hear "The Birks of Aberfeldy" with a terrible burr anymore,' Professor said, like he was saying holy words over a coffin.

From their pillbox, the Germans had splattered the mud

around us, told us to get off no-man's-land because someone in authority on their side was coming. *Twick twick* the bullets went as they spurted into the soft earth, twicking as fast as a child's lips making a fart sound.

'The fuckers could have given us a minute,' Dave said, a touch of hysteria in his voice. 'Trossachs got it with the second burst. Guts out the back and the wire around his legs like briars.' Devonshire Dave; Trossachs had been his partner.

Even though the water was two feet below the rim of the shell hole, we were submerged to our chins, afraid of a sniper's bullet as much as the chunky soup lapping against our bottom lips. The sides of the hole were shiny-black like wet coal, and as soft as dough before it's put in the baker.

'His guts went flying out,' I said. The sight of Trossachs' guts in the wind was nightmarish in my brain.

'Bird!' Professor commanded, his tone telling me to calm down, to back away from the hysterics. 'It's the usual story. An officer came along and they had to put the shift on us. Their man on the gun could have killed all of us as easily as he killed Trossachs. The gunner is probably taking a tongue-lashing right now for bad shooting, for allowing us out in no-man's in the first place.'

Within this group of stretcher-bearers I had acquired Bird as a nickname by way of Wrenn. Having a nickname meant you were trusted to do the right thing in every situation. 'Brotherly' could not have been used to describe the relationship among the men with nicknames for each other. But without it ever having been said, we knew we could depend on each other for a bullet in the head if that ever became a necessity. It takes something beyond the love of brothers to depend on each other to that extreme—maybe it's just an emotionless acceptance of reality, maybe it's just behaviour born of unabating extreme conditions.

Two hours earlier, we had been in another hole, a dry one, waiting for 'an isolated spasm of hostilities', as Professor called it, to run its course.

When the hostilities did stop we sat for another ten minutes. Then we pushed the three stretchers up over the rim, one man holding a handle each, the canvas stretched taut—our way of asking for German permission to go into no-man's for the wounded. A one-shot signal that didn't put a hole in a stretcher meant we could come out. But the one-shot signal was not a guarantee that an officer wouldn't come on the scene and change the situation in an eye blink. That's what had just happened without any of us having found even one chap who would survive his wounds. The shooter had allowed five of us to jump into the nearest hole, three of us clutching a rolled-up stretcher each—*Never leave your stretcher behind you. You're as useless as tits on a bull if you haven't your stretcher. Leave your rifle, leave your drawers, leave your balls, leave your wife but never leave your stretcher.*

We had gone into this new hole with our noses pinched between thumbs and fingers, eyes closed, muscles squeezed tight against the bullets with our names on them. But, despite my own fearsome expectation, before the soles of my boots touched the water, I had glimpsed Con and Kitty and myself coming out of the bushes at the Bridge, screaming, and leaping into the water at the perfect angle to drench the courting man and woman who had wandered within range on the far side of the Canal. 'You little hures! If I catch you, I'll pull the balls off you.'

Down into the hole I sank, not afraid at all of drowning; stretcher-bearers did not carry heavy backpacks or rifles when they went looking for the wounded. But I was afraid of what I might bump into in the dark water. Shell holes were places where terrible things dwelt—bits of men, bits of horses, the newly dead and the long dead; ropes of guts, soggy flesh held to bone by thin strings of sinew, bloated rats floating, too fat to climb out of the hole.

I was hysterically afraid of touching water-logged dead flesh in the dark—the sponginess of it. I wasn't as repulsed by it in the daylight, had been wading in it for two years; it had even got into my boots sometimes. But in the dark, my fear of touching meat of dead man or animal was paralysing. I imagined rottenness that had once been a horse's tongue or a man's liver getting into my mouth, my nose, my eyes, my ears, my hair.

When all the vomiting was over, Professor's calm voice was a whiff of reassurance, a wafting of emotional smelling salts. Even though he held the same rank as the rest of us, Professor was our leader when there was no officer. Before the War he had stood in large lecture halls and set fire to hundreds of young minds. He had been a conscientious objector, but he did not shrink from doing his duty. 'I am a slave to duty, like Frederick, so I became a stretcher-bearer,' he had said once, his hand in the air and his index finger wagging. Professor was tall and thin and no matter how dirty, tired, or bedraggled, he always managed to look as if he just stepped away from a mirror. He had a thin moustache and a long face. He was a likeable and patient man who I couldn't imagine as a teacher, but maybe university professors hadn't to be as cross as the teachers of young boys.

And now, Con and Professor swam out into the middle of the hole and retrieved the three floating stretchers. After rolling the canvas around the handles and tying the thongs, they cautiously pushed them over the rim of the hole. 'There's always a sniper, lads, in war or out of it,' was Professor's warning.

With the stretchers rescued, Professor said, 'This is a deep hole, lads. We can't hold on with our fingers for long. We should find something to stand on, and at the same time, we must be careful of snipers. Anyone got an idea?'

'We could use our knives to carve nitches in the walls,' Owl said, 'like the things for statues in churches.' Owl was Welsh, with eyes too big for his face. He could see in the dark and boasted that he'd never been in a coal mine or a church choir. He was a thatcher.

'Niches,' Professor said. 'That's a great idea, Owl.'

For a long time in silence we sat in our niches, the black and lumpy water at our chins: five heads, each wearing its tin helmet despite the plunge. Our five niches took up half the circumference of the hole, our backs to the German trenches. All we had was our lives and our sopping uniforms and whatever was sopping in our sopping pockets—no water, no food, no cigarettes. There was nothing to look at besides each other. We couldn't sleep. Once, I shouted out, 'Jesus Christ!' and splashed away a mat of human hair floating into my space.

'Easy, Bird,' Professor crooned. After a while he said, 'We're here until darkness, lads. We'll have to talk about something.'

'Trossachs' guts in the wind!' Lard burst out, and the sound that came out of him was a sob being wrestled to the ground. 'His mum, no one's left for her. Husband was a piper in South Africa.' Lard had been thinking too much. Men disturbed other men when they talked too much about friends dying.

Professor tried to force Lard off the road that led to dark caves for everyone. 'Maybe you could write to Trossachs' mother, Lard,' he said, 'tell her about Trossachs, what a good chap he was, how he died.'

'Will you write the letter if I tell you what to say?' Lard asked.

'Of course, Lard,' Professor said. 'Every mum wants to know how her son died, else her imagination will torment her forever. It's best if she hears from someone who was with him. That way she won't be hoping till she dies that the army letter was wrong, that someday he's going to walk in the front door and say, "Hello, Mum."'

'For a second before he fell, his guts was blowing in the breeze,' Lard said. 'At first I thought he had ribbons caught on the back of his coat, but I won't say that to his mum.' Lard was Dave from Devonshire who got his nickname by way of a Devonshire 'delicacy', as he called it. After hearing about pasty once too often, Professor said the 'delicacy' had more lard than anything else in it.

151

The big guns were still drumming in the far distance.

'Fucking Belgium,' Owl said. 'Who'd have thought this is how a war would be fought—guts shooting out your back when you're helping your mates? I never thought war would be sitting in a hole full of black water with bits of dead men and horses making a soup of it, and we pissing in it in our trousers and shitting in it too, if we don't get out of here soon.'

'This won't be a good war story to tell if we ever get home again,' Con said. ' "Tell us about what you did in the War?" the people will ask. "We sat in a water hole keeping bits of rotting man-meat and horse-meat out of our mouths," is all we'll be able to say.' His hand came up out of the water and, careful not to create a wake and make matters worse for himself, he slowly pushed a lump of grey something away.

'I can say I saw Trossachs' guts blowing in the wind through a hole in his back while he was still standing,' Lard said, 'and everyone will think I'm mad.'

'Lads,' said Professor, 'when you joined up you thought you would fight the War running across daisied and buttercupped and sun-bright fields shooting at Gerry, while all the bullets and shells that Gerry threw at you missed. In-between-times you'd cavort with French maidens in the grass while they served you wine and bounteous views of their suntanned bosoms.'

'Cavort?' Con asked.

'Oh, Vanderbilt,' Professor said. Con got his nickname by way of Cornelius. 'You know—play around with the maidens while accidentally touching them in the places maidens like to be accidentally touched in. But stop! I will not be led down that track. Our notion of war changed the minute we landed in France, if only because it was raining. War is hell, is what an American general said after three years of civil war.'

'You're right there, Professor,' Con said. 'Just look at us. It's not as if we're sitting in a bathtub of warm soapy water. We're in a devil's bathtub.'

'At least we're alive,' Lard said. 'Trossachs will never say Burns again for us. I never thought I'd see a man's guts blowing in the wind and the man still alive, standing.'

Professor moved in again to push the dark thoughts out of the shell hole.

'Lads,' he said, 'exactly five hundred years ago today, on the twenty-fifth of October, 1415, a famous battle was fought very near where we are right now. On this very day, Saint Crispian's day. And there was another great battle fought near here on the eighteenth of June in 1815, just one hundred years ago.'

'And now we're fighting here,' Owl said. 'What I want to know is why in the name of the good Christ would anyone fight over this shitty place? What does Fucking Belgium have that's worth fighting for, besides muck and shite?'

'It's not a question of what Fucking Belgium has, Owl, as much as where Fucking Belgium happens to be,' Professor said. 'If you have a big army, the easiest way to get from Germany to France is through Fucking Belgium. That's exactly why we're in Fucking Belgium.'

'They should put up a sign: You Can't Get to France This Way,' Con said. 'Who fought here in 1415?'

'The English and the French, but it was just over the border in France, about fifty miles from here in a place called Agincourt, and the wrong side won. That's why it's so famous. The French had six times more soldiers, but the English won. Henry, the English king, was a religious fanatic and he firmly believed he was doing God's work. That helped him to win.'

'Isn't that what every side in every war ever said,' Owl said. 'God's on our side.'

'But Henry hadn't to depend too much on God for help. In those days war was the most dangerous sport of all, and kings liked to show how good they were at it. The kings and princes were the generals in those days, and they wanted to be out in front so they could win all the honour. They wanted to be the ones to kill or capture the important people on the other side. Henry was every bit as interested in honour as he was in taking over large areas of France.'

'What's honour?' Lard asked. 'Having your guts floating on the breeze?'

'Honour is the right to brag about the great things you did. This war we're in will be over sometime; the Germans will be gone home with their tails between their legs. And in years to come we'll be able to say, "We were there. We did our bit." And the pride we will feel and the way people will look at us when we are old men parade-marching in uniforms too small for us will be our small cloud of honour or glory. We will be given special distinction and people will clap their hands as we stumble by and they'll say, "You helped to keep the Germans out of our homes, and we thank you."'

'I'll tell you one thing, Professor,' Owl said. 'If I live to be a hundred, I'll never feel there was anything honourable about sitting in this shite-hole, waiting to crawl out like a garden slug in the dark. We're not even defending this miserable muck hole, we're just sitting in it. We don't even have guns, for Christ's sake. There's nothing about this that's worth remembering. As a matter of fact, the sooner I forget about this hole the better. I'd be ashamed to let anyone know that I spent even five minutes of the War like this; sitting in a shite-hole. People would laugh at us if they knew about it.'

'You'll remember this hole, Owl, and we'll all remember it and we'll tell our grandchildren about it. And if you don't believe me, then think of this—here we are sitting in a shite-hole in the middle of Fucking Belgium, and we are remembering the men who fought in a battle five hundred years ago. We don't know the name of one common soldier who fought in that battle. Their fight only lasted three hours, but all the pain and suffering they endured for months in order to attain their victory was part of the battle. We don't know what any individual man did at Agincourt, but we do know what all the men did together. No one will know in a few years that we sat here in this stinking hole, but they will know we were part of the War. We are as important to the War as the men on the big guns or the ones bringing all the stuff over from England on ships, or the ones charging out of the trenches, or the doctors and the nurses back at the stations. When they put up monuments to the men who died in this war, those will be our monuments too.'

Professor's little speech made me feel not as bad as I'd been. I remember there was a pause for a few seconds, as if we were storing Professor's words in a safe place from which we could bring them out again and listen to them for the comfort they would give.

'Is there a monument for the men at Agincourt?'

'Shakespeare wrote a play about Henry and the battle,' Professor said.

'That bastard,' Owl spluttered. 'I got more beatings at school over that bastard than I did from all the bullies who beat the shite out of me in the schoolyard. I could never learn his bloody poetry, it was all so awkward and full of words nobody ever heard of. I couldn't ever spell the fucker's name right and got punished for that too. And don't tell me, Professor, you're going to sit here in this horses' grave and say some of the fucker's poems.'

'Just a few lines, Owl,' Professor smiled. 'In Shakespeare's play, one of Henry's men wishes out loud that they had ten thousand more soldiers on their side. But Henry says, "The fewer men we have the greater will be our share of the honour when we win. As a matter of fact, if any man here has no stomach for the fight, he can go home and we will give him some money for the journey. I will not die in the company of a man who is afraid to die."'

'That's a bit mad,' Lard said, 'facing a big fight with not enough men, and telling your lads they can go home if they want.'

'If Haig said that he wouldn't have one man left in this

Fucking Belgium in five minutes sharp.'

'Henry wasn't really offering to pay a man's way home,' Con said. 'He was saying, "You can go home if you like, but if you do you're a real shite to leave the rest of us here to die; you're a coward and I hope a wild pig rips the balls out of you on the way home."'

'But Shakespeare said it nicer, Vanderbilt, don't you think? And Henry was obsessed with winning glory and honour. He said, "If it's a sin to want all the honour in the world, then I am the biggest sinner in the world."'

'I can't understand that,' Owl said, 'wanting glory. All I want is a good wash and then a plate of eggs and rashers and sausages and lashings of bread and butter and a mug of sweet tea strong enough to trot a mouse.'

'You must remember that in the play Henry is trying to encourage a ragtag group of hungry and exhausted men who have just laid eyes on an army six times as large as theirs. He's trying to keep his men from running away, from fainting with the fright.'

'He's trying to stop the scutter from running down the backs of their legs,' Con said.

'Poetic, Vanderbilt, poetic,' Professor said. 'So, to keep the shite from running down the backs of their legs, Henry says, "Today is the feast of Saint Crispian. Every one of us who survives this battle and lives to old age will stand proud every year from now on on Saint Crispian's day. We will roll up our sleeves and show our scars and say, I got these wounds on Crispian's day. Old men get forgetful, but every one of us in our old age will remember what we did on Saint Crispian's day, and we'll exaggerate too, and tell of doing things we never did. No matter how useless any of us feels about ourselves right now, we will all be changed forever by what happens today, we will never again think of ourselves as useless. In years to come, the good man will teach our story to his son, and every Saint Crispian's day from now to the ending of the world, we will be remembered, we few, we happy few, we band of brothers; for he today who sheds his blood with me shall be my brother."'

'Happy, my arse!' Lard said. 'How could anyone be happy about maybe getting a blunt spear through the guts?'

'Band of brothers,' Owl said. 'That sounds nice and cuddly, but since I've been in the army I've never felt like I belonged to a band of brothers.'

'Right now I feel, a little tiny bit, like I belong to a band of first cousins, maybe,' Professor said, 'but only because we are all up to our necks in this shite-hole together, and we're all stretcher-men. And this is something I will tell my grandchildren when I'm old and doddery, if I ever get back to Blighty, that is. And the grandchildren will say, "Gads! Here he goes again, gassing on about that stinking old 'ole in Fucking Belgium." ' I saw smiles flickering on a couple of faces. Professor had moved us all away from Trossachs' guts in the wind, had even taken us out of the hole for a few seconds.

'Henry got exactly what he set out to get—remembrance and honour. Here we are today in a hole on Saint Crispian's day remembering him.'

Con said, 'If Shakespeare wrote a play about five men trapped in a black hole full of rotten men and horses, would he have written a speech as high sounding as the one he wrote for Henry?'

'Oh, Vanderbilt! You sceptical Celt! Before Agincourt, Henry's army was as helpless as we are now. When the time is right, when it gets dark, we'll climb out of here and make our way back to the lines. And when we are back on our feet, washed and dry, we will come back to the front again and we will rescue the wounded, and some of the wounded will go home and recover and they will get married and have children and those children will have children and we will be giving life to genera-tions of people we will never know and can't even imagine.

157

Some of those children will be doctors and nurses and soldiers and leaders and farmers and engineers and mill workers and architects and Irish storytellers ...'

'... and professors,' Owl said.

'... and roof-thatchers, Owl, and poets. And some of the poets and writers and historians will look back at this War and they will tell the stories of the soldiers. Books and plays will be written about the War, and monuments will be built to the men who died, and every year there will be a special day to remember all the men who fought and died or survived. And for a few years, for as long as we live, we'll be able to pull up *our* sleeves and show *our* wounds and we'll exaggerate a bit and maybe even tell a few lies, but we will know that we were here, that we spent an afternoon in a rank grave so we could crawl out in the dark and come back to save generations of men and women.'

'You think so, Professor?' Lard asked.

'I know so, Lard. Our misery today will be our honour and our glory when stories of the War are written down. Remember the condition of Henry's men when he was giving his speech and look at what they did. They fought and won. One of our brothers got killed, but we have survived an afternoon in a hole of liquid, dead, stinking flesh. We will crawl out, but we will come back. We're doing a good job. We're fighting our part of the War. For every man we save we have won his war for him. And yes, Vanderbilt. Yes, yes and yes again. Shakespeare could easily have written a speech about us, and it would have been every bit as heroic and every bit as moving as the one he wrote and put into the mouth of Henry the king.'

There was nothing but the sounds of the big guns for a long time. As I sat there up to my chin in the liquid grave, I heard a faint echo of joy in the chambers of my heart for the first time since our ship had turned around in the Mediterranean two years earlier.

The light faded. When it got dark we crawled out of the hole looking like creatures from a swamp. We got back to our own lines and we washed our clothes and ourselves. Lard spoke his letter to Trossachs' mother and Professor did not change a word.

We came back to the front with our stretchers. We saved men we thought would make it. We put out of their misery globs of guts with nothing human about them but their screaming mouths.

Lard got a new partner, but on that first day, before we even had time to nickname him, before they had even unfurled their stretcher, the new man was killed and Lard lost a hand—an expensive blighty. Professor and Owl carried 143 men out of no-man's before they were killed by the same shell. Before Con died two years later, we carried 1683 men to safety. I kept count with scratches on the handles of the stretcher, the way my father had shown me how to keep count of the fish caught on the hazel rod when I was small; the side of a tiny box for one point, the bottom for two, the other side for three, the top for four and from one corner to the other for five, and then onto a new box. On our stretcher handles there were 336 boxes, two sides and one bottom.

I sent Kitty a picture of five heads sitting on black water in a round hole with the word Agincourt under it. I knew I'd have to explain it when I came home.

Coming Home

Billy Simkins

dear mrs Hatchel,

if you had a son by the name of Cornelius Hatchel killed in
the war write back to me. I would write to you about him if he
was your son, he was called Con and his middle name was
Francis, my name is Billy Simkins 62 Fairmount bldv Mans-
field Beds England.

Signed,
Billy Simkins

Jer Meaney

I was the one who seen him first the day he come home.

I mean, I was the first one seen him and *knew* it was Matthias. People over at Marbra Station must have saw him, and at the Dublin station too, but they only seen him the way you'd see someone you don't know; just another person, unless of course the person had something wrong with him like a glass eye or only one arm or a burnt face like the Hodgkins one behind her mask.

But there wasn't anything wrong with Matthias's body when I caught up with him on the Bog Road, no wooden leg like Mick Nolan, no shakes like Ownie Egan roaring in his house in the middle of the day or night, his burned lungs making him sound like a calving cow in trouble—frighten the shite out of you—and eyes bulging forever against the green gas snaking across no-man's-land, screaming at it to 'Stay away, stay away, ya hure,' shouting, 'Piss on me hanky, piss on me hanky, will someone for the love of Jazus piss on me hanky? I've not a drop left in me.'

That was the first time, on the Bog Road, I ever saw Matthias by himself. It was always Matthias and Con and the girl Kitty since they were small childer down at the Canal. The Hatchel triplets. Poor Con didn't come back at all—buried a million miles away, in France somewhere, too far for anyone to go and cry at his grave, may the Lord have mercy on him.

By the walk of him from behind it never crossed my mind it was Matthias—he'd always walked with a bit of a stoop to the left, and this fella was as straight as a telegraph pole. And when I did pass him and looked back, it still took me a second to recognize him. Compared to the well-fed Matthias that left Enderly to join the army, he was a skeleton: sunk eyes, grey hair made all the greyer with the fierce black eyebrows, cheeks sucked in like when you bite into a sloe after your mother telling you not to, so purple you couldn't stop yourself. Matthias was twenty-two years younger than myself but he looked twenty-two years older.

Of course, he wasn't wearing the uniform. I wouldn't have been wearing it myself neither, if 'twere me, never knowing when you'd run into a Fenian or some other bugger who'd give you hell for joining the army—'Took the king's shilling, didn't ya?'—accusing you, not asking you a question at all. Ireland had changed since Matthias went off to join up. Them lads in Dublin in 1916 had seen to that; suddenly you weren't a real Irishman if you'd fought in the English army. It was a terrible mix-up—most of the lads out in the trenches fighting for a daily wage on the English side, and suddenly at Easter, the English soldiers in Dublin shooting the yobs in Kilmainham. If you ask me, they got what they deserved. Of course, I'd never say that out loud, or I'd get hit by someone sooner or later, most likely in the back in the dark.

'Good God! It's you, Matthias,' I shouted, when I looked back at him, and I was all excited to see him, because he was the last one from the town to come back. There was great excitement in Ballyrannel when the two of them went off to see the world. Most of the lads in the town were jealous, sorry they hadn't whatever it is that gets a young fellow up and moving away from the homeplace. Of course, when the War started a year later and Mister Redmond began speechifying, about thirty lads from Ballyrannel joined up. There was a great severance pay for the missus and the childers.

A whole lot of stories came back from France and Belgium about Matthias escaping getting killed a hundred times, or half blown to bits, or legless at least, or armless. He was in the papers a whole lot of times: 'The Scarlet Pimpernel of the Stretcher-Bearers'. This French reporter picked out six soldiers at the beginning of the War and every month wrote about what was happening to one of them, all the while the War was on. After two years of seeing how Matthias was still carrying out the wounded, he called him the Scarlet Pimpernel because there was a man by that name who was always having narrow escapes from the English in the Boer War, and Matthias was like that. Of course, in Ballyrannel we all knew about the first miraculous escape he had when he was a chap and the rest of the family got burnt to death down by the Canal; only Matt was wearing the Franciscan scapular that day he'd have been burned with the rest of them.

The Dublin paper translated the Frenchman's stories about Matthias. The other five soldiers were killed and then the reporter himself was killed the week before the War ended just after stepping away from the spot where he and Matt had their picture took together, Matthias tall, the Frenchman a bit of a runt. They say a lot of quare things like that happened all the time, mostly to the Germans—two lads talking and a shell would blow one to bits and not touch the other; even stories of chaps getting their heads took clean off their shoulders and they still taking that last step forward when they fell. There were stories about bodies blasted into nothing and the heads left there on the ground with the strap of the tin helmet still under the chin, and the butt of a fag in the mouth still lighting.

It made us all feel important that Matthias and Ballyrannel were in the papers.

I was so excited to see him that I blurted out, 'Janey, Matthias, I thought you were dead a hundred times, and here y'are home from the War safe and sound.' I pulled on the reins and the pony stopped, and the half-blind mare behind hit her chest against the tailboard.

To tell the truth, the next minute the hairs stood up on the back of my neck. Not only did Matthias not answer me, he didn't even see me. He didn't even veer to one side to walk around the mare and the cart and the pony. He walked through the whole lot of us like he was a ghost; never even changed his step, just kept going like we wasn't there at all.

The eyes of him!

'Matthias,' I called weakly, 'it's me, Jer. Jer Meaney.'

He didn't look around, and the hairs on my arms were up like the hairs on the back of a frightened dog trying to make himself look bigger to a bigger dog. To tell you the God's truth, I was certain sure I'd seen a ghost—all those stories in the papers from the War, about angels with bows and arrows in the sky on wild horses beating back the Germans so the English could escape, and the Blessed Virgin Mary herself hanging off the spire of a church and not falling no matter how many times they fired at her and the baby in her arms and the War supposed to stop when she fell, and miraculous medals stopping bullets in front of men's hearts; God rolling the sun around in the sky trying to stop the men from killing each other; and two aeroplanes fighting in the sky and everyone on the ground seeing the shape of a heart around them—God telling them that he loved one as much as the other; people all over England getting in touch with their slaughtered husbands and sons and brothers through people who can talk to the dead. So, it wouldn't be strange at all if Matthias had been killed and I was seeing his ghost walking toward home, or at least toward the place where he had lived once, just a few walls now like black tooth stumps in a terrible mouth, nettles and dandelions and docks growing in the kitchen floor, tom-tits building in the walls, yellow and black.

I sat there in the pony's cart looking after him, shaking from the fright and I said to myself, I'm not going to catch up with him again; I'm going to wait here till he gets so far ahead I won't catch him till he's in Ballyrannel. Without me telling her to, the pony pulled over to the side of the road to graze, and the mare behind jerked on the reins till I let her graze too.

We were on our way home from the stallion in Duff's yard in Marbra, the mare behind the cart as calm as any mare can be after getting herself well and truly poked, and me a shilling the poorer after paying Pat Cullen for the use of his stallion's balls and mickey.

While the two animals grazed, I watched Matthias disappearing around the bend at Cork Corcoran's house and at the same time I fretted that there was great news to tell and it wouldn't be me who got to tell it. He got smaller and smaller and then I heard the rhyme in my head. I wondered if it had been there all the time only I hadn't noticed it.

My side, my side.

It kept going around and I couldn't shake it out of my brain.

My side, my side. Come to my side, where the peasonlee is yellow. Where the peasonlee is brighter. Come to my side, my side, where the plover is golden and linnets fill the sky with green. What the hell is peasonlee?

I waited another ten minutes after he disappeared, thinking I'd arrive in the town just in time to see all the excitement. But I waited too long, and when I did catch up, he was at the far end of the town standing on the coping stones at the Harbour with a small crowd around him talking and children touching him.

I stopped the pony and stood up in the cart to see over the people.

Matthias's cap was on the back of his head, the angle a man shifts to when he's faced with a question he can't answer. Even though they were talking to him and touching him, it didn't look like Matt was hearing them or feeling them. He was looking around, like he was looking for something or someone. You could say he was glassy-eyed like a dead man, just like he was out there on the Bog Road when he walked through me and the cart.

My side, my side, the daisies dance on my side. Dancing in the grass on my side, my side. The green lapwing, black and white grazes in the yellow daisies on my side. My side. The lapwing's horn is in the dandelions on my side. My side. The bloody song just wouldn't go away. And as the words went around like a spinning top in my head, didn't Herby Kelly come along on his bike and pull up at the side of my cart, kept his feet on the pedals, and put his hand on the wingboard for balance.

'What's going on, Jer?' he asked. Runty Herby was the nosiest man in Ballyrannel, and thicker than a double ditch.

'Matthias Wrenn just came home from the War,' I said.

'He didn't!' Herby said. Then after a few seconds, 'Pity he fought for Dinglish.'

I didn't say anything because Herby had plunged into dangerous territory. Herby would run bare-balled into a growth of nettles and dead briars if he thought someone would look at him. As sure as shite, Herby knew less about politics than I did, and he was only saying what he'd heard some scuttered Fenian saying in a public house, believed by saying it himself he was being a patriotic Irishman.

'Took the king's shilling,' Herby said, and he spat out over the front wheel of his bike, but he couldn't even do that right. The spit got caught on the handlebar and stretched its way down to the ground like a string of afterbirth hanging out of a cow after calving. Herby didn't notice.

That's when I saw Kitty Hatchel running like a hare, coming up along the Canal bank in strides that only her long legs could take, her hair and her dress looking like she was out in a storm and facing into a fierce wind. The dress was the yellow of a primrose with spots of red the size of a crow's eggs.

Kitty Hatchel

The heart in my chest jumped when I heard Sonny Mack shouting in his thin voice from the Bridge.

'Kee-teee. Kee-teee. Kee-teee.'

It was a Saturday afternoon. I was just after dipping the scrubbing brush into the basin to start on the last chair outside the back door. There were soap bubbles on my knuckles and fingers.

'Kee-teee. Kee-teee. Kee-teee.'

Even though I knew for a certainty it was Sonny, even though I knew for a certainty why he was calling me, I still ran to the corner of the house and looked. And Sonny was there, exactly where I knew he'd be, standing on the parapet in the centre of the Bridge, his two hands cupping his mouth, his head bent back and he throwing out my name with all his might.

'Kee-teee. Kee-teee. Kee-teee.'

Sonny on the Bridge was a Russian wolf howling at the moon, its pewter hide inlaid with a streak of moonbeam from nose-tip to tail-tip; he was a caribou of pure silver with its mouth open at the end of its taut-stretched neck, its tilted antlers touching the strong shoulders behind, and it baying at the world from a high crag; he was a calling child carved from shining marble, the sun sparkling off the polished stone like light coming out of God's hands when he created the world on the green cover of the catechism.

I thought I'd have a heart attack.

The instant Sonny saw me seeing him, saw me jumping up and down like a mad frog with its front legs over its head, he shouted, 'He's this side of Cork Corcoran's.' I waved, and he waved and stepped off the parapet, disappeared, and I knew Sonny was already on his way, running barefooted, betattered and bespattered back along the Towpath to the Harbour so he could tell everyone in school he was there when Matthias Wrenn came back to Ballyrannel after walking home from the War, that he'd been on the lookout for a month and that Kitty Hatchel had paid him tuppence with the promise of another tuppence if he got word to her before Matthias reached the Harbour.

Fourpence, lads. Fourpence.

And I came back to myself and found myself standing there, my finger in my mouth and Mammy at the kitchen door asking, 'Was there someone?'

'Mam, he's home! Matthias. Oh, Mam.' And I burst out crying and fell down on my knees beside the rosebush and put my hands to my face and bawled as if I'd been told that Matthias had been killed in France, sobbed like I did when the army letter came about Con. I bent down until the top of my forehead was on the ground and my hair got caught in the rosebush, but I didn't know that till Mammy started lifting me to my feet, and she had to run into the kitchen to get the scissors to cut the strands in the thorns. She brushed the flower-bed soil off my forehead, told me to wash my face before I put on the dress that Missus Hodgkins gave me so I'd look nice if Matthias came home on a Saturday afternoon or on a Sunday and I wouldn't be able to use the dress she had hanging for me in Enderly if he came home during the week while I was working there.

I fled in through the kitchen and into the room, and ripped off my old work apron. I was pulling on Sarah Hodgkins's dress, the colour of beastings with drops of blood in it, when I realized Mam had followed, that she was wringing her hands and crying and I knew she was crying for Matthias being home—and for Con not being home. 'Oh, Mam,' I squeaked out and I put my arms around her and the two of us sobbed and sobbed. And we kept sobbing even when we heard Daddy shouting from the yard, 'Did you hear? Did you hear?' And when we heard his boots in the kitchen, Mam pushed me away and said, 'Kitty, you have to wipe your face before you let Matthias see you, before you let Dad see you.'

'Did you hear?' Daddy called from the doorway.

I dipped into my washbasin and scooped cupped hands of water onto my face. Mam was holding the flour-sack towel for me, she after wiping her own face in it before Daddy saw her.

'It looks like you heard,' Daddy said.

Mam waited until she had cleared the sticky strings of crying out of her throat before she spoke. 'Run your fingers through your hair,' she said to me, and to Daddy she said, 'Get out of the door, James, or she'll knock you down.'

But I didn't run past Daddy because I had to bring him into my happiness. I put my arms around his neck, my head on his chest. 'I'm terrible glad, Kit,' he said, and he stroked my hair. But then he couldn't help himself. 'Poor Con!' he blurted out in a shower of tears, and I felt the pain in his heart. Then he whispered, 'Poor Con, poor Con. Run, Kit. Run, Kit. We'll be all right. Run,' he said, and he pushed me away, turned me toward the kitchen door.

And I ran and ran and ran, but Con's tears kept up with me and Daddy's and Mammy's tears kept up with me, and I knew they were holding each other in a whirlpool of sadness and gladness for Con and Matthias. With my face full forward I ran along the Canal bank, and I heard the keening sounds of Mam-dog running to her hungry pups; heard the sounds of a bewildered sow looking for the place where her piglets squeal in fear of a knife; I heard the fierce clucking of a hen when she sees a remembered shadow in the sky and her chicks are scattered all over. And all those sounds of fretful Mamness were keening out through my own tight lips.

I ran onto the coping stones at the Harbour still keening the sounds of an anxious animal, searching for a glimpse of the family member it believed had been lost forever.

A gap opened in the circle of people surrounding Matthias, and there he was in his cloth cap, the peak broken in the middle and it pointing to the sky like the beak of a bittern. And in my forward lunge I was stunned by the sight of him so skeletal, head all skull, unfocused eyes deep in sockets. But he was Matthias, home, with folded jacket over his left shoulder and canvas bag hanging out of his right hand. His collarless shirt was unbuttoned. I recovered from the stumble and flew off the ground, attached myself to him with such force that someone stepped forward and kept him from falling backward and everyone cheered. But in that split second between jumping and landing, I had been stricken in the heart every bit as much as if I'd run at full gallop onto the blunt, wooden handle of a plough in the dark. I knew before my arms were around his neck that this was not my Matthias who'd gone away to India.

This Matthias didn't drop his short coat and bag and squeeze me. He didn't twirl me around in a dance of mad gladness. He didn't shout and cry and bite my ears and devour my lips and run his fingers through my hair and feel the shape of my skull. He didn't shout out. He didn't say anything. And I knew that this absence of greeting was part of what I had not seen in his eyes. And I was bewildered. And then I was disappointed, terribly wounded. A storm of feelings swept through me, and I thought I was going to lose control, become a blabbering idiot in front of this audience. All the nighttime terrors that I'd buried, and all the fears and hopes that I'd pushed behind a dam in my head and all the imaginings of the last four years came washing over me like a brown flood roaring down the narrow Owenass River, washing everything before it after a week's rain in the peaty mountains. And through the roar of the flood I heard for the first time the words Missus Hodgkins had said to me a hundred times: 'You must prepare yourself, Kitty. There's more ways of getting killed in a war than by bullets.'

Kitty Hatchel

On the coping stones at the Harbour the people of Ballyrannel saw the enthusiastic girl launching herself onto her soldier home from the War and they were unaware of what the girl had not seen in her soldier's eyes. And it suddenly became very important to me that the people of Ballyrannel not know how cruelly disappointed I was, but I did not think I had the strength to behave so opposite to what was going on in my insides.

But as I released my arms from Matt's neck and slid down to the ground, I remembered how I had made myself walk around the damaged wall at the top of Knockmullen Castle, terrified, but wanting to show Con and Matthias that a girl could do it. By the time my feet were back on the ground, I had steeled myself against the staring faces, the pitying faces and the satisfied faces and I performed for all of them.

Instead of collapsing in a puddle of pain and tears and confusion on this public stage, I took Matt's hand and caressed his cheek like I'd caress the cheek of a frightened child. Matt's lips were just barely open, his eyes were almost focused on me, and I could almost see the curtain of gossamer hanging before his eyes.

'Come on, Matt,' I said. I squeezed his fingers, and he obediently followed. Sonny Mack ran into the circle, picked up Matt's cap, and handed it to me. I pressed it to my nose and smelled the sweat, and hid my face in a moment of weakness.

But I whipped the cap away and, bare-faced, I led Matt toward the Canal bank, people calling out to him to welcome him home, telling him it was good to see him and wishing him well. I made my face smile thanks to them for him. And a man was standing up in his pony cart looking over the heads of the people at what was going on—he was one of the Mad Meaneys from out on the Emo Road—and your man, Herby Kelly, was sitting on his bike keeping himself balanced by holding on to the wingboard of Meaney's cart. As we walked past the cart, Herby shouted to Matthias, 'You fought on the wrong side, ya hure!'

No matter how stupid the remark and no matter how stupid the man who made it, it contained enough begrudgery to crack the dam inside me, and the mixture of anxieties and disappointments was unleashed from behind the collapsing wall. I raged at the world, raged like a winter storm in the tossing, screaming, and bare branches of the elm tree near the still-blackened ruins of Matt's old house.

Spurred claws leading the way like the feet of an attacking game cock, I lit onto Herby and dragged four fingers down each side of his face. And the terrible expectation and excitement that had turned so sour so suddenly gave me such detestation for the old fool that I kept my nails buried deeply in Herby's skin all the way down to his chin. My face, inches away from his, screamed screams that were made by jagged, unravelled nerves that had been compressed for years and when I'd finished scraubing and screaming, I jerked his hand off the wingboard of the cart and made him fall over while still sitting up straight on his bike, the four streaks of blood on each side of his face overflowing into each other.

I turned back to Matt and took his hand, and I pulled him towards the bank on our side of the Canal. Our side. Our goddamn side. Goddamn you, Herby Kelly. Goddamn you, Mister Kaiser Bill, Goddamn you, King George.

Our Goddamn side. Our side.

Con's and my side when we were small before the fire in Matt's house.

His side. Matt's side.

My side, my side where the mayweed's sweeter, the daisies big as eggcups.

My side. My side. A girl on my side has tiny feet and wheenshie toes. My side, my side where Con and Kitty live in a castle small, with a Daddy tall, on my side, my side.

Crucified Christ!

That's what was in my head as we went along the bank without speaking, arm in arm. I couldn't think of one word to say to him. After all the weeks and months and years, here he was home and I had my arm in his and I could not think of one word to say to him. Maybe I was afraid of what he would say back to me. Maybe he would even ask my name. Oh sweet Jesus! If that happened! If that happened I don't know …

Matthias stopped walking and I took in a sharp breath of expectation. But he hadn't stopped to talk to me, nor even to look at me. He stared into the water at a small shoal of silvery-red roach suspended above the green-green weeds, their gill-wings spinning silently, keeping them steady in their places.

I looked at Matthias looking, examined his face and saw many small white scars on his cheek and skin. Except for his eyebrows, his hair was grey. And I saw too that there was no gossamer veil obstructing his eyes, that Matt's eyes were simply old before their time.

Four years had passed since I'd promised to marry him that day he left for India in 1914, but Matthias had lived several lives since he'd sailed from the North Wall with Con beside him waving. He was like Oisín who went to Tír na nÓg where everyone stayed young forever. But everything was backward for Matt. He was the one who had grown old, while it was the people he'd left behind who'd remained young. Matthias had aged decades while we had aged years.

It was only now that I knew the circle of welcoming and smiling faces at the Harbour had been overwhelming for him who had lived so long in the company of filthy, stinking, comforting men who had sunk within skin-depth of savagery. The greenness and the levelness and tidiness of the fields must have been a shock for him who had lived four years in destroyed and poisoned landscapes without trees or grass; the silence of the countryside must have been deafening to him after years of guns and rifles and screaming horses and pain-roaring men; the body of an excited and happy woman clinging to him was probably too much for him who had just stepped out of sewer trenches where lice had clung to every bit of flesh and rats gnawed at sleeping fingers in the dark.

As I looked at him, I comforted myself with the thought that time was all that Matthias needed to bring his spinning world to a stop, that the passing of our countryside time would bring Matt back to the people and the place he had left a million years ago, that he would finally fit back into the notch the fates had wrenched him from all those years ago. His pre-War memory would have to be resurrected, and his War memory would have to fade away into dimness. When Oisín had begged to visit the land of his own people, he was warned not to get off his horse, not to touch the ground, else he would lose his youthfulness. But with Matt, it was going to be the opposite; he would have to fall back into the land of his own people, he would have to immerse himself, dive head first back into the people he had left, so he could regain his own self. I knew a long time would have to pass before the scales would begin to fall from his eyes.

And my hopes were confirmed when Matthias said, 'Roach.' His voice was rusty, sounded like the axle of the bog-barrow on its first day out of storage before Daddy rubbed on a swipe of goosegrease with his finger.

'I never thought I'd see ... Nor the green weeds. Roach and perch.' He stared down at the shoal of roach like a man feeding something inside himself, like a man rebuilding his memory, I wanted to believe. 'We fished in the Somme,' he said, as if talking to someone else.

He stood there staring for a long time, but when I gave his arm a tender tug he came back and walked on with me.

I rubbed his arm as we walked, caressed his arm through the cloth of the sleeve. For a hundred yards at a time I closed my eyes and let Matthias guide me beside the water, while I tried to convince my brain that he had indeed come home. I stroked his upper arm with gentle fingertips, followed the bend of his elbow and slipped down to his naked wrist and hand and fondled his fingers. Not once did he return my touch, not once did he sigh, not once did he say my name.

I had always known that Matthias would come home, was always afraid that Con wouldn't. I had always believed that neither Lionel nor Sarah Hodgkins would come back, but Sarah did even though it would have been better for everyone, including herself, if she'd been killed. I didn't know yet how much of Matthias had been left in France and Belgium, didn't know if the best part of him had been burned away in the hell he'd visited. I didn't know yet if it was only a damaged piece of Matthias that had come home, damaged as bad as Sarah, only not so hard to look at.

In the rushes and long grass beside the one-person track, the swish of Matt's feet was the only sound for a long time. And then he stopped again. At first I thought he was whispering, but it was singing he was, and he was singing the Canal Song, lines he and Con had made up one time to tease me. 'My side, my side where girlie's cheeks part for the fart of the onion she eats for breakfast. My side, my side where girlie's smile beguiles Mad Meaney in his cart.' And then he was staring into the distance at nothing, the way your eyes sometimes take off on their own. He took a deep breath and sighed, 'Jesus, Con.'

When we came to the Bridge, I followed the tug of Matt's

arm and we crossed over the Canal, steep climb up, steep climb down the other side and then around the end of the parapet and down to the Towpath. Under the half-moon Bridge, Matthias stood on the coping stones looking down through the four feet of water where fish seldom swam because of the shade of the Bridge. Without stooping, he dropped his bag onto the shining granite. He slipped his jacket off his shoulder and let that fall to the ground too. Without caring where it landed, he knocked his cap off the back of his head. He sat down on the coping stones and lowered himself, boots and clothes and all, into the water. In the water, under the Bridge, facing away from me, Matt said something that got blurred in its own echo. What I heard him saying was, 'Will you wash me, Kitty?'

I went around to the loose stone in the side of the bridge where we'd always hidden a bar of green Lifeguard, where I still kept one for washing myself in the dark during the summer.

When I came back, Matt was sitting on the bottom of the Canal, his nose between his thumb and finger. He looked up through the water and beckoned at me to come in with his other hand. That's what I thought, but I wasn't sure because I wasn't sure of anything. When he surfaced, he rubbed the water away from his eyes and said, 'Will you wash me, Kitty?'

He might as well have said, Will you marry me, Kitty? Will you be the mother of my children, Kitty?

I hesitated for a second about Sarah Hodgkins's dress and the baggy blue knickers I was wearing under it, the only thing I was wearing under it. I started to look around and then I thought to myself, I don't give a damn who sees me. I bent down to the hem of Sarah's dress, pulled it up and over my head and let it fall on Matt's bag. In a big splash I landed beside him, the bar of soap held tightly in my right hand.

Kitty Hatchel

In the clear water of the Canal I stripped Matthias and scrubbed him till he was as pink as a baby dripping over a steaming basin in its mother's hands. With studied slowness Matt followed the directions I gave him through my fingertips and whispers. Every part of him I washed, and there was no response from his adult body.

'Lift your arms, Matt.'

'Close your eyes.'

I washed between his toes, behind his knees, between his legs back and front, all over his front and back, saw how the hair at his belly and under his arms was as grey as the hair on his head, softly poked my finger into the crevices of his ears, caressed his face with soapy fingers, imagined I was transferring healing strength to him when I pulled his face between my breasts and soaped the back of his neck.

When the cold got to us, I threw on my dress, left him sitting naked on the coping stones. I ran home for a towel and the work clothes he had left behind when he went off the join the army. Of course, Mammy and Daddy couldn't figure out what was going on, me being away so long, no Matthias with me and my dress wet in some spots and dry in others. I said he'd gone for a swim, that we'd be home in a few minutes, and I flew back to the Bridge. I dried and dressed him as if he were a three-year-old. He didn't speak.

Daddy and Mammy met us near the rosebush, and when they saw him, they stopped and gaped, Mammy bringing her hand to her face, unable to hide her shock at seeing how his body had aged and changed, the thinness of him, the greyness of him, the eyes of him. Matthias gaped at them, pursed his lips, and moved his head up and down as imperceptibly as a piece of blanket fluff stirring in the breath of a sleeping baby. He had the look of a man trying either to cry or not cry.

Daddy and Mammy went to him, linked their arms in his, and brought him into the house as if he was their child returning from a long stay in the Scarlet Fever Hospital in Abbeyleix from which they had believed he would never return alive. And Matthias said nothing.

On the wall below the high mantelpiece I had hung some of the sketches Matt had sent me. The most obvious one was of two stretcher-men, their backs to the artist, one end of their stretcher's handles stuck into the mud between them, each man with an up-reached hand holding the handles. In the near distance was a standing cartwheel, its rim gone, the spokes like the rays of the sun in a child's drawing. In the distance was a huge snipe with its beak sunk into the soft earth in search of food. But it wasn't a snipe at all. It was an enormous gun on wheels that had been heeled up, its barrel buried in the black earth. It was Matt's best and I had always imagined the two stretcher-men were Matt and Con. Matt didn't see his drawings, didn't see anything, when Daddy and Mammy led him into the kitchen.

That first hour around the kitchen table—two rabbits, cabbage boiled and chopped fine and fried in butter, boiled potatoes, butter, and mugs of milk—was torture for everyone. Matthias did not speak. Daddy and Mammy made small talk and longed to hear about Con. I looked at him and wondered if he was home from the War at all. Here he was with the people who'd worried about him every second of every minute of every day for four years, and he had nothing to say. He owed us something in return for the suffering we had done for him, I thought. I was beginning to get cross with him.

As the small talk went on, I realized that Mammy, Daddy and I were trying to convince Matt that nothing had changed, that everything was the same as it was four years earlier. We grew silent.

While he nibbled absently at his food, Matthias stared into the far distance or the far past, or he could have been looking at the broken wheel and the snipe in the picture. When he put down the rabbit's leg that he didn't even know was a rabbit's leg, his eyes fell onto his plate. Daddy and Mammy and I looked at each other, raised our eyebrows to each other in helplessness. The burning turf in the fireplace made noise as it fell down on itself, and without looking, I knew a cloud of white ash was floating up the chimney on the draft.

I dearly wanted to kneel on the floor beside Matt and press his head between my breasts like I'd done in the Canal. I wanted to give him anchorage, to convince him he was here, home in the kitchen, that the War was over, that we had become used to the idea that Con had died. But I couldn't do that, could not be that intimate with him in front of Mammy and Daddy.

Because I couldn't comfort Matthias physically, I frantically scoured around in my brain looking for something to say that would blow to pieces the dam that was blocking the flow of Matt's words. I wondered if Con's absence and Matthias's presence were the two logs locking up everything behind them. And the more I thought of it, the more convinced I became this was the obstacle that needed removal.

I said, 'Matthias, you mustn't think for one minute that Con's death …'

But as the first words came out, Matthias moved his chair on the hard floor. The grating of the chair legs was as tooth-shaking as a nun's fingernails on a blackboard trying to get another few letters out of a stub of chalk. The harsh sound not only cut off my words, it made the silence in the kitchen louder. And into this dark silence, Matthias launched three lifeless words: 'I killed Con.' His eyes did not leave his plate.

Mammy reached out and put her hand on top of Daddy's, and tears fell on the table in front of her. Daddy reached across the table and put his hand on Matt's hand. 'Don't say that, Matthias,' he said. 'It was the lad firing the gun who killed Con and not anyone else.'

More silence. No noise of collapsing fire, no sigh of wind in chimney. Immense silence. Mammy's hand squeezing Daddy's on the table, me with my eyes about to spill over. And I prayed that Matthias would go on, that he would say what he was trying to say and release us all.

He slowly pulled his hand from under Daddy's. '*I* killed Con,' he said.

'Tell us, Matthias,' Mammy said. 'Tell us why you think you killed Con so we can tell you that you didn't. We have the letter ...'

'The letter ...' Matthias pursed his lips. He sounded like a man dredging words up out of a dark cloying hole. 'I killed men to save them. Bundles of guts. A doctor showed me how.' I heard Mammy gasping. 'I killed Con to save him from a firing squad.'

I heard Mammy and Daddy trying to keep Matt's words away. I heard myself cry out.

Together, the three of us began to speak, but our voices faded into the silence before a sentence was completed. Mammy began to sob, did nothing to hide her face, sat there with her hand on Daddy's hand, and did nothing to stifle the sounds welling up out of her. Daddy looked like he had aged twenty years. My throat was aching from keeping my crying controlled.

Daddy said, 'Matt, how did you kill Con?' and in his tone was the knowledge that Matt had not physically killed Con, that Matt was blaming himself for something that indirectly caused Con's death.

The way Matthias spoke made me think he was just saying words, that he wasn't answering a question. 'I killed Con with a knife over his fourth rib into his heart,' he said.

'No, Matt, no,' Mammy cried out. 'No, Matt, don't say that.'

Daddy put his arm around Mammy's shoulder, but she drew away from him like she'd been burned. 'Matt,' she cried loudly. 'Matt, Matt, Matt. You loved him. *You loved Con,*' she shouted, and her voice collapsed into the bawlings of a calf that can't find its mother. Daddy had his hands clamped to the side of his head, looking like he was blocking out Mammy's grief and Matthias' words. But even if he'd been stone deaf, he would have heard the new wail that rose into the kitchen from the far side of the table.

Matthias' face was screwed up in a terrible agony, his eyes sightless. His hands on the table were balled into blackthorn knobs, and out of his mouth was coming a sound that could only have been forged in hell; the sound of a million pieces that had been individually buried and hammered into compression for four long years; it was the sound of pain and agony and death and terror and sadness and starvation and boredom and fear and despair that had been compressed that was now escaping with the terrible admission of what he'd had to do to save his brother.

Like the blood-curdling braying of a donkey in distress on a dark night, the agony poured out of Matthias. His fisted hands shook on the tabletop, water ran from his sightless eyes and down his face into his twisted, fully open, unsightly mouth. His chin trembled like the chin of a singing woman holding on to a high note. He was completely gone into his own head, gone to the world, gone to us, gone back to the War. And he didn't stop.

At last I did what I should have done an hour ago; I went to Matt, knelt on the floor beside him and held his upper arm. But I couldn't control myself any longer, and my own years of worry for Matt, all the heart-twisting sadness for Con, for Mammy grieving Con, for Daddy grieving Con, all the pain and anger and sadness I'd kept locked up came loose and I got swept up into the release of Matt's agony. But even when my grief had spent itself, Matthias was still crying the horrors out of his head. I pushed my arms around his chest, pulled my face into his side, and I felt the horrors convulsing up through his body, heard them roaring out through his mouth; he cried, he bellowed, he laughed, he sobbed, he whispered.

No person's body and soul could endure such a cleansing for long, and gradually Matthias began to collapse. The braying slipped down into body-shaking sobs. And when the sobs eased still further, I saw Mammy kneeling on the floor at the far side of Matt's chair holding on to him. Daddy was kneeling behind the chair, his hands on Matt's shoulders, his forehead pressed into the back of Matt's neck. We knelt on the cold floor for a long time. The fire had gone out. The wick of the wall lamp began to smoke as it ran out of oil.

Daddy and Mammy almost carried Matthias into the room, Matt's head resting on Daddy's shoulder. While Daddy removed Matt's clothes, Mammy came back to the kitchen, and we put our arms around each other, our heads on each other's shoulders, neither of us crying, neither of us saying a word.

Daddy came back and wrapped his arms around the two of us. I had never felt this intimacy between us before. 'We'll never know how terrible it was. Even if he told us every detail we'd still not know.' Then after a while he said, 'He'll sleep for a week.'

When Matthias woke up after a day and a half, Paulie Bolger, the postman, had brought Billy Simkins' second letter.

Billy Simkins

Dear Mrs Hatchel,

My cousin, J. R. Lowndes, is writing this letter for me because he works in an office and he can spell better than me. I wrote the last letter myself.

I knew a chap in the War called Professor. He was one of the stretcher lads, as tough as six-inch nails. Before the army saw that I was smaller than Haig, we were billeted together once in Dicksmood, lying in a hay barn on the way back from Ocean Villas after a great wash with soap. This professor said it is a good thing to write to the family of soldiers we saw dying. Getting their address is the hard part, one of the lads said, and Professor said, no, the hard part is writing the letter, and a letter from a mate is better than an army letter that says nothing but 'Killed in action.' But the real hard part, the professor said, is knowing what to leave out. If you saw a lad stuffing his guts back into his stomach there's no need to put that in a letter.

I must have seen thirty lads getting killed if I saw one, and the last thing a few of them was doing when they died was stuffing their stomachs back in, or trying to hold them from sliding out any further. It wasn't easy sometimes to look for a lad's army book in the muck, with Gerry still firing his machine guns and a lad's blood making your hands all slippy and the steam from his hot guts fogging up your glasses. Most times, in the end, the book in a pocket was falling apart with water and blood. I wrote to five families since the War ended and you are the last. My cousin, J. R. Lowndes, wrote them all, once I found out who to write to.

I got your address from Con that night in the cellar in Ocean Villas. The cellar was being used as a dressing station, but that night there was no fighting and no casualties were coming in. If you ever went to Ocean Villas and found the cellar, you'd find a picture cut into the plaster above the arch that once led to the stairs to go up into the house, but the house got blown away a long time before we got there. There's a bridge in the picture and a river flowing under it and swans. The bridge was like a circle because you could see its shadow in the water. There was a little man standing on the bridge wall with his hands over his head like he was going to dive into the river. A frame was carved around the bridge and the river and the swans and the exact words under the picture are, 'In memory of Con H. 1918. He jumped off bridges and faced up to Haig. Your side was better, Con.' I wrote them down on the inside of a Woodbine box, and my cousin, J. R. Lowndes, is looking at it right now along with the message Con wrote on it. I can tell you something, Mrs Hatchel: Con H. did face up to Field Marshal Douglas Haig and told him a thing or two before the guards dragged him out of Haig's parlour. How the picture of the bridge and the river and the swans and the writing got on the wall frightened all the lads and the nurses because the picture wasn't there the night before, and Con was alive the night before so it had to be made in his memory after he died. A nurse said Con carved it himself after he died—his soul was so brave for facing up to Haig and telling him a thing or two. A lot of strange things happened in the War, like all the lads who saw angels with bows and arrows shooting out of the sky at the Germans to keep them back and to let our lads escape once near the start of the War. Some lads got saved because something their mother's gave them in their pockets stopped bullets, like little Bibles with the words so small nobody could read them except a midget.

I'm not good at telling things in a way that takes the hardness out of them. Like the professor said, I'm never sure what to leave out, but I can say at the start that I didn't see Con getting shot, or blown up, or run over, or drowned, or dying of the flu, or stuffing his liver back into its place, nor his stomach, because none of those things happened to Con. I slept in the same cellar with your son on the night he died, but when the lads came in to get him at dawn he was dead beside me on the floor and this lieutenant was shouting at me for dereliction of duty because Con was dead. I got so twisted about the whole thing—Con dead and all, and he such a brave man—that I shouted at the lieutenant, 'What difference is it that he's dead in his sleep when you were going to shoot him when the sun rises?' Only I'd seen Con facing up to Haig the night before I wouldn't have shouted at the lieutenant. But the lieutenant shouted back, 'Dead in his sleep, my arse. Strip him.' The lads with the lieutenant didn't move. Neither did the nurses, nor the orderlies, nor the few ambulance lads who'd been wakened out of the first good night's sleep of their lives to hear this lieutenant shouting for someone to strip the clothes off Con. Then he shouted at his sergeant get down there and smell his mouth, meaning Con's. The sergeant got down real slow like he had the pains of an old man in his knees. He put his nose near Con's face and made a snuffle noise.

'Well, sergeant,' the lieutenant shouted, 'was this man drunk?'

'There's no smell of liquor off him,' the sergeant said.

'Don't stand up, sergeant,' the lieutenant said. 'Cut his clothes off him.'

The sergeant nicked off the buttons of the terrible dirty tunic, and when he pulled it apart his hands got all red from the blood and dirty from the muck. Then he cut apart the gansey that someone had knitted for Con and made diamond shapes in it with different coloured wool, and it was as soppy as a biscuit that was dipped for too long in tea. The more blood the lieutenant saw, the more his feet twitched on the floor, me still lying down beside Con but up on my elbow. Then the buttons of the shirt got snipped off, and then up the middle of the vest went the blade of the sergeant's knife. The sergeant was wet to the wrists with blood the way you'd see a butcher on slaughtering day at the back of his shop after sticking the hanging pigs. When the sergeant pulled everything back off Con's chest there was nothing but blood, and the lieutenant shouted at one of the nurses to wash it away. When she did, there was a small hole in Con's chest just like the hole you'd see in Christ's side where the soldier stuck in the spear and blood and water flowed out. The lieutenant got me by the eyes and started shouting at me like I was a dog. I told him I didn't do it and I didn't know who did it.

'Someone did this to save him from the firing squad,' the lieutenant shouted, and he looked all around the cellar. 'Everyone who spent the night in here up against the wall,' the lieutenant said, 'and you hurry them along, sergeant.'

The sergeant gave a few shouts, and the orderlies and the nurses and the drivers and myself went to the wall, but no matter what the lieutenant said no one said anything because no one had anything to say. Everyone was dead asleep in chairs, or cots, or on the floor, and no one heard anyone moving around in the night. The lieutenant made the sergeant take down everyone's name and number and said there would be an investigation. Then he saw the picture with the words under it cut into the white plaster over the arch, and he looked at it for a while. Then he said to the sergeant 'What's that man's name?' and he pointing to Con on the floor with his stick.

The sergeant pulled the papers of transference out of his

pocket and said, 'Sir, his name is Cornelius Hatchel.'

'Was he Irish?' the lieutenant asked me, and I said he was.

'What did he call himself?'

'He went by Con,' I said.

'Who drew this?' the lieutenant asked, and he touched the picture with his stick and nobody said anything. 'Do you lot mean to tell me that someone came in here last night, killed this man and then cut a memorial stone to him here and no one heard anything? Is that what you're telling me? Everyone stick out your hands,' the lieutenant said, and he walked along looking for plaster dust from the arch. Then he said to his sergeant, 'I want an investigation started right away, and the first thing I want to know is the name of this man's closest friend.'

But I'm ahead of myself altogether, Mrs Hatchel. I have told you the end of the story before the beginning but it doesn't matter now. One way or the other, the lieutenant who came to shoot Con at dawn said Con was murdered, and it doesn't matter if you know that at the start or the stop of the story.

For most of the War I was not at the front at all, and one of the times was that one night in the cellar in Ocean Villas. That wasn't the name of the place but no one could say its name in French. Myself and a few other lucky lads worked around the headquarters where all the big knobs hung out. We were shorter than Fem that was eff and emm together for Field Marshal. Talk about luck getting born short and getting pulled out of the trenches because of it, and all my life in school getting picked on because I was small. We kept headquarters clean and took out the ashes and lit the fires, and emptied the poes, and made the beds, and stuff like that, and went for the coal and food. We were a few steps under a batman; skivvies I suppose we were most of the time. The worst part was we had to be spit and polish all the time, but that was better than the trenches. We got the food that was left and sometimes even a drop of wine out of a glass, but I never understood wine because I'm a Guinness man myself.

Fem had a toady working for him who was called Uphis-arse, and most times Uphis for short. There never was a man more like a dog than Uphisarse and he was under Fem's feet all the time with his tongue out waiting to be told what to do, or to get kicked, or to get his paws stepped on, or to get shouted at, or to get his belly scratched with a good word. Uphisarse, with his wet eyes and the look on his face of a dog wanting to do anything to please—even jump into a fire—used to make my skin feel like there were maggots squirming all over me. It was a real pitiable sight to have to look at Uphisarse being so far up the arse of Fem, if you know what I mean.

On a night around eleven in 1918, I was damping down the fire in Fem's bedroom with the man himself scratching his chest and belly after being in his woolly uniform all day. The sound was like the scratching of fingernails on a taut bed sheet. I hated that sound. Uphis came knocking and whined at Fem for permission to speak and said there was a messenger who'd come a long time ago and wouldn't go away. Fem growled like a lion frightening off a mouse and told Uphis to find out what the message was and to tell him in the morning—in other words telling Uphis to bugger off. Uphis scraped his arse along the floor like a dog scratching his itchy piles and said the mes-senger wouldn't talk to anyone, only to the field marshal; that he'd come hours ago and wouldn't go away because it was urgent and the guards had him. The guards were afraid he had some-thing important for the field marshal because he wouldn't stop telling them the message was very important. Fem growled again, and Uphis scraped his arse on the floor again and said nothing. Then Fem stood up and pulled on his tunic with all its accoutrements. His medals jangled like pennies in an empty bucket, so loud that it was like Fem was shouting at Uphis that this better be important or I'm going to send you yelping through the nearest wall with my boot up your arse. Fem even

put on his Sam Brown because he never let anyone see him not
in full uniform except me and his batman. Maybe that's why
he was growling so much at Uphis because Uphis saw the great
man in his vest and with his galluses down around his arse.
Himself and Uphis went out into Fem's parlour, and I stole over
to the door to listen and look. Uphis was loping for the outside
door but Fem growled at him to hold his horses until the tunic
was buttoned all the way to the neck, and Uphis nearly broke
out in the mange the way Haig snarled at him. When Fem was
all ready he gave the nod, and Uphis fell over himself trying to
get to the knob and there were the guards right outside the doorway with the messenger between them. The guards always
stayed outside because they were a couple of feet taller than
Fem and twice as broad. They were there to stop anyone who
tried to get in and ask them their business and then they told
Uphis and Uphis said yes or no. This night the guards came
into Fem's parlor because they were treating the messenger like
he wanted guarding.

I suppose it was because the guards and Haig and Uphis
were so clean and creased and polished and spitted and relaxed
and well fed, that the messenger looked like a madman, so
dirty and thin and hungry. I could get the stink of him the
minute he came in and it was worse than the worst onion-and-
porter fart I ever smelled. He was covered from head to toe
with wet muck and his uniform was a sopping rag. His face
was wiped the way a boy wipes his nose with a belt of his
sleeve that drags the snot across his face from nose to ears. He
wanted a good shave and there was a lot of white in his eyes
and a lot of muck in his hair. He had no helmet or rifle the
way a soldier always has. The soldier looked like a human rat,
if you know what I mean. You would cross to the other side of
the road if you saw him coming. Uphis and Haig looked at
him the way they'd look at a steaming horse dung served to
them on a dinner plate with gold paint around the edge. Uphis

told the messenger to salute and the mucky soldier gave a snort that sounded like 'fuck you' in snort language. Uphis said, 'Are you a soldier or what?' and the messenger said, 'I am a what, your honour.'

Then Uphis said, 'Salute Field Marshal Haig.'

The messenger saluted like he was in a show on a stage having a go at the army and said, 'Does that make you feel any better, your honour?'

'This man is mad,' Haig growled at Uphis. 'Why is he so dirty, and why was he allowed into my presence stinking like a pig?'

'I'm not mad at all,' the soldier said, 'and I am dirty because I have come from the place you sent me to. I came from the trenches and no-man's-land, and there's bits of dead soldiers in my boots and on my uniform and in my pockets, and that's why I stink like an open grave but that's all beside the point. The message I have for you is what's important, Mr Haig.'

'He is Field Marshal Haig,' Uphis said, 'and you will address the field marshal properly.'

'Why was this madman allowed into my headquarters?' Fem snapped at Uphis.

'Because I kept asking to see the great man because I have an important message for you, Mr Haig,' the soldier said.

'I am *Field Marshal* Haig,' Haig roared, 'and you are insubordinate. Take this man out of my sight; you will hear from me in the morning, Cheeseman'—meaning Uphis, and Uphis whined and protected his balls by pulling his tail between his legs.

The soldier slipped out from between the two big guards before they could grab him, and he ran behind Fem's big desk that was bigger than most people's kitchens. He had a revolver in his hand and he clicked it ready with his other hand. Fem turned around the way a man turns around when he hears a noise behind him when he's walking along a lane in the dark.

A sound even came out of Fem like he expected to get hit. The two guards were stuck to the floor by their flat feet, and Uphis had his fingers at his open mouth with his eyes as big as two ripe plums.

'Look at me, *Field Marshal* Haig!' the soldier shouted. 'Look at me. I am one of your soldiers. Look at me, goddamn you. Look at me. I am the message,' he shouted. 'Look at me. Smell me. It's me in the state that I'm in that's the message. I am the message and I am from all the lads.'

'What lads?' Uphis shouted at the soldier like he was trying to be brave in front of Fem.

The soldier waved the revolver in Haig's direction. 'What lads do you think I'm talking about only the lads in the trenches with the rats, and the lads dead and the rats eating them?' the soldier said. 'The lads out in the land rotting under their packs or drying out like mackerel on the wire; the lads floating in the shell holes all swelled up like drowned dogs in the Canal with a rock tied around the neck waiting for a tench to burst them so they can sink again; the lads in the trenches waiting to go over the top with their feet rotten in the rotten water standing on last week's corpses and wading around in their own shite and piss and vomiting on each other with the fright.'

'You will stop this,' Uphis shouted, like he was afraid the soldier's words would splash onto Fem's immaculate uniform and dirty it.

The soldier didn't hear Uphis and said, 'As well as a message I am an invitation to Field Marshal Haig to come up to the trenches to enjoy the muck, and the rats, and the shite, and the piss, and the rotten corpses, and rotten horses. The lads told me to invite you to the picnic they're having and you're to bring your camel loaded with claret to give the lads a toddy. They want the impeccable field marshal to go up to see the view from the grand places you keep sending them to. The lads said to bring your impeccable wife with you to the trenches.'

Uphis ran over and slapped the flat of his hand on the top of the desk and at the same time shouted at the soldier to shut his mouth, but he nearly fell when he was backing away real quick when the soldier pointed his gun at him.

The soldier looked back to Haig and said, 'Your wife would love to see the way the rats use their little claws to hold onto a man's face when it's eating his cheeks, when it's sucking the eyes out of him.'

'I'm ordering you to shut your mouth!' Uphis shouted across the room, but the soldier never even blinked.

'If your wife wants to swim before the picnic she can hold onto the lads who have floated to the top, use them to hold onto when she gets tired.'

Uphis could do nothing but stand there and cringe and shiver like a dog that knows a hobnailed boot is on its way to its arse. Fem had to take over and he barked, 'Where's your unit?'

The soldier said, 'Near Ocean Villas where you sent all the Newfoundlanders to fall like a lost herd of crying, cornered caribou in front of machine guns.'

'And is your commanding officer aware of your where-abouts?' Haig asked.

'I didn't tell him I was coming to see you, if that's what you mean. I know that if he had known he wouldn't have said, 'Say hello to Haig for me.' He'd have said, 'Shoot the fucker when you see him.'

'You are a deserter,' Haig said, pretending the soldier hadn't a gun. 'There will be no orderly room for you, Mister.'

I nearly collapsed onto the floor when Fem shouted out my name at the top of his lungs without even looking over his shoulder at his bedroom door. For a second I thought he'd caught me listening and was going to court-martial me. I wasn't able to get myself moving quick enough, and he shouted out my name again. I came out with the coal scuttle still in my hand and I wanted to go to the lav badly, I was so frightened.

'You are a witness in a court martial, Simkins. This man is guilty of desertion by his own admission.'

Fem sat down at his smaller desk at the wall and took a piece of paper out of his drawer, and took one of the twelve pens he had in twelve inkwells on his desk. As usual he looked at the nib before he started to write, hoping he was going to find a hair in it so he could shout at his batman. Fem took in a breath like he was going to say something when the soldier said, 'Cornelius Francis Hatchel. That's spelled C-o-r-n-e-l-i-u-s F-r-a-n-c-i-s; not 'es' like a girl's. I'm called Con by my familiars. H-a-t-c-h-e-l, as Irish as Paddy's pig, is my last name and as old as a Roman emperor is my first.' Then he told Fem a number and a stretcher unit that I can't remember because I was never good at sums.

While Haig wrote, Con said, 'The wife will have to be careful not to swallow any of the stuff in the trenches because its full of shite and piss and vomit and rotting feet and rotting horse flesh and rotting man flesh. I've heard it said by lads who got a mouthful of the stuff that German soldiers taste better from all that beer they drink; it gives their meat a nice flavour, like the taste of the sun in barley-fed bacon. During the picnic she'll have to make sure to keep the flies off her little sandwiches and to hold them up over her head, but even then the rats might run up along her and out along her arm. She'll have to hold her water for a long time because there's no place for a woman to go unless she does it when she's halfway up her belly in trench water.'

Haig stood up from his desk and his chair fell over behind him. It made a loud noise, and Uphis made like he was going to get the chair but then thought better if it. Haig roared, 'Shut your mouth. Shut your filthy mouth. As field marshal of the British Expeditionary Force I find you guilty of desertion. You will be brought back to Ocean Villas, and Simkins will give this envelope to your officer. You will be shot at dawn.'

Con didn't hear Haig, and he said, 'The lads will make a path of duckboards for your wife so the hem of her dress won't drag across the piles of rotting guts and disturb the flies mixing their dinner with their own shite between their front legs.'

'Shut up!' Fem bellowed, like a lion with its paw in a spring trap, and everyone in the room except Con shook. 'Cheeseman, arrange a detail to take this man back to his unit. Simkins, you will deliver the papers of transference.' When he stuck the envelope out at me, I didn't know what to do with the coal scuttle and it fell on the floor. The coal went everywhere, and when I went down on my knees to pick it all up, Fem roared at me, 'Get off the floor, you buffoon,' and when I did he stuck the letter in my face.

'You're a cavalryman yourself, Mr Haig,' Con said. 'Surely they'll make a statue of you on a horse after the War to pretend to themselves how great the War was, and when all the people are cheering you, Mr Haig, it's not cheering you will hear but only the hisses of the men you sent to hell while they were still alive. Remember me, Mr Haig, when they pull the cover off the statue and you see yourself up there being proud on the horse's back, and listen to the hissing and the booing of the young lads you sent to the butcher, not for a pound of beef, but to get butchered themselves.'

'Take that man out of here!' Fem shouted, and when the two guards didn't come to life, Fem shouted at Con, 'Give that revolver to me, soldier.' Con looked at the revolver like he'd never seen it before, and he let it fall onto the top of the big desk in front of him. The gun went off and the bullet hit the row of inkwells and pens on Fem's other desk and everyone jumped.

The two big soldiers ran over and grabbed Con. They dragged him out through the door with Uphis and myself after them. Uphis was running so as to get out of Fem's sight as quick as he could.

That's how I was one of the lads in the detail that brought Con back to his own unit about six miles in the dark to Ocean Villas. That's how I come to have slept beside your son that last night and how he gave me your address, and he wrote on the inside of the Woodbine box a message for me to put in the letter. 'Matt, we got to the far end of the Mediterranean, and we saw Africa. Remember the Canal. Marry Kitty. Tell them all I love them. And Sarah. Your brother, Con.' That's exactly what he wrote, and I'd send you the Woodbine box only I promised it to the lads down at the legion hall as a bit of the war.

That's all I can tell you, and I hope I have done right what Professor said to do.

Billy Simkins

Kitty Hatchel

For the first few weeks after his return I did not believe the old Matthias could ever catch up with the body that had come home from the War. He didn't know when he was hungry. He was barely able to take care of himself in the other departments, sometimes coming out of the bushes with dribbles on his trousers from crotch to ankle. We had to tell him when it was time for bed. He seemed unable to take his eyes off the past, to pull them back and put them on my face, on anyone's face. Many times, when riding home from Enderly, I'd find him leaning on the parapet of the Bridge, staring down into the calm water. I could be leaning on the smooth stones beside him for five minutes before he'd notice me.

In our efforts to rush him back into our world, we couldn't see that Matt was not able to put one foot in front of the other. We did not understand at all that he had just stepped out of a gargantuan, screaming meat grinder, as Missus Hodgkins called the War; that he was still hearing the crunching gears of the grinder, still seeing the feeding of soldiers into the machine's gaping mouth by the thousands, still smelling the freshly spilled, cloying intestines of young screaming men, still inhaling the steam that rose out of the ever-fresh streams of hot blood. We just did not know that Matt was still in Belgium or France, that we only had his body. He was a child still seeing whiteness no matter where he looked after lying on the Canal bank staring into the sun for ages, imagining the sun was a hole in the sky, an opening to be flown through on the quick wings of a woodquest.

Without having been told, I knew Mammy and Daddy were keeping a wary eye on Matt, afraid he would do himself harm, afraid he would drown himself. Several times, Daddy had 'accidentally' met up with him in the fields, had tried to get Matt to talk, had tried to talk to him. But Daddy told Mammy, 'It's like the time the house burned down and I found him sitting under the elm and when I said where's the others he didn't answer because he'd only have to hear what he'd have to tell me. I'd say he can't talk about the War now because he can't bear to hear what he'll have to tell.'

But as the long days went by, bits and pieces began to come out of him. Daddy and Mammy and I, and eventually Missus Hodgkins and Sarah, told each other what we had heard. When we put them together we began to have some inkling of how he and Con had lived and survived among the tumbling blades and milling rollers of the grinder.

It had taken a week to decide whether we should show Billy Simkins's letter to Matthias. In the end, with encouragement from Missus Hodgkins, we decided that if Matt saw Con's death from another man's point of view, it would help to lighten his load of sorrow and remorse.

And the reading of Billy Simkins's letter was to Matt what the first unaided step is to a child learning to walk. His face didn't light up with surprise and delight; he didn't seek the applause of encouraging parents, but it brought a change. He straightened up, confidence seemed to have seeped into him. He combed his hair.

But still he was mainly silent. After more futile interceptions in the lonely fields, Daddy said, 'We know what he had to do to take care of Con. He told us he used the knife on others. We can only imagine how many.'

On my way home from Enderly a week after he'd read the Simkins letter, I found Matt on the Bridge staring down. For many long silent minutes I gazed with him at the comings and goings of two eels in the coping stones under the Bridge; the playful slithering in and out of the openings between the stones was hypnotizing. As usual, it was difficult to tell if Matt was seeing what I was seeing or if he was looking at the War. I turned to him as if his face might give some inkling about what he was seeing. I might as well have been looking at a weather-worn stone.

The newspapers had never told us what the War was like for the ordinary soldier and even the 'Pimpernel' reporter had spared us the truth about the trenches. All during the War, we had read of great victories and small defeats, of explosions in Belgium that were heard in London. The papers had told us what the governments had wanted us to hear. We had no idea at all what the state of the fields was after a battle, what they were littered with. We didn't even know about the barbed wire.

Without turning his head away from the water below, Matt said, 'I have to tell you something, Kitty.' His use of my name upset the even rhythm of my heart.

In a voice he had not owned before he went away, Matt spoke with deliberation, with the gravity of a man who would not be interrupted by priest or nun. 'Killing Con in that house in France was the right thing to do at the time. But now that I'm back home where Con always was with us, I can't see how it was the right thing to do at all. I should have taken hold of him and run.'

What was there for me to say? I couldn't think of anything. I could have said, 'It was the circumstances of the times that were in it, Matt.' But I didn't know to say that. It was Missus Hodgkins who suggested I say that to him in the future if he spoke of rights and wrongs in the War, rights and wrongs that couldn't be measured against the ordinariness of everyday life in Ballyrannel.

The eels chased each other, head to tail, in and out of the coping stones. They looked like the rim of a bike-wheel spinning on its side in the water, and I saw a barefooted boy with the tail of his shirt flying in the wind, a short stick in his hand and he joyfully running at full tilt beside a spokeless bike-wheel.

Finally, I put my hand on Matt's shoulder—the first time I'd touched him since we'd knelt around him on the kitchen floor that day he came home. He didn't shrug me off. Very gently, like I was lowering a baby into sleep, I moved my hand around Matt's back. His shoulders heaved when he took in a deep breath. 'I don't know how many men I killed. Most of them were bundles of guts with a beating heart and maybe an arm or a leg sticking out.'

I wanted to hide my face, turn away from his words, but I kept my hand on him.

'I'd poke around looking for the heart in the mess. Sometimes I could see it, beating away like it was hoping the body would put itself back together again. I'd stick them with my knife the way I'd poke a pointed stick into soft clay to make a hole for a cabbage plant. Thousands of them, and that's not a lie, not an exaggeration. The dying lads, more or less recognizable as men and still conscious, I'd lie down with, snuggle up to them, and sing while I was slipping the knife into their hearts so they'd know someone was there with them while they were dying. Knifey was what I called my knife. She was a nurse, a nun, a Sister of Mercy.'

With my right hand I kept a grasp on the capstone of the Bridge, my knuckles white, my eyes on the side of Matt's aged face. He was speaking in a distant voice, no ups or downs.

'Do you know what I sang to them, Kitty?' He turned as slowly as a loaded barge turning in the Harbour and he looked at my face for the first time in four years. I had to make myself not turn away. His eyes were still far away but he was making a huge effort to pull them home from the War, to focus them on mine, to speak to me the things he didn't want to look at anymore. He moved his face flesh like a drunk man trying to show he wasn't drunk. 'Do you know what I sang to them, Kitty?' And quietly he began to sing, so quietly, that if a man had been standing on the Towpath below he could not have heard. His eyes sank into mine and mine sank into his and I felt something like I felt the first time I stripped off my clothes with Matt looking at me all over. 'Here comes the pony, his day's work is done, And down through the meadow he now takes a run. Up go his heels and down goes his head, It's time little children were going to bed.'

Before he got to the last line, Matt's face had begun to change, his eyes had flowed over, and streams were trickling down his face. Like he had his mouth full of sticky Bullseyes, he said, 'Mammy used to sing that to me on her lap in front of the fire before putting me to bed.' He lost all control over his voice and he cried out the agony of a big animal in pain; and I knew the sound of his anguish was speeding along the top of the water to the Harbour in one direction and on past the Supply in the other. He leaned into me, nearly fell. I took his head onto my shoulder and pressed the side of his face into my neck. He cried from the depths, as the *De profundis* says at the end of Mass. We both sank to the ground at the foot of the parapet, and I held him there until Daddy came looking, thinking someone was in the Canal and shouting for help. I moved my hand at him and he went away.

Missus Hodgkins

During the War I often thought that Kitty and I should have been sisters-in-anxiety because of our common fears. But the anxiety I suffered for Sarah and Lionel during the War did not get its grip on Kitty until Matthias returned from Europe; it was only when he got back that she became anxious about his survival.

Before he got home to Ballyrannel at all, while he was still off out there someplace picking his way homeward across the terrible fields of Europe, I had told Kitty I wanted him back working at Enderly. 'Getting back into the routine of a workday will be the best thing for him, will get his mind off what he's seen,' I said. And when he came home and Kitty told me she wasn't getting anywhere with Matthias, I told her that in three days' time I would go out to the house and speak to him myself.

The three days' notice was my way of warning Kitty's mother that she would be having a visitor; a rich visitor was about to descend on a poor house. Poorer people get embarrassed when someone they imagine to be of higher status comes into their houses. God forbid that the priest or the doctor is suddenly summoned to a poor house; the sweeping and the scurrying that goes on, the hiding of old boots and coats and the throwing of buckets and baskets into the nearest hiding places, the dog shouted out from under the kitchen table. I know the poor do it because I do it myself whenever someone, rich or poor, is on their way to visit Enderly.

But, even if a poorer woman has time to prepare for a visitor, there is no way to change the things that speak of poverty: a front door that's scarred and holed from the teeth and claws of generations of dogs frightened of thunder; a cement floor with the swirls of the smoothing trowel still in it; a thatched house without ceilings that dropped bits of ancient straw into tea mugs; homemade furniture that can never be made to shine like ancient, tooled and polished oak; walls that begin to turn brown from turf smoke on the same day they are freshly white-washed; a kettle-and-pot crane over the open fire thickly enam-elled in years of black soot splattering down the broad chimney whenever it rains. No visitor, except for doctor or priest, ever gets further than the kitchen.

Most better-off people respect the pride of the poor and never put themselves in the position of having to be invited into the poor person's house. But even if I say so myself, I have the knack for fitting into a poor woman's kitchen; instead of arriv-ing grandly in the pony and trap I use the infernal cycle, wob-bling all over the place. I wear clothes that have seen their best days a long time ago; I plunk into the homemade kitchen chair, take off my headscarf, stretch out my legs with their good but worn shoes, accept the offered tea and eat the homemade bread. I admire knick-knacks that deserve admiration and compliment by talking about the never-ending job of keeping a house clean.

Kitty said that when she told her mother about my impend-ing visit her mammy got into a flutter, got as fussed-up as a brooding hen, as agitated as a sow making a nest for the arrival of her litter. When Mister Hatchel suggested that Matthias should 'accidentally' intercept me on the Bridge and in doing so keep me away from the house, he believed he had relieved his wife of the need to clean the house from top to bottom.

And so it was that I was accidentally 'come across' by Missus Hatchel after I had accidentally 'come across' Matthias on the Bridge that day. According to Kitty, 'Mammy' had been on the lookout for my arrival. When Mammy 'coincidentally' went for a walk and began to cross over the Bridge, she pretended to be surprised at the sight of Matthias and his visitor.

I dislike the name Mammy. It reminds me of a pair of old, overused mammaries hanging down around the navel.

'Oh, Missus Hodgkins, it's grand to see you,' Missus Hatchel said, and she had a little chat with me about the weather. She finished up by saying, 'Maybe you'd like to call in for a cup of tea on your way home.' And Missus Hatchel was so excited that she forgot to cross the Bridge. She went home and buttered the slices of bread she had carefully cut, making sure they were the same thickness at the top and the bottom. And she peeked under the spread-over tea towel to make sure there were no bits of straw in the cups she'd got for a wedding present from Poor Meg, decorated with yellowhammers in leaf-bare, red-berried winter bushes.

On the Bridge, Matthias did not turn to look at me when I propped the Raleigh against the parapet. He glanced at my face when I began to talk, as if the voice was familiar and he was trying to place it.

I never dreamed that the steely self-control I'd manufactured and wrapped around myself like a suit of armour would come apart at the rivets that day. I did not even suspect that instead of giving comfort and encouragement to Matthias, it would be he who would give those things to me.

For a few short minutes things went as planned. I told Matthias how Charlie Coffey, our foreman, and his wife had died of the influenza. 'I need a good man to take over the farm, Matthias. I think you'd be a better organizer than any of the other lads, and anyhow, they're all afraid of the job; none of them will take it on. If everything works out all right then you can have Charlie's cottage in a few months. We'll give it a new coat of whitewash, paint the windows and the door.'

And suddenly, for no discernible reason, my suit of armour collapsed around my feet and my brain escaped, took off on its own. 'Oh, Matthias, they said Lionel got lost between Ypres and Passchendaele. And there's Sarah ... Oh, Matthias.' And then I was crying with my forehead on Matt's shoulder. And I pleaded, a fistful of Matthias's jacket in my clenched hand, 'Tell me what it was like. Tell me about the place where my Lionel died. I know from the "Pimpernel" stories that you were at Passchendaele too.'

Matthias peered down onto the smooth surface of the Canal as if he were reading the mysterious tracks of the water striders. After a long, long time he spoke unhurriedly.

'Passchendaele was higher than Wipers and the Germans were up there with their guns. Our lads were always trying to capture it.' He paused so long, I was afraid he'd come to a full stop. 'If a soldier went missing in action there, it meant he'd gone down into the mud somewhere in the seven miles between the two towns. Besides all the other lads who got killed and were found, eighty thousand lads disappeared between Wipers and Passchendaele and were never heard of again, not a trace of them ever found. Eighty thousand.' He stopped, as if trying to imagine eighty thousand men.

'Con would have said ... I was there in 1917, lying on my back on the edge of a road just below Tyne Cot. I was getting a rest after pulling myself out of the muck the way a nearly drowned man would put his hands on the bank of a river and pull himself out shaking all over. There was a dressing station in Tyne Cot beside the old German pillbox. Rain, not heavy, was coming down onto my face, and the clouds were low, like home, like we were on our backs on the Canal bank, Con and Kitty, looking up at clouds so low we could reach up and make swirls.'

Matthias went silent again and I wanted to shake him, to keep him going, to hand me whatever little scrap he had to tell me. 'Everything was the colour of wet turf, brown-black, not a green leaf, not a blade of grass. The man on the stretcher had gone quiet, and I thought he might be dead after all our trouble, eight of us after carrying him out, sometimes with the muck up to our bellies, the stretcher up at our shoulders. But I didn't care enough about the stretcher-case to bother myself with him. The other seven lads were lying down on the road too, catching their breath, trying to get the blood back into their shoulder muscles.'

Oh God, I thought, will you keep going and tell me something about Lionel.

'I was so dirty, so wet, so hungry, so tired that I did not believe I would ever get myself going again. I hadn't been able, or maybe it was that I wasn't interested enough, to unbutton my trousers for a long time, days, maybe a week, and I'd been doing in them what I had to do whenever I had to. I must have stunk worse than rotten potatoes.

'I don't know if I took out Knifey, but I do know that I thought about her, about how nice and easy she could do for me what she'd done for all the other lads. All I'd have to do was set her handle in a little hole in the road, put a slant on her blade, and roll onto her. And while I was thinking about Knifey, one of the lads said, by way of warning, "Staff car coming." But no one moved, no one looked up. The car had nowhere to go unless it ran over us first. It stopped within inches of the lad who'd warned us. "And fuck you too," the lad said, his arm a pillow to keep his head off the road and the wind-up handle of the car six inches above him. "Why don't you just drive on over me and put me out of my misery? I don't care a shite."

'My arm was a pillow too, and I was facing the car. The driver jumped out shouting, "Party, 'shun!" No one gave any sign that they'd heard him except the lad under the wind-up handle. He said, "And fuck you too," and he didn't know or care if anyone heard him. The driver didn't know yet that he had crossed the boundary into hell a few miles ago. He roared at us again to jump to our feet for inspection. Then the car swayed on its springs and two more pairs of feet stepped out of the car. One of them could have been a lieutenant, from what I could see of his patches. The other one had so many stripes and ribbons and medals that he must have been someone near the top.

'In my eyes, close to the road, he was standing ramrod straight, his high leather boots shining, his hands behind his back. The driver shouted, "Party, 'shun!" and this officer said calmly, "It's all right, driver." He looked at us, from one to the other, scattered about on the road. He looked at the man on the stretcher who was, in fact, dead.

'The officer put his hands on his hips. He looked at the lake of porridge we had just crossed, saw teams of plunging horses, saw other teams of stretcher-bearers wading their ways toward us carrying their loads at chest level. The muck-covered men and animals were moving slowly like ants after their nest has been flooded with treacle by a cruel child.

'The officer's hands fell to his sides. He took a few steps forward as if he were making sure that the muddy lumps were really the bodies of men and horses, that the big things poking up into the sky were once shining guns that had shot one-ton shells two miles into the distance. And his eyes went all the way to the village on the hill, Passchendaele, and he seeing for the first time what the hell-fields of three battles look like.

'He joined his hands at his crotch, laced his fingers together like a man who knows he has to protect himself. He turned and looked back toward Wipers. In his spit and polish, his ribbons and stripes, he looked down at us; none of us wearing a helmet, our hair matted and stuck to our heads, the rest of our bodies coated in wet mud, the whites of our eyes all the whiter in our black faces. We were more like dug-up corpses than soldiers of the king. We were men exhausted beyond exhaustion, too exhausted to show him respect, too exhausted to talk to him. He looked again at the awful mud, six feet deep in places. The ground all around us, from Passchendaele to Wipers, was churned up, loose and watery like what comes out of a sick animal's hole. The shell craters were lakes, and in the lake-water terrible things floated and at the bottom of the lakes terrible bits of things lay piled up. Bodies that had been buried here at Tyne Cot earlier in the War had been ploughed up in bits and pieces by the latest shelling. To this officer of rank, the smell of the rotting flesh must have been sickening.

'When he looked down again and saw what we had become, a sob shook his whole body, shook him violently because he had been fighting against what he knew what was going to come out of him in front of subordinates. He stumbled back until he was leaning against the car. He snatched his hat off his head, and said, "Good God. Good God, did we send men to fight in this?" He didn't try to hide his face in his hands while he cried. Then he turned around and laid his forehead on his arms on the car's edge. The sounds of his other fist pounding the roof of the car were mixed with the strange sounds coming out of his mouth, the high-pitched, sad sounds a pig makes when the long knife is pressing on its flesh above its heart. Then he threw up and his shining boots got splattered with his own vomit.'

Matthias stopped talking there, just like that, and I waited in vain for him to go on. But he was finished talking about that place called Passchendaele where my child had either drowned, been shot, or blown to smithereens. And I knew that, no matter what had happened to him, no part of him would be found and that he would never be tenderly buried, like a son should be, showered with tears. Somewhere in Belgium, beneath many feet of soil, my Lionel lay lost like a drowned swimmer, arms and legs stretched out in the clutching, hardening clay that pressed into his unprotected face.

On the Bridge over the Canal, I grasped Matthias's upper arm and cried for Lionel and for Sarah, for my David, for Con, and for every young man who had died at Passchendaele, for every young man who'd been wasted in the War, for their mothers and fathers. I cried in shame, too, for making Matthias revisit that place whose very name spoke of the last passions of so many young lads.

Kitty Hatchel

Two mornings after Missus Hodgkins's visit, Matthias was in the kitchen when I got up. Hope welled in my chest. In sleep-raspy voices we good-morninged each other. Silently, we drank tea and ate buttered bread. When I took my coat off the hook at the back of the door, Matt stood up and followed me into the yard. He already had Daddy's battered, big-framed BSA bike lying against the gable end of the house when I wheeled Mammy's bike out of the turf shed.

'Please, God,' I prayed.

While I freewheeled down the far side of the Bridge, I slyly cast an eye back across the Canal, and he was there on the other side, off the saddle, pushing down on the pedals with all his weight as if he'd forgotten that the only way to beat the steep slope was to go at it with speed already gathered on the flat. Then I promised myself I wouldn't look again till I got to the Harbour but I couldn't bear it that far. As I was passing the entrance to the Lamberts', I glanced over my shoulder, pretended to be looking at the pile of ashes that had lain in the foundations of the big house since it was burned down by the IRA. Like I always did, I shivered at the remembrance of the two old brothers, struggling to escape the flames but dying inside—the pain, the screams.

In the corner of my eye, Matthias was two hundred yards

back. By the time I wheeled off Harbour Lane onto Bops, I knew I was letting myself get carried away, that in reality Matthias still had years to travel before he finally came home; I knew he'd look at me again as if I were a stranger; knew I had to dampen my galloping hope that he had suddenly snapped back into our world. And what I hoped for outweighed what I knew.

When I was on the Marbra Road for a mile, he began to catch up with me. Just as I steered into the Hodgkins's avenue he drew level and his fat tyres made a grinding sound in the gravel. My heart was pounding, the palms of my hands so damp that they slipped on the handlebars. He said, 'Kitty, I'm going to work for Missus Hodgkins and I'm going to marry you when I get better. I'll be seeing Con all over Enderly.'

I got into such a wobble that I nearly fell off my bike. By the time I got around the last bend on the avenue, Matt had gone through the green wicket gate in the Famine wall surrounding the farmyard and the house.

Exactly one month later, on a wet day, Sarah Hodgkins went out to the farmyard just before dinnertime. She stood in the doorway of the Machine Shed and looked at Matthias, fat drops dripping onto her rain hat off the wooden lintel above her.

Missus Hodgkins had seen Sarah passing the kitchen window, and now she had her nose pressed against the glass, rubbing away the fog of her breath every few seconds with the corner of her floury apron. She was making little noises as she spied on her daughter, and her fingertips played against the glass as if she were a wild animal not knowing it was clawing for its freedom. She said later that she was suffering from the hope that this might be the beginning of the moment when Sarah's mind would be snapped off whatever it was that was holding her in the past.

When Sarah darkened the doorway under the dripping lintel, Matthias glanced up from his work and said, 'Come in out of the rain.' She did, and it was twenty minutes more before she spoke, asked Matt where Con was and he told her he was buried in a cemetery near Ocean Villas in France. She asked him how Con had died, and he told her that he'd been shot while loading a casualty onto a stretcher.

'At the time, I thought it was the easiest thing for her to hear,' he told me many months later.

Silently, Sarah looked at Matt shaving a new wooden handle for a drill harrow. He knew she was weeping but he didn't do or say anything, kept shaving the handle as if she weren't there. After a long time, she went away.

Missus Hodgkins didn't stop talking that day after Sarah came back from the Machine Shed. She dusted every piece of furniture on the first floor while she talked to me through the open kitchen door. Her speech was full of 'maybe this', 'maybe that', 'I hope', 'I pray', 'Poor Sarah', 'Poor Lionel', 'David'. Then she said Con's and Matt's names, because she never recited her list of losses without remembering them.

On the day after their first encounter, Sarah suddenly appeared in the Machine Shed door again. It wasn't raining, so she didn't have to go in. It took her a long time to ask Matt if he'd been wounded.

'Just these,' he said, and rubbed the side of his face, 'from tiny bits of a hot shell.'

After a long time Matt asked her, 'Why are you wearing that veil?'

Her face had been burned in the same fire that burned five other VADs to death in a dressing station in France, she said.

'How long were you in hospital after the fire?'

'About nineteen months.'

'Where?'

'Pine Haven.'

'In Scotland?'

'Yes. Edinburgh,' Sarah said. She stepped into the shed and moved her fingers over the nearest of the centre poles that held up the roof of the wide shed. She looked at the barkless, age-polished, pine pole the way a woman looks at a baby's face while she traces her fingers over the soft flesh, as if she loved the wood like a woman loving the face of her baby. 'I knitted a jersey for Con while I was there, diamonds in four colours.'

'He was wearing it when he was killed,' Matt said. Sarah brought her hands to her face like someone who's heard something they don't know what to do with.

Missus Hodgkins stayed at the kitchen window until she invented a reason to go out and walk past the Machine Shed door. When she came back she was almost grinning. 'She's only ten feet away from Matthias,' she said, 'and they're talking.'

A black and spikey feeling swept around my chest.

Matt said to Sarah, 'I was in a hole near the very end with an officer who'd just come back from Pine Haven, "And here I am," he says, "in a shell hole on my first day back with a dead horse and a live Irishman." I asked him would he like it better the other way around—dead Irishman and live horse? He laughed with every part of his face except his eyes. He had dreadful eyes. His name was Owen, first or last I don't remember; his name reminded me of Owen Egan. Poor Ownie's all shell-shocked. I asked him about his wound and he said, "Pine Haven is for the head, not the body." '

Matthias didn't tell Sarah that when Owen said Pine Haven was for head injuries, that he'd put the tip of his index finger against his temple, twirled his hand and said, 'Dottyville.'

Soon Sarah was finding Matt every day and staying near him. The long silences of one didn't seem to bother the other.

And I knew what I was feeling was jealousy.

'Did you kill anyone?' Sarah asked Matt when he was putting in a new stile for the Lower Paddock.

And Matt said, 'I did—men so wounded they had no chance of living.' He thought the conversation was over, but a long time later Sarah asked, 'What about God?'

'What about God?'

'Only God has the right to kill.'

Matthias rested the heavy head of the mallet on top of the stile post. 'I saw what was on the battlefield when the shooting stopped. God wasn't there. I was. I killed men who were better dead than alive.' Matthias hammered the post down into the earth to the eighteen-inch notch he had cut with his knife. 'There is no God, Sarah, that's why he wasn't in France or Belgium between 1914 and 1918.'

Sarah went over to the wooden paddock fence, put her hands on the top and looked for a long time across the field to the trees where the flocks of crows came home to roost every night.

Matthias used the partially constructed stile to climb into the paddock. With the crowbar, he pierced the earth and twisted it around in the hole. Before he pulled it out he said, 'I am not a murderer, Sarah. I saved men. I saved the ones I brought back, and I saved the ones that were too bad to bring back.'

Sarah turned away from the tall trees and looked at Matt. For the first time, they looked at each other's eyes, stayed looking for a long time. Then Matthias told me they heard me whacking the gong to tell them dinner was ready.

Another day, Sarah and Matthias were coming back to the farmyard after moving sixty-two yearlings into a field of aftergrass. From one corner of the Big Pasture to the other, they were almost walking side by side, she a few steps behind.

'Did you know that Con thought you were a goddess?' Matthias asked.

Sarah said nothing, almost stopped walking, felt her veil to make sure it was tied properly.

'Con said you were the most beautiful girl in the world. When you were near him he couldn't talk because you were so beautiful, and he said if he lived in a fairy tale you would kiss him and he'd turn into a wartier frog than the one he was already. He'd say, "Whenever Sarah came near me I couldn't talk and all my warts lit up like the Christmas lights we saw in the Liffey that time."'

Sarah made a noise and her veil swelled out in front of her mouth. 'Con hadn't warts,' she said.

'He felt he had when you were near him. Many times when we hadn't spoken for a long time, one of us would ask the other what was he thinking about. Con had two answers; Sarah or The Canal, but most times it was Sarah. Under hedges, in trenches, under stretchers, on our backs looking up at the stars, looking at the faraway War at night, once in a shell hole where we'd been for five hours, it was always Sarah. He was in love with you, or at least he imagined he was, and you were someone for him to hold on to. You were with him all the time, Sarah, keeping him going. The only time he took off the jersey you knitted for him was to wash himself or it. Sarah's diamonds, he always called it.' When Matthias came to the Back Gate he began to hold it open for Sarah but when he stepped aside for her, she was standing twenty feet back. She was turned away from him. He knew she was crying and he didn't know what to do. He went on and let the Back Gate swing shut after him.

Two months later, shortly after moving into the foreman's cottage, Matt was sitting up with a mare, waiting for her to foal. It was two o'clock in the morning when Sarah quietly opened the stable door. In the light of the yard lamp she quietly placed a mug of tea and a buttered scone on an upturned bucket. Matt was lying in an armful of straw in the corner of the stall. Sarah went to the opposite corner and sat on the ancient crushed-oats chest, coated with the dried drool of fifty years of passing horses.

After a while, Matt whispered, 'Is that for me?' meaning the tea and the scone.

'It's not for Jackdempsey,' Sarah whispered back, the first glimmer of lightheartedness that Matt heard from her. The giant horse, Jackdempsey, was two stalls away, standing as he slept.

Quietly, Matt rolled out of the crinkling straw. When he

finished eating he hung the mug on a hook in the door and sat on the upturned bucket, nearer to Sarah. He leaned back against the door. They looked at the big-bellied mare lying in the straw, her short, irregular pushes trying to get her foal started on its journey. Matthias already had the mare's tail wrapped in sacking and binder twine.

'Do you ever feel bad about the lads you killed?' Sarah whispered. She waited the long time it took for Matthias to line up his words. 'Guilty?' she prompted. 'Do you ever feel guilty?'

When he finally answered, Matt spoke like a man in the confessional but it was only because of the nervous mare that he was whispering. 'I could have brought them back to the dressing stations to get patched up. They'd have lived the rest of their lives in pain and blindness and deafness and crippleness and loneliness, sides of faces gone, jaws and chins shot away, faces wiped clean by red-hot shrapnel, no noses, no eyes. There and then, at that moment when I was pushing Knifey into them, I was saving them from surviving another few hours as bundles of pain till all the blood soaked out and they roared with thirst, if they had tongues or throats to roar with. If I feel any guilt, it's because I didn't save more of them. I brought back too many that were stitched together like rag dolls, like worn sacks patched on a winter's night, and sent to old soldiers' homes to stare at white ceilings for the rest of their lives while someone else fed and wiped them because they were paid to do it.'

The mare made a sudden move with her head, made the pruttering-smuffering noise horses make with their big lips that sounds like they're asking a question. Then the mare's bag broke, and the water ran out of her like a big splash flowing out of an overturned bucket. Jackdempsey rattled his lips in his sleep.

'It won't be long now,' Matthias whispered.

'That's what the monkey said when the train ran over his tail,' Sarah said. Matthias looked at her as if he was looking at a cat standing on its hind legs with a fiddle under its chin and a bow in its paw. Sarah didn't turn her eyes away. Matt told me that it was because he believed she was smiling behind her veil, that she was strong for a moment, that he asked her, 'Were they able to do anything at Pine Haven? Patch you up?'

Sarah felt the edges of her veil, satisfied herself that it was in place. The mare groaned. The two white hooves of the foal had appeared in the blackness of the vulva. Sarah whispered, 'I know how to help. Daddy always let me clean the new foals.'

The legs slipped out and the nose was exactly between the legs near the knees. They sat and waited and watched and let the mare push out her foal before they stood, then made quiet noises to let the mare know they were close by. It was after four o'clock when Matthias and Sarah said goodnight to each other, sounding like two normal people.

It was a long time before I heard about the foaling, but even with all that time gone by, a cold, thorny, iron bar turned around inside my chest, tore at the strings around my heart.

Kitty Hatchel

Missus Hodgkins had not taken Jackdempsey out since Sarah and Lionel went to the War. She said she had lost the will to enjoy herself. Jackdempsey had grown fat and wild, and Phil Kelly had tried and failed to gallop him back into shape.

Seeing Matt stepping into Enderly that first time since he'd gone away with Con must have touched something inside Missus Hodgkins, maybe rekindled the joy she'd once known when the farmyard was all abustle with men and animals. The first thing she told Matt he had to do was bring Jackdempsey out for long rides to drain all the built-up energy out of him, to retame him.

Not long after her first few encounters with Matthias, Sarah was out at the early-morning stables holding Jackdempsey by the bridle while Matt saddled the horse and cinched the leather girth into its big buckle, Jackdempsey not needing to be held at all.

Then, one morning at the sink, while trying to keep my eyes away from the kitchen window, out comes Sarah with her mother's quiet old mare, Timahoe. Sarah was wearing riding trousers. I stood there astonished, mouth open, jealousy fanning itself into flames as big as the ones on Easter-candle wicks. Sarah brought the horse over to the saddling stile, climbed the three steps and gently placed herself onto Timahoe's back. The second her far foot went into the stirrup, Sarah trotted off with Jackdempsey following and Matt's long, untrimmed hair floated on the gentle wind.

My once-upon-a-time prince had ridden off with the princess, and the scullery maid was left holding a bucket of dirty water. What could I do? Red hot tears came out of me, ran down my face. I made a loud sigh of despair. Then I felt a hand on my shoulder, and I stiffened like I would if I felt something crawling across my face in the bed in the dark.

'Kitty, Kitty, Kitty.' It was Missus Hodgkins. She moved her hand around my upper back, what I'd often seen her doing to calm a frightened animal. 'What is causing you terrible pain is giving me great hope.'

I didn't turn around, didn't want her to see my twisted face.

'Kitty, I'm going to say this even though I don't think you'll hear me; at this time, neither Sarah nor Matthias is capable of what you are afraid is happening. They are two very damaged people.' Her hand lightly circled around from my waist to my shoulders. 'I think you'll agree that since Matthias came back to work, Sarah has shown the first signs of coming out of herself. You yourself have said Matthias is holding his ground, holding on to the few forward steps he's taken. Kitty, please try to hold on, please try not to say anything that will stop them from helping each other. It's hard. I'm not the one in love with Matthias, but I do love my daughter and I want her back every bit as much as you want Matthias. She's all I've got left, Kitty. The jealousy will flare up in you, I know, but I'm asking you not to put words on it for Matthias or Sarah to hear. Please come to me, I beg you, please come to me and tell me whenever you think you're going to explode. Don't go to them, please. Please, Kitty.' She stayed there touching my back for a long while. I couldn't turn around to reassure her because I did not think I could hold my tongue after seeing Matt and Sarah riding off together into the fields of Enderly. Missus Hodgkins went away.

Since she'd come home from the War, Sarah had worn

clothes that gave her the look of a VAD: dark green wool skirt far below the knees, lighter green blouse tucked into the top of her skirt, narrow black belt around her waist. She kept her hair enclosed in a green knitted cap. The top strings of the veil went over her ears with the knot tucked under the cap and the bottom strings tied in a bow at the nape of her neck. She had fourteen veils, two for each day, all white and shaped like the Vicks-soaked masks the VADs used to kill the smell of gangrene and spilled stomachs.

When May came around, Sarah was out on the farm more than she'd ever been since coming home. Besides spending all that time, silent or talkative, with Matthias, she had started giving me shy little waves of her hand, the kind small children give when they're told by their parents to wave goodbye. I wondered if my jealousy was obvious to her and if she was trying to reassure me, telling me she hadn't any designs on Matt, or maybe even thanking me for the loan of my Matthias.

Then for the first time Missus Hodgkins asked Sarah to do something, asked her to take the four-o'clock tea out to Matthias in the fields. But that was my job. I was angry. I was ashamed of being angry. Sweet Jesus! And Missus Hodgkins's nose was stuck to the window when Sarah walked down the yard toward the Back Gate, the black cloth bag with its bottle of sweet milky tea, a mug, and the jam-and-butter sandwich. When Missus Hodgkins finally unstuck her nose, she came into the kitchen where I was rolling out the makings of the next day's brown bread.

'Kitty, I'm beginning to hope too much,' she said. 'I'm setting myself up all over again to be completely despaired. I just have to keep telling myself that she's never going to be a hundred per cent.'

For Missus Hodgkins's sake, I made a huge effort. 'Six months ago you never thought she'd get this far,' I said. 'Another six months and she'll be talking to you and maybe me.' Making a bigger effort, I said, 'Matt told me yesterday that Sarah made a little joke a while ago.'

And then, of course, I had to tell her about the mare foaling and Sarah with the tea at two in the morning and the little joke about the monkey's tail and Missus Hodgkins went around the house saying, "It won't be long now said the monkey when the train ran over its tail," and sometimes saying, "It won't be long now," like it was a prayer.

When Sarah arrived in the Back Batens with the four-o'clock tea, Matt was at the far end of the field coming toward her on the metal roller. Where he had already rolled the young barley, the field was striped in straight, eight-foot swaths of dark and light green. The horse Matt was driving, Ballyadams, saw Sarah first, cocked his ears forward, and softly snickered. The horse and Sarah had known each other since he was a foal— Sarah had dried him when he was born. Now she stood in the horse's path, and when Matt brought him to a stop beside her, she stroked his neck. With long lips smacking as he sniffed in expectation of something sweet, the horse nuzzled her in the chest and belly. Sarah was good with horses, even the bad-tempered ones that laid their ears back and showed their teeth to everyone else. And as she scratched around the butt of his ear, the horse raised his head in pleasure, and in passing Sarah's face his smacking lips caught the veil and took it clean off her face. Sarah cried out and turned away, dropping the four-o'clock tea and covering her face with her hands. But Matthias had seen her face, had seen the same face Con had been in love with. He saw no scars, no disfigurement. He got out of his seat and stood on the iron frame of the roller.

Sarah kept her back to him, held her hands to her face as she looked around desperately for the veil. She snatched it out of the horse's mouth and ran to the field gate, trying to tie on the veil as she fled. Matthias leapt down from the shafts of the roller and shouted, 'Sarah.'

Sarah kept running. Matthias followed. He caught up with her as she was trying to undo the gate-latch with one hand while keeping the veil pressed against her face with the other.

'Go away.'

She could not undo the latch. She whirled around on Matthias and, with hands and crumpled veil spread over her face, screeched at him to go away. Matthias threw his arms around her like the Christian in the Colosseum throwing a net over a lion in the picture in the penny catechism, and Sarah hid her face in his shoulder and she kicked his shins and struggled in his arms like a turkey with its legs tied for weighing upside down at Christmas time. When she became quiet enough to hear him, Matthias said, 'I told you lies too, Sarah. We told lies to each other.'

'We stood like that for a quarter of an hour,' Matthias told me the next Sunday at Knockmullen Castle. 'Just the two of us in the ten-acre field with Ballyadams grazing the sweet spring grass on the headland after pulling the roller over the four-o'clock tea bag. The rattling bit in the rings was the only sound except for the excitement of small birds building their nests.' I couldn't have cared less about rattling bits or building birds; Matthias had no idea how I was burning on the inside while he told me about Sarah and himself. All I could see was the intimacy between them. I thought of Missus Hodgkins's hopes and my more noble self reminded me that the two of them were recovering invalids, were helping each other in ways that only they themselves could.

At last Sarah spoke, sounding like she had six inches of scarf in her mouth because she would not take her face out of Matt's shoulder. 'I didn't tell lies,' she said. Matthias ignored Sarah's protest and talked about the lies he himself had told. 'I told you lies about Con,' he said. 'He didn't get killed in no-man's-land. I killed him, Sarah.' He felt her body tensing 'like the first spasm of a man having a fit'. Then he told her the

224

whole story about Con making his way to Field Marshall Haig and about Knifey in the cellar in Ocean Villas, and about the letter from Billy Simkins and how Mammy and Daddy and Missus Hodgkins and me and now Sarah were the only ones who knew what had really happened to Con. And Sarah cried.

'And she cried and cried and cried,' Matthias told me, as we leaned on the ivied walls that I had walked around twelve years ago, a century ago. Despite my crossness, I turned to Matt, put my hand on his upper arm. 'I cried too,' he said, 'and do you know who I cried for, Kitty? For Mammy and Daddy and the girls in the fire. I never cried for them before, and here I was, what, thirteen years and one war later crying for them for the first time.'

Eighty-seven feet up in the air, on the only remaining floor of Knockmullen Castle, we stared across the miles of flat land. With its roof gone these hundreds of years, the floor was covered with grass; stunted whitethorns, too sickly ever to produce haws, grew near the walls. It was a warm Sunday afternoon, and there wasn't a stir in the countryside, no farmers in the fields, no wind in the bushy hedges, only grazing cattle spotting the distant fields, barely moving in the rich grass of spring, no flies out yet to be swished away with annoyed tails. I pulled on Matt's arm and turned him until he was looking at me. I laid the side of my face on his chest and put my arms around his middle. It was a long time before we sank down onto the grass, and after terrible clumsy fumbling, we made love for the first time, and I have always wondered did I do it to assure myself that Matt was still mine and not Sarah's.

Matthias Wrenn

At the gate of the Back Batens in the shadow of the grove of pine trees, we cried for Con, wetting each other with tears. When we stood away, separated, Sarah's hands fluttered to her face. With her fingertips, she touched her cheeks and nose and neck and forehead and ears and hair. She took off her knitted cap. Even as she stepped over to the shallow dry drain that surrounded the field, she kept her hands out in front like a man in the dark afraid of walking into the edge of an open door. She stepped down and sat in the rich green grass on the bank scattered with long-stemmed dandelions and foxtail, the dark grove of pine trees at her back. When she put her elbows on her knees, she finally lowered her hands.

Sarah was pale, her hair short and hacked as if she'd cut it without looking in a mirror. Her face was thin, but she was still the lovely Sarah she had been before the War. All she needed was a little weathering, a little eating and a few months of hair-growing. The one big difference was in her eyes; they did not sparkle like they had when Lionel and Con and her father were still alive, when the boundaries of her world had been Enderly and her boarding school in Dublin.

I sat down near her.

'I did tell you lies, Matt,' she began. 'The five VADs in the fire that night were Vera, Eleanor, Flora, Jane and Izzy. All the casualties had been moved out on the trains that day, and we were organizing the place; we were always organizing the place whenever the War took a rest. A falling flare started the fire, and bottles of ether and the wells of the oil lamps exploded and made the whole thing worse. I was coming out of the latrine about twenty yards away and, in a second, the whole tent became a soaring flame. It was the screams—that was the worst part; the high-pitched screams. Four of them stumbled out, all on fire like their hair and clothes had been splashed with flames. I was transfixed, paralysed by the horror of it, standing there looking at them falling down over each other.

'And I stayed transfixed while their flames were beaten out by people swinging coats and towels. People were pouring out of the dark, out of the other Red Cross tents, and all running around in circles and shouting. The four of them lay there like bits of burnt wood still smoking. I don't remember the next few hours, but at some point before morning I ended up in the tent where they'd been brought. The four who'd come out of the flames were still alive, blackened lumps that had been their heads sticking out at the end of the white sheets. I couldn't tell one from the other: no hair; cheeks and lips and noses and ears gone; eyes blinded; rows of teeth all the way back to the molars bare and clenched; the neck skin black and as fragile as what's left when you burn a page of a book.'

Our house, the night I sank the dog in the Canal, came into my head, but I would not let Sarah's picture of the burnt VADs resurrect my memory of Daddy and Mammy and the girls.

'Their internal organs were still going strong. Their breath made whistling noises through the holes in their faces. A nurse came and stood beside me and she said, "We're waiting for them to die." I said to the nurse, "I'm not waiting." She must have thought I was leaving, and she went away. All the Red Cross dressing stations were laid out exactly the same so that anyone new could walk in and know where everything was stored. I filled a syringe with morphine four times, and one after the other stuck the needle through the sheets into their bellies. The very second I'd done the last one, before I'd even pulled the syringe back out, two orderlies came and took me by the elbows. They had been watching, glad I was doing what they were afraid to do. They took me out of there and brought me to another tent a long way away. About a month later I was in Pine Haven wearing the veil. But Pine Haven did nothing for me. I was as daft coming out of the place as I was going in. The only good thing about my nineteen months there was that I knitted the jersey for Con.'

Sarah became silent because she was trying not to cry. She took the crumpled veil out her coat pocket and pressed it into her eyes.

'Con told me one time my eyes were full of diamonds. That's why I knitted the jersey in diamond shapes, to tell him that I remembered what he'd said, that I'd heard what he'd said in the garden that day when he was thinning the strawberries and I was going to the wedding. Poor Con. If only the two of us had known how much we thought of each other during the War.'

She couldn't go on. She lowered her face onto her knees and wept, put her hands under her knees and pressed herself into her thighs, brought her finger-laced hands to the back of her head, elbows down each side of her knees, bawled like a calf, shuddered like a fish out of water, threw her head back until she could see the tops of the pine trees behind her, and opened her throat to the anguish welling up, erupting from her insides.

What does a man do when a woman cries? When anyone cries? What did I do when a man roared in pain in no-man's-land? Cried for his mother?

I touched Sarah's shoulder and she fell over onto me, fell face first onto my thigh. I rubbed her back very gently like I'd touch a horse's rump so he wouldn't lash out with a killing hoof. Then my other hand was on her hair. Then I was humming and gliding my hand between her shoulder blades and letting her chopped hair slip through my fingers and I thought of diamonds and Con and I was glad he'd known that the tender feelings he'd had for a girl had been recognized and reciprocated. He had kept from me the secret of the pattern of Sarah's jersey. I was glad for Con.

Sarah cried herself out and remained on my thigh for a long time. I thought she might have fallen asleep, but when I looked down, her eyes were open and gazing on the long grass three feet away on the other side of the dry drain. She sat up and touched her face with the damp veil.

'I suppose I had a relationship with Con the same as he had with me: two young people in love with each other, but neither telling the other and neither knowing. It would have been romantic but it would have never gone anywhere—there was too much social and religious stuff between us.' She looked at me. 'Even if we never told each other, the romance was there and, as things turned out, it never had to be destroyed on the rocks of reality.'

We sat again without words for a long time until Sarah began to flatten her veil out on her thigh. She brought it to her face and tied the strings at the back. 'It's going to take me a bit longer to walk around without this. I'm forever afraid something bad is going to happen to my face, and I've persuaded myself that the veil keeps me safe.'

Kitty Hatchel

'Not beside her, Kitty; near her. And Kitty,' Matthias said and paused as if what he wanted to say next was hard to say. He put his arm across my shoulders. 'There must have been times when I talked too much about Sarah.' And, quickly, I thought, How right you are, Matthias. But I held my tongue. I was too happy for Missus Hodgkins.

It was on the Bridge that he told me about Sarah and the fire and how the veil might be coming off soon. I was so happy for the happiness Missus Hodgkins was going to have that my jealousy went puff. I wanted to run to Enderly, go to Sarah, beg her to take off the veil this very minute and go to her mother, let her mother know there was still the possibility of grandchildren who would play away and sing away and squeal away and laugh away from Enderly the grief laid down by a faraway war, by young death and old death. I wanted to fly to Enderly and put my arms around Missus Hodgkins and tell her there was going to be a miracle, that her own Sarah was almost home from the War, and that when she finally arrived, she would be every bit as beautiful as she had ever been, every bit as sane. I wanted to tell her that children would come back to Enderly and that she would be there to hear them and hold them. Oh, Missus Hodgkins, if only I'd had wings on my feet that night, nothing would have stopped me from flying to you and stopping your pain at that very moment. But I had to wait, we all had to wait, until Sarah went to you herself.

And then, where else but on the Bridge in the same few minutes, did my own Matthias give a sign that he too was almost home. As he did on every Tuesday evening since he'd moved into the foreman's cottage, he came home with me to see Daddy and Mammy. As usual, when we got to the top of the Bridge we got off the bikes and leaned over the parapet to view the kingdom of our childhood.

Matthias pointed to three bored roach roughing up the surface of the Canal for scooting water striders. 'There were times I thought I'd never see the Canal again,' he started. 'Con said it was full of sanctifying grace—sanctifying grace as smooth as mercury in a glass and as warm as custard on apple cake in winter.' Matt paused and stared at the roach. I had learned not to push Matt when he paused in his speech; he would continue in his own good time.

'We fished in the Somme, Con and myself. We skinned hazel poles for rods. Unravelled a reins to make the line. Bent strands of barbed wire were the hooks. Con cut meat off a dead horse for bait. We caught nothing. No fish could be that stupid to be fooled with barbed wire and horsemeat, Con said. But we fished. That's all we wanted to do. Fish. It didn't even matter if there were fish in the water. We were terrible tired from carrying all the bodies out, and when we wakened it was the next morning and the rods were gone.' He paused for a long time again. These pauses, I'd decided, were for Matthias to give himself time to poke through a huge mound of memories, to carefully unravel the ones he wanted to look at. 'Con said he didn't know the names of all the fish till you wrote that composition for the school in Marbra; where the nuns wouldn't take you for saying the sound of the Canal Song was better than Sheila Feeney singing at Benediction. Roach, perch, eel, pike, bream, carp, rudd and tench.'

I was very happy to slip into the memory he was in. 'That's

what Daddy said. Mammy said it was because I wrote what Uncle Martin said about swans' names—pens and inkwells. But it was just that my composition wasn't good enough.'

'Con imitated Sheila Feeney singing *Tantum Ergo*,' Matthias said, 'went up on his toes on the high notes and made the desperate faces she made like she was trying to keep in a fart. He made his jaw tremble and joined his hands at the belly. We'd be in stitches, even the lads who didn't know what he was doing. Once he sang it in a shed with hay. A billet. Ah, the smell of the hay ...' Matt paused again, and when he resumed talking I had to make a ninety-degree turn in my brain to catch up with him.

'Do you think I've recovered enough from the War to be your husband?' he asked. My faltering brain took a few seconds to recognize the question as a marriage proposal.

Even though there had been times when I was very cross about Matt and Sarah I could have burst into green flames, I always knew Matt and I would get married sooner or later. Even so, now that Matt was beating around the bush in his attempt to propose to me, a weakness visited my knees briefly, but I had the presence of mind not to shout out my joy; there should be a little romance in a marriage proposal, I thought. I leaned over the parapet and looked down at the three roach.

'If I was a roach I'd die of the hunger,' I said. 'I'd never be able to eat flies.' The roach had had their fill of flies; they had tired of upsetting the striders and were now bunking each other with their heads.

'Do you think your parents think I'm good enough for you?'

I dribbled a spit over my bottom lip and dropped it within an inch of the smallest fish. It flew away in a flash of silver as if the dragons of fishwater were after it. Matthias didn't take his eyes off the water. 'Would you mind living in the Enderly cottage with me if we got married?'

The roach began to circle, trying to figure out what direction would take them toward the Harbour. 'That small fish doesn't know his way home,' I said.

I could feel Matthias looking at me, could see him frowning, even though I wasn't looking at him. 'Would you stay working for Missus Hodgkins if we got married?'

Twilight had crept in, and the bats were skimming along the water in their unbalanced way, as awkward as bottom-heavy mice learning to fly. It was a year and three months since that day I'd washed Matthias in the Canal.

Without Matthias even noticing, I picked a flat stone off the road and dropped it into the water. The fish fled in three directions and Matt looked at me. I looked at him.

'What?' he asked.

'What?' I asked him.

'Are you listening to me at all, Kitty?'

'Are you asking me to marry you, Matt?' I said.

'I suppose I am.' He looked back to the water.

'Matt, look at me.' I put a hand on each side of his face and twisted it toward me. 'If you want me to marry you, then ask me to marry you.'

'I'm afraid you might say no.'

'*Matthias!*' I shouted in exasperation, and the word went skimming among the flying mice along the top of the water. 'Ask me if I'll marry you.'

'Will you marry me?'

'Who?'

'What?'

'Who are you asking to marry you?'

'You.'

'And what's my name?'

'Kitty.'

'Then ask me again.'

'Will you marry me, Kitty?'

'When?'

'Soon.'

'Next month?'

'That would be nice.'

'I'll think about it, Matthias.'

'You will?'

'I just did.'

'And?'

'YES YES YES!' I shouted so loud that my voice boomed along the Canal to the Harbour. And I already had flung my arms around Matt's neck by the time the yesses came echoing back over the still surface to the Bridge.

Ralphie Blake

I didn't sleep for ages after the Lamberts' place. God, the nightmares when I did sleep! The two of them would be on the floor beside each other on their backs, their faces melting and little rivers of fat flowing out and their flesh spitting and hissing like rashers and sausages in a frying pan on a Sunday morning. Jesus! I'd wake up paralysed with the fright and for a minute I wouldn't know where I was, the two of them still on the floor beside the bed and the smell of burning meat in the room. The state of huffing and puffing I'd be in, and the missus asking me what was wrong. The sweat would be running down my face and my feet freezing in the bed at the same time.

Since the catechism and Cain and Abel in the school, I thought Murder was the worst thing; the very worst sin. Even the sound of it is terrible. You can feel the fear of the one getting murdered in the word and hear the evil of the one doing it. Murder. Murder is a Roman soldier sticking his sword through a baby in its mother's arms in the Massacre of the Innocents, or Cain bringing down the branch of a tree on the back of his brother's head. When Murder is done the sun should not be shining. And here I was in my bed in the dark and me, myself— me, Ralphie Blake—was a Murderer. I'd be lying there on my back looking up into the dark and saying, 'Murderer, Murderer.'

I didn't light the match that lit the fire that killed the

Lamberts, but I was down near the Canal Bridge with a whistle to blow if anyone came along. Protestants or not, the poor bastards were going to see their entire lives go up in flames. Even though they weren't supposed to die, Father Kinsella said I was guilty of Murder because I was a helper. He told me, too, that if I kept on hanging out with men who might commit Murder again, his absolution would be no good because I wouldn't be having a firm resolution to avoid the same sin in the future. 'No resolution, no absolution,' Mister Bennett the teacher used to say.

Like an eejit, I told Johnjoe Lacy what the priest said and he nearly ate the face off me, called Father Kinsella a fucking eejit of a priest and said if I became a traitor to the IRA I would be shot like a deserter. 'In for a penny, in for a pound,' Johnjoe said, and he took delight in saying it, like he had me by the balls.

So when Johnjoe leaned on the wingboard of the cart fornent the Quaker Meeting House and said, 'Enderly's soon, me lad,' I got such a bubbling in the guts that I wanted to find a bush to shite behind. I knew this day was coming because Johnjoe had been often landing lately on the wingboard like a grey crow that eats dead animals 'to keep my patriotic spirit burning hot for future forays for Ireland'.

'Your man, Wrenn, will be our man on the inside,' he said.

I didn't look up from my brushing. I was so staggered with a sudden rush of fear that I had to squeeze my grip on the brush handle as well as tighten up my arse. I was between a rock and a hard place. I knew it would be suicide to try to burn down Enderly because Matthias Wrenn wouldn't let it happen. There I was, Johnjoe behind me pushing, and Matthias in front ready to kill.

The Lamberts' place had been so easy that Johnjoe and the lads thought all they had to do was waltz into Enderly and light a match. They were all so cocksure of themselves because the wind happened to take the fire through the Lamberts' house and the out-buildings in a flash. To hear them talking you'd think

God had something to do with it, had raised the wind and steered it to destroy what had taken hundreds of years to build. To hear Johnjoe you'd think God was a Catholic who hated Protestants and England. I always thought the catechism was wrong where it said man is made in God's image and likeness; it should have said God is made in man's image and likeness.

When I'd lie awake in the dark after a Lambert nightmare, I'd start thinking about the burning of Enderly that I knew was coming. The way Johnjoe talked about it, you'd think Matthias Wrenn was a child, like Johnjoe didn't know that Matthias going through the War was the same as a piece of metal going through a four-year furnace.

There was something about all the lads who'd been in the War. It was like they'd seen things, had apparitions like the girl at Lourdes and been changed, made different from the rest of us. Some of them were more than a bit touched, like Mad Bill Goodwin with the cat in his coat pocket, its head sticking out and it mewing—some people said it even pissed in the pocket; Joe Lawless snaking around against the walls of the houses like he was dodging bullets; Shaky Dick Porter shaking all the time and falling down in a fit when he heard a door banging in the wind. Most of them didn't even know what the weather was doing, walking around in the spills like the sun was shining, or out cutting hedges or spreading dung in a farmer's field in the middle of winter stripped to the shirt with the sleeves rolled up and the buttons opened down to the navel while the rest of us shivered in the frost. Some of them were such hard chaws that they could knit socks out of barbed wire and then wear them. And the way they'd look through you when you'd be talking to them, looking like they were looking at something forty miles away or a hundred years ago; none of them giving a shite about the IRA or about what happened in Dublin at Easter in 1916, except for being annoyed to hell with the Sixteeners for doing what they did when they did it.

Matthias Wrenn was the hardest chaw of all the War lads. He was no relation of the Matt who went off to see the world with Con in 1913. His long hair and that headband of his gave him the look of an old warrior on the cover of a book wearing skins; all he needed was a shield and a sword. There was no knowing when Matthias would slip back into the state he was in when he came home, mad as a coot. And here was Johnjoe Lacy saying Matthias would be our man on the inside, whatever the hell that meant. I knew, sure as be damned, that Matthias would take the side of the Hodgkinses if for no other reason than that he was living at Enderly, for Christ's sake, with Kitty and the child in the foreman's cottage. And talking about Kitty! She wasn't going to be darning her husband's socks while we were outside running around setting fires, burning her house out from under her. Herby Kelly's face still had the scars of her nails from the day Matthias came home from the War and Herby opened his mouth to let some of his old Fenian shite out. And as well as that, she'd been with Missus Hodgkins all during the War, and the two of them with men in the trenches. If two women spend time together in the same ditch fighting off the same enemy, they quick get more related to each other than sisters. Kitty would be as fierce fighting for Enderly as Matthias.

Johnjoe Lacy said Matthias was just lucky, that it was luck that had kept him alive for those four years. Once Johnjoe got an idea in his head he used every kind of stupidity to back it up. Everyone said he'd got worse since the beating he'd taken from Dan Griffin that Fair Day a couple of years ago. Of all the people in the town it was only Johnjoe who saw his beating as heroic; the beating was his martyrdom for Ireland. Ever since the Fair, he used his face to draw more attention to himself, forcing people to look at him while he went on with his long-winded speechifying, the jaw all crooked from the three breaks, the wrecked nose twisted off to one side. Everyone in the town knew that Dan Griffin left Johnjoe nearly dead in the cowshite of the

Fair Day. But many times from the wingboard of my cart, John-joe told me he had risen up out of the cowshite and it was this rising that had proved he'd been right to tell Dan Griffin he wasn't an Irishman at all. Johnjoe was proud of his injuries; he believed the nose and the jaw made people think that if only he'd had the chance he would have got the same wounds in Dublin in 1916, that he would have been out there in the front lines laying down his life for Ireland twenty times over. He always managed to put his scars in front of the burning General Post Office with guns shooting all over the place.

One night I was staring into the dark in the bed terrified that Johnjoe might be thinking of shooting me because I'd told him about confessing to Father Kinsella. The thoughts of getting a hard bullet in the head were enough to make me throw up; the noise of the shot and the burning of my skin from the powder! I knew I had to show Johnjoe I was a true IRA man, and it took an awful lot of thinking before I thought of something; I'd start acting like I was as good an IRA man as Johnjoe; I'd start talking about 'us' and 'we'.

Every day after that, while I swept and shovelled along the town roads, I practised in my head how I'd talk to Johnjoe.

So now fornent the Quaker Meeting House I went around the ass and cart to where Johnjoe was leaning on the wingboard, and I hoping I wasn't walking like a man with the cheeks of his arse pinched together looking for a bush. I leaned on the wing-board beside him. I spoke softly, almost in a whisper like I was a conspirator.

'We'll have to be very careful with Wrenn, Johnjoe.' I used Matthias's last name so Johnjoe wouldn't think I liked him. 'The lads from the War can't be trusted. They're not Irish any-more after being in the English army so long. Some of them talk like they're English. They don't believe in God anymore and they don't care if the Hodgkinses are Protestants or Catholics or pagans. Wrenn is the worst of them.'

'He's our man on the inside, Ralphie, and he'll do what I tell him to do because he won't have a say in the matter.'

'We'll have to be very careful about the way we get him to help us, Johnjoe. The Hodgkinses were in that house for two hundred years before the Famine, and they've always been good to the people of Ballyrannel. I've thought about this, Johnjoe. We have to remember that Wrenn worked for years for the Hodgkinses before the War. And the very minute he came home, when he was still going around stupid, Missus Hodgkins herself asked him to go back to work for her. She went down to the Canal Bridge on her bike. I don't think he's going to let anything happen to Missus Hodgkins or the daughter, or any part of Enderly for that matter.'

When Johnjoe answered me, he was whispering too. 'Wrenn and his ilk are only waiting for the chance to redeem themselves for fighting for the English. He'll be glad we're giving him the chance to fight for Ireland.'

'But are we sure of that, Johnjoe? We have to remember that Wrenn lives in Enderly. His own father worked in Enderly from the time he was a chap to the day he got burnt to death. He worked the harvest from the cutting of the hay to the picking of the spuds; he ploughed for weeks every spring in Enderly. I think we'll have a hard time getting Wrenn on our side.'

In other words, I thought to myself, if we go to Matthias expecting him to help the IRA burn Enderly or harm anyone in it, he'll run us off the place with the five prongs of a dungfork up our arses and you're an eejit, Johnjoe, if you can't see that.

Johnjoe couldn't see it. He said, 'Them lads can't forgive themselves for fighting for the English at the Somme when they should have been fighting against them at the General Post Office. The likes of Wrenn are all ashamed. They're all panting, all waiting for the chance to fight the English to get forgiveness from the real Irish—the anti-English, patriotic, and Catholic Irish.' Johnjoe started fiddling with the buttons of his fork. I didn't look down but I knew he was going to take a slash up against the wheel of my ass and cart right there in the middle of the town. Johnjoe's water started sloshing through the spokes of the wheel onto the road. He was worse than a dog.

It's funny how you can listen to a man saying words and hear him meaning something different altogether. I was only hearing Johnjoe talking about himself, that he was going to burn Enderly so he could show Ballyrannel that it wasn't fear that had kept him from doing something against the English when the doing was possible and dangerous to do. Johnjoe was safely jumping up on the bandwagon so that at a future time when land was being divided, he would be able to say, 'I fought for Ireland. I'm entitled.'

Johnjoe talked like he knew Matthias, like he knew what went on inside Matthias's head. 'We'll be offering Wrenn the chance he's frothing for. I'm telling you, Ralphie, he'll help us to burn down Enderly. He might even do it on his own without any of our lads having to go up there at all, if I went up there and explained things to him.'

Dan Griffin must have damaged Johnjoe's brain as well as his face when he'd battered him into the cow dung that time.

'We still have to be careful, Johnjoe,' I whispered, and I pretending I couldn't see or hear Johnjoe's rush of yellow water. 'Wrenn and Con Hatchel spent too many good years in that house. They played with the Hodgkins children, went hunting with the son. I think if Wrenn finds out we're going to burn down Enderly he'll kill every one of us.' Johnjoe must have had a bladder like a sow's. God, the water that came out of him!

'Maybe we'll only tell him some of the plan.' I could hardly believe that Johnjoe had listened to me.

'I don't think we should bring him into this at all, Johnjoe. I'd say he'll even go to the RIC for help if he has to.' And the minute I said that, I was afraid Johnjoe heard fear leaking through my pretending.

'Maybe he won't be able to go anywhere, Ralphie. If what

you say about him is right, then maybe it would be better not to ask for his help until we knock on the wicket gate and he answers it. Then we'll give him a choice: help us or we'll kill him on the spot.'

'Will we have a gun, Johnjoe?'

'There's no guns, Ralphie.'

'Then how will we kill him?'

'There's more than one way to skin a cat, Ralphie. A piece of thin wire around his neck is one way.' Johnjoe gave his thing a terrible shaking, and I knew some of his drops fell on my boots. The ignorant fucker.

'Who'll put the wire around his neck?'

'You sound like you're afraid of Wrenn, Ralphie.'

Sweet Jesus tonight! I got very nervous and tried to cover up by making a joke. 'If he was dead I wouldn't be afraid at all to put the wire around his neck. But to tell you the truth, Johnjoe, Wrenn is the last man in the world I'd pick to have a fight with.'

Johnjoe slapped me on the shoulder. 'No one's going to ask you to kill him, Ralphie.'

'But what's to stop him from killing us, you and the lads and myself?'

'Six to one, Ralphie. No man could beat odds like that. Wrenn will back down very quick.' Johnjoe folded his thing back into his trousers.

'Don't you think that depends on what he's fighting for, Johnjoe?'

'Ralphie, I hate saying this, but it sounds to me like you're getting afraid again to strike this blow against the English.'

Again! I felt my arse tightening up. 'Fuck the English,' I blustered. 'It's Wrenn I'm afraid of, one of our own.'

'A little fear never hurt anyone, Ralphie, as long as it doesn't make him so weak that he'd betray his friends.' He fiddled with the buttons in his fork and sent a watery spit across the cart into the street. 'When you get the call to arms, Ralphie, be ready to answer. I'll go over the plans with my second. We'll be striking before Christmas.' Johnjoe pushed himself off the wingboard and went off to sweep his chimleys, leaving me and my guts as shaky as frogs' spawn in a ditch.

That night I couldn't sleep until I convinced myself that Johnjoe would never find out if I became an informer, and that Matthias would kill me for a fact if I did anything against Enderly. Murder is the worst word for me. But for a lot of people in Ireland, 'informer' is the worst word. When Christ told everyone to love each other, he pointed to Ireland and said informers were not counted. When an Irish informer dies there is only one road for him to travel.

It was because of how the Irish think of informers that it took me two days to go up to Enderly in the dark to tell Matthias what Johnjoe was going to do. In the end it was either be a live informer or a dead IRA man killed with a terrible lot of pain. Imagine getting stuck through the guts with a five-pronged dung fork.

Kitty Hatchel

Two months after Ballyadams had snickered off her veil in the Back Batens, Sarah went to the door of the Machine Shed after the men were gone home for the day.

I was finishing up my work, and Missus Hodgkins was at the window again. 'She's gone in,' she said.

In the Machine Shed, Matthias was lifting a pickaxe off its place on the wall. When he saw Sarah, he said, 'You look different.' And being a woman, Sarah asked, 'How?'

Matthias banged the end of the handle against the floor and the loose head of the pickaxe slipped down along the smooth wood to the floor. He went to the workbench. Then he said, 'I don't know. You just look different.' He put the handle in the vice and picked up a handsaw.

When Sarah spoke next she had walked over to the bench. 'Do I look much different now?' she asked, and when Matthias turned around she had removed her veil and her knitted cap. To Matthias it looked as if Sarah had been secretly letting the sun shine on her face. Her freckles were back, and the paleness of the Back Batens was gone.

'She had the wool cap in one hand and a comb and a scissors in the other. Her hair had grown to her shoulders since I saw it in the Back Batens, but it was still chopped like a child after getting hold of a scissors when the mother wasn't looking.'

'Will you cut my hair, Matthias?' Sarah said, and she touched the bunches of uneven strands. She held out the comb and the scissors.

'Besides clipping a horse for the winter, I've never cut hair in my life,' Matt said.

'All you have to do is even it up all around, make it all the same length.'

They looked at each other for so long they almost entered a staring match. Then Matt asked, 'Who cut it for you the last time?'

'Can't you tell? I did it myself. I looked at myself in a mirror for the first time in four years that day Ballyadams pulled off the veil in the Back Batens.'

Matthias finished sawing the notch into the end of the pick handle. He said, 'You can't blame me if I make it worse.' He took the comb and scissors.

'You'd have to be blind to do that,' Sarah said, and she sat down on the round slice of beech, eight inches thick, that Charlie Coffey had put legs in years ago.

Missus Hodgkins came into the kitchen. I was straightening my hair to look presentable for Matthias when I said goodnight to him before going home on my bike. Missus Hodgkins said, 'Wait a minute, Kitty. I'm going out to look into the Machine Shed.'

'What excuse have you this time?' I asked her.

'There's a goose hatching in the Turkey House,' she said, and she left. She was back in less than a minute. 'You can't go out to Matthias, Kitty,' she said. She was agitated, breathless. She sat down, put her elbows on the table, and put her face in her hands. Missus Hodgkins was not a woman to let anyone see her being less than strong. Her shoulders shook and she sobbed once. She took a deep breath, wiped her eyes with her fingers. 'Matt was between Sarah and the door, but I could see she was sitting. Matt's cutting her hair. I saw the scissors in Matt's hand and I heard the snipping.' And then Missus Hodgkins sobbed. I stood behind her and put my hands on her shoulders while she wept in relief for the recovery of her lost daughter. Even though I knew Matt and I were about to be married, even though I knew he and Sarah were recovering from the War, even though I knew Sarah had helped to bring Matt home as much as he had helped her, my jealous self almost drove me out to the Machine Shed to scream and cause havoc.

Missus Hodgkins put her hand on my hand as she calmed down. She said, 'I know this is driving you mad, Kitty, this thing of Matthias and Sarah, and I thank you for being so strong for the two of them.' She stood up and took both of my hands. 'Most women wouldn't have been able to stand by and let them help each other this way. You have been very selfless. Do you mind if I hug you?' And she held me for a long time. And then I put my arms around her, and we stood at the kitchen table like that for ages. When we let go, the green dragon had retreated, but he hadn't disappeared. Sharp nails were still clawing at my insides.

It was two weeks later that Missus Hodgkins found a note on the table when she came down to the kitchen in the morning. 'Dear Mama, I'm almost home. Today I will not be wearing the veil or the cap. Sarah.' Ten minutes later, as she raised her cup to her lips, she looked up and Sarah was in the doorway and she was beautiful and she was smiling and she was crying and she said, 'Hello, Mama,' the first time she'd spoken to her mother since she'd gone away to France six years ago.

When I came to work a while later, I swept up the broken pieces of Missus Hodgkins's tea cup.

During the week before our wedding, I talked to Matthias about my jealousy. It was my roundabout way of telling him that once we were husband and wife, I would not be able to endure that kind of distress. We were lying in Ali Baba's Cave at the time, each of us fully dressed, each of us exhausted. Matt got up on his elbow and looked down into my face.

He said, 'Kitty, Kitty, Kitty,' and his voice was full of love and sorrow. 'I've tried to figure out Sarah and myself in my head, because I wanted to tell you what went on. I don't want even a shadow of Sarah to ever come between us.' He placed the flat of his hand on my belly as if afraid I might not stay to listen. 'Let me finish what I have to say, even if I say it wrong. At first I was afraid of Sarah. I thought she was madder than me. Then I saw we were two people quare in the head and still injured after being in the same train crash together. Then I was afraid you would start thinking wrong things about us. The only time she was womanness to my manness was the time she stood before me without her veil and cap and asked me to cut her hair.

'The second time she came to the Machine Shed, in some strange twist in my brain, Sarah became Con. The rest of the time, me helping to bring Sarah home from the War was me holding Con after Knifey went into his heart. In some way, Sarah let me see that I had helped Con home from the War. I helped him home because I couldn't let him be dragged out there and be shot like a dog for standing up to Haig. Getting Sarah away from the War is exactly what I did for Con. Sarah escaped out of the fog, and Con slipped away into it. And I am happy that Sarah let me see what I did for Con was exactly what I was doing for her—there was no difference, and I will never be sad again for what I did for Con. I will always be happy, always glad that I helped him home from the War.'

Missus Hodgkins

Everyone said the horse's name as if it were one word—Jackdempsey.

Dempsey was in the papers when the horse came into his prime, that's why David gave him the name. 'Big' was the word to describe Jackdempsey, but if the boxer had been as gentle as the horse when I got him, he wouldn't have fought his way out of a paper bag.

When the children went away, I couldn't enjoy riding any more, not with them facing the hardships of war. So Jackdempsey got fat and uppity—a little bit nasty. But when Lionel was killed and David died and Sarah came home, I had to start riding again, had to get out there and gallop away from it all. It was the old mare, Timahoe, I took out. By myself, in the depths of the countryside, I had to drive poor Timahoe too hard to get her into a gallop. So I told Phil Kelly to do something with Jackdempsey, bring him out every day until the horse was back in shape.

Jackdempsey smelled Phil's nervousness from the beginning, and instead of the man taking the horse for gallops, the horse took the man on wild rides, one of which ended with Phil going over the horse's head and landing on the flat of his back, the wind knocked out of him. He could have broken his neck.

That night after Matthias told me about Passchendaele on the Bridge, I found myself awake and in my head was the idea that Matthias and Jackdempsey would be good for each other: at full gallop on a horse with a nasty attitude, Matthias's mind would have no choice but to be engaged with the present moment. And it worked perfectly. I firmly believe it was the wild gallops on Jackdempsey that cleared Matt's mind of the War for a while and allowed him to be home, if only for the duration of the ride. And I believe, too, that it was through this new opening in Matthias' mind that Sarah slipped. When they quickly realized they were both still plunging around in the muck and death of Europe—that each had even killed friends to save them—Sarah and Matthias, together, started the long climb out of the guilty trenches of their own minds. Poor Kitty; she was so selfless, so strong for the two of them. I know she suffered from painful jealousy. What woman wouldn't?

A few months after he began work, Matthias had subdued, retamed and retrained Jackdempsey; after his long hiatus, the big beast was gentle again and he was mine to ride. And two months after Matthias had cut Sarah's hair in the Machine Shed, I galloped Jackdempsey across the far fields, pushed him to the point where he was quivering when I let him turn around to begin the canter home.

I suddenly had the feeling that I had skipped forward in time, that I'd missed something. I wasn't surprised at all that my eyes were full of blue, that the blue was framed in the stems of the long grass swaying around me. Not one cloud was visible, nothing but blue. A blue dress fluttered into my head, the one I had given Kitty that day she went to Dublin to see Matthias and Con off to India. The dress had been bought out of a London catalogue for my own nineteen-year-old Sarah to wear to her cousin's wedding one year earlier.

Sarah at nineteen!

Sarah, home at last!

The blue of her eyes, the blue of her dress, the tone of her skin, the russet of her hair. And she carried herself at the wedding in a way I had not been aware of before—I was seeing my little girl as a fully grown woman for the first time. All eyes were on her, and I was anxious, afraid the bride might think the groom's relatives were trying to upstage her. The way David beamed every time he looked at her, his eyes wandering back to her all day. And to think that within a year of the wedding she would have begun the journey in which she would become so lost.

I fell asleep in the long grass with the sun warm on me. In a very quick dream I saw Matthias, as lost himself as was Sarah, plunging back into the bloody mist of the war and bringing Sarah by the hand out of the gun-flashed fog, a whole person. And there she was, Sarah standing in the kitchen doorway more beautiful than she had ever been. 'Hello, Mama,' she said. We ended up on the kitchen floor, me with my back to the wall, Sarah with her head on my breast, the two women of the family wailing in an ecstasy of joy and pain; out of Abattoir Europe we had snatched this remaining piece of our family; Enderly would have children again, children for David and Lionel and Sarah and me; the next generation would not know, could not know, the pain of the Enderlies who'd gone before them. We were the unlucky generation.

The blueness was disturbed by a wandering crow flapping its black trail across the sky. *As the crow flies*, I thought, is not the best way to describe the shortest distance between two points. Any crow I ever watched wandered around in the air from one curious sight to the next—just like a solitary dog wandering from one tantalizing sniff to the next.

September 1917. It was in September our Lionel was killed near Passchendaele; in January 1918 the Hatchels got news of Con, wrapped in protective lies in a letter from Matthias; in March 1918 our silent Sarah came home—brought home by two other VADs—wearing a headdress like Moslem women wear, only her eyes showing. Her blue eyes! Poor silent child. In her damaged mind, the VADs told me, Sarah was covering the disfigurement she had seen in the disfigured faces of her friends when their dressing station caught fire. Sarah, the VADs said, might or might not regain her sanity, might or might not speak again—nobody knew. They told me about Pine Haven's failure to get through to her. Poor Sarah: she fled when strangers came, avoided the workers, even hid herself from Kitty; didn't leave the house at all; only reluctantly allowed David and myself to touch her shoulders. A month after her return my beloved David died of a heart attack in the kitchen. Lionel's death and Sarah's madness were so visibly dragging him down that I knew he couldn't go on.

The crow sank out of my eyes and I heard Jackdempsey close by, the metal of his bit rattling in its iron rings. It was then I suspected I had fallen off the horse. But I had no memory of it—the falling—didn't remember if I'd tried to save myself with desperate grabbings at mane and saddle. I did remember that I'd been cantering along with Kitty in my mind. Later in the day Sarah and I were planning to visit Kitty in the foreman's cottage. Kitty's mother was coming to hold Cornelia and I had baked a dozen scones first thing that morning, had put the two jars—clotted cream and blackcurrant jam—in the basket, each covered with butter paper held on the rims with double-bowed pink yarn.

The magnificent details a person remembers: double-bowed pink yarn.

In August 1918 Kitty ran wailing along the Canal bank to meet her returned soldier, her Matthias who had survived four years of shells, bullets, disease, drowning, influenza, fleas and rats. 'Le Pimpernel irlandais', as the French journalist called him, had finally come home. 'Does a stretcher-bearer in no-man's-land worry all the time about getting killed, Monsieur Wrenn?' 'No. Out there, you only think about what you're doing at this very moment. The notion of getting killed belongs in the future. So, if you're alive there's no need to worry. If you're dead you can't worry. The ones who did worry went mad quickly.' Our very own Matthias speaking like an ancient sage, and all Ballyrannel proud of him. Matthias and Con, for four years, had danced together on the steely, interlocking, razor-edged blades of the War, while all around them—in their very close presence—men were unlegged, dearmed, eviscerated, blinded, unmanned, evaporated, made mad, exploded into red mist, made part of the mud in which they had learned to live like some unclassified species of animal. Matthias had scraped other men's brains, other men's eyes, other men's blood, other men's warm viscera off his face so many times that he simply wiped his hands clean on the seat of his trousers. 'Le Pimpernel irlandais' came home and immediately plodded back into no-man's-land to save our Sarah.

Jackdempsey's big bewhiskered nose was six inches above my face, the green juice of the munched grass oozing out at both sides of his mouth. His nostrils were two black holes against my face. When he sniffed, he made the noise of a windstorm in a winter's chimney. He went away and I heard him manoeuvering the sweet grass over the piece of iron across the back of his tongue. I was very comfortable lying on my back in thick grass, not concerned at all that a one-ton horse was stepping carelessly nearby.

The big ship made the long slow turn away from the Suez Canal, back into the Mediterranean, but the implications for Con and Matthias meant nothing to Kitty. How could she have seen the connection between the killing of an Austrian prince in an unpronounceable city in an unheard-of country and the turning-around of a ship full of British troops bound for India? The going to India was far worse for Kitty than was the turning-around in the Mediterranean. She didn't care if India meant adventure more than it meant danger. She could not accept that the young men had been handed the chance of a lifetime, were going on a poor-man's Cook's Tour of the world at the expense of the king. When she read Matthias's letter about their ship pulling out of the queue within sight of the Suez Canal, she squealed with delight—Matthias was not going to be eight thousand miles away—he would only be in Belgium or France for a few months while the War lasted. 'How can Matthias and Con be in danger? They're only stretcher-bearers and nobody shoots stretcher-bearers.' That's what she said when I told her about that first day of July in 1916.

'King's Clothing Tattered at Somme', as one newspaper imperiously put it, trying to put a brave face on a terrible man-made disaster, trying to cover up the monstrous failure of leadership. And behind the headline of the tattered clothing was the image of the king and the Kaiser—two haughty, arrogant, self-centred, removed men sitting on horseback—tearing at each other's clothing by sending their own children out to play in their war games, sitting there overseeing a hunt in a Bavarian forest on a Sunday afternoon, each waiting until the other had no children left to die. I read everything about the War to keep myself prepared; I wouldn't be clattered straight in the face when the bad news came. My tactic didn't insulate me against the grief, but it buffered me against total breakdown when I saw Lionel's envelope in Paul Bolger's hand, Paul already weeping for me, not able to look at my face. When I put my hand on his shoulder, Paul may have thought I was comforting him but I was only trying to stay on my feet.

Jackdempsey came between me and the sun, raised his tail into the familiar pre-relief arc, and unloaded himself of twenty pounds of processed grass. There should have been steam, there should have been that fresh smell that can sometimes sink into the lowest, tiniest pockets of the lungs, but if there was steam and if there was smell, neither registered with me. Jackdempsey moved away, and the moment the sun touched me, I went off again into my bubbling memory, looked at whatever came to the surface.

'Officers are the last to get killed,' Kitty said whenever I mentioned Lionel. Our Lionel had been in the Officers' Training Corps when he'd been in Trinity, and in August 1914 he was a reserve officer. His regiment was already on the move to

Europe while most of the world was still looking for Sarajevo in tattered school atlases. He was meeting up with the Old Contemptibles in their retreat from Mons, while Matthias and Con were disembarking at a rainy Boulogne, when they should have been near to stepping off their ship in a sunny Bombay.

'Oh, Missus Hodgkins. Sarah's taking care of wounded soldiers. Nothing bad can ever happen to her. It would be too unfair. And as well as that, she has a red cross on her white smock.' Kitty spoke these fairy-tale thoughts when she knew I was worried about our Sarah. Sometimes there was impatience in my responses. 'Red crosses are not miraculous medals, Kitty. Sarah may have a red cross on her white smock, but blind machines throwing bombs over the horizon can't see red crosses on white smocks.'

Catholics were always passing around stories of lives being saved in France and Belgium by miraculous medals deflecting bullets. Catholics believe in many strange things. Miraculous medals! Who thinks up these things? Medal-makers maybe, when the medal business is slow, when there are no wars and the generals have no need of medals for all types of stupid behaviour? What is it about soldiers and their medals? Medals and marbles! 'I have more marbles than you.' 'I have more medals than you.' Even when the wounded and shell-shocked young men began turning up in Ballyrannel before the War was even half over, Kitty kept her eyes closed, refused to believe in the possibility that Matthias or Con could be wounded or killed.

Even when Con's death-letter came, when her house was full of the worst kind of grief, she still fiercely held on to her belief that Matthias would be restored whole to her. He was, after all, 'Le Pimpernel irlandais' with the stretcher, Monsieur Wrenn. And then for Matthias to come home—to skip untouched out of that grinder, to walk unscathed out of Europe when around him eight million young men had been wantonly slaughtered—was Kitty's triumph. She had endured the War her way, and she had got Matthias back. I had endured the War my way, and I had bent before the terrible fierceness of the death of one child and the insanity of the other.

In the tall grass I didn't know if I'd had my eyes closed for a time, didn't know whether I'd been lying there for two minutes or two hours. I still felt no need to get up and look for the horse. The stalks of grass stood erect all around the edge of my body in the shape of a coffin, narrow at the feet and widening out as they came up to the shoulders. I thought about the jam I was bringing for Kitty's high tea in the afternoon—the previous autumn, Kitty herself had made the jam, her swollen belly touching the edge of the range as she stirred the boiling pot.

And why had Matthias survived and our Lionel …? I had been driving that selfish question from my mind ever since Lionel's letter came. And suddenly he was there, my Lionel, standing there looking down at me. 'Oh, Lionel. Oh, my Lionel,' I cried out. But when he came down out of the blue sky onto his hunkers, it was Matthias. He said my name and put his hand on my forehead. He whispered, said he'd be back, and I felt myself slipping away.

When I came back it was Sarah who had her hand on my forehead. 'Mama,' she whispered. She put one hand each side of my body and leaned in over me. 'Mama, you've had a fall. Are you in pain?'

'No pain at all, Sarah,' I said, thought I said, because she spoke again as if she hadn't heard me.

'Mama, can you hear me?'

I said, 'Of course I can hear you, Sarah. Why are you whispering?'

'Mama, I want you to do something for me. Shut your eyes for a second.'

I went along with her, closed and opened my eyes.

'Mama, shut your eyes once if you have any pain. Close them twice if the answer is no.'

Twenty years, I thought, twenty years ago I was lying on my back on a Scottish blanket on the mown grass in the garden with Sarah astride my chest. She was examining my face, telling me to move my nose, close one eye, purse my lips, move my eyebrows, wiggle my ears, wrinkle my forehead. She looked into my ears, looked up my nostrils, felt my teeth with her little fingers, asked about the red drop at the back of my mouth. And here she was, playing her little-girl game again. I played along and closed my eyes twice. Sarah smiled and I fell asleep, couldn't keep my eyes open all of a sudden. And then I heard someone calling me from far away, calling and calling. And when I opened my eyes, Lionel was there above my face, but it was Phillip Sutton, the doctor I couldn't call 'Doctor' because he was too young and we'd known his family before he was born.

He turned his head and said, 'Do it again, Sarah.' He turned back to me and said, 'Did you feel that, Missus Hodgkins?'

'Feel what?' I asked him. 'Are you playing too?'

'You've had a fall, Missus Hodgkins. Jackdempsey came home and we've been out looking for you. Matt has a board, and we're going to slide it under you in case you have broken bones.'

Kneeling on one side of me, Phillip and Sarah held me from moving while Matthias grunted and pushed the board under me. I was glad I was wearing my jodhpurs. I didn't want Matthias and Phillip, nor Sarah even, seeing what an older woman doesn't want anyone to see, even her husband.

They tied me onto the board like I was a shot deer. Matthias and Sarah carried, Sarah at my feet looking at me. Phillip, MD, walked beside the stretcher holding my hand.

The board was as comfortable as the grass. When Matthias and Sarah got their rhythm down I swayed gently from side to side and I was in the swing in the apple tree in Daddy's garden, that lolling time, after an hour of high soaring, when the swing takes forever to come to a stop, the bright sun squinting through the tiny gaps in the leafy boughs above. Through the fields of

Enderly they carried me and I thought it was ironic that the War stretcher-bearer and the War VAD were carrying one more casualty home. And then I tried to call Matt to tell him the joke I'd just thought up: Wasn't it a good job I was all in one piece when he found me, otherwise he would have sung in my ear and slipped Knifey in between my ribs. Then I thought, Dear God, that's not funny, not funny at all—what are you thinking, woman? When I came to again, I wasn't swinging under the apple tree any more. It took several seconds to recognize my own room from my own bed because there was no pillow and I was looking straight up.

'Mama, you're home in your bed,' Sarah whispered. 'Mama, I want you to do something for me. If you can hear me, blink your eyes.'

I decided if I pretended not to hear her, she might speak louder.

'Mama, I'll speak louder. Now can you hear me? Blink if you can.'

I blinked.

I blinked and it dawned on me that when I'd been speaking no one was hearing me; Sarah was asking me to move my eyelids because that was all I could move; Sarah hadn't been whispering—it was me, my hearing was damaged. Sarah was probably shouting. I wasn't alarmed at all.

'Mama, you've been hurt. I'm going to ask you a question. Blink once if the answer is yes. Blink twice if the answer is no. The question is, can you feel any pain?'

I blinked twice.

'Mama, Phillip Sutton's here. He's going to talk to you.'

I don't know how long I went away, dreamed about the birth of Lionel, saw him for the first time, wrapped in a towel and he as ugly as any newborn baby, face all scrunched up after being pulled through the tunnel too small for his head. I held up my hands to take him and the doctor said, 'Missus Hodgkins, open your eyes for me.' And opening my eyes was laborious because

Lionel was within inches of my fingertips, my son was coming into my arms for the first time. 'Missus Hodgkins, please try to open your eyes.'

'My eyes are open,' I said.

'Mama, it's me, Sarah. Please open your eyes for Phillip.'

I saw the ceiling above my face. The palm of a hand moved before my eyes.

'Missus Hodgkins, this is Phillip. It's very important that you try to stay with us for a few minutes. Blink once if you can hear me.'

I blinked and told him I was getting too tired to do much more blinking. 'Missus Hodgkins, you have suffered an injury and I need you to stay awake to tell me some things. Answer yes with one blink, no with two blinks. Do you have any feeling in your body?'

One blink for yes, two for no. I blinked twice.

'Is there any way we can make you more comfortable?'

'I would like my pillow under my head to help me see the photograph in the silver frame on the far wall. But don't bother— you can't hear me and, anyhow, I know the picture so well I can see it without looking. Lionel's on David's knee, Sarah on mine. David in his Sunday tweeds, me in the dark blue velvet dress Mama gave me when I got married, white lace collar. My travelling dress, Mama called it. Lionel's in his first suit made by Miss Bowe, complete with peaked cap with cloth button on top. Sarah is all white, except for her shoes, and Poor Meg tied the bow on her ribbon. The picture was taken years before the War damaged us all. But look, David; look, Lionel!—Sarah came back from the War and the sadness is fading out of the silver frame.'

'Missus Hodgkins, please try to keep your eyes open.'

'Oh, Mama, oh Mama. Mama. Mama. Mama.'

'Missus Hodgkins, can you feel this?'

'Missus Hodgkins?'

'Oh, Mama, Mama. Don't go, Mama. Don't go, Mama.'

Sarah Hodgkins

On the first anniversary of Mama's death I was on the second page of a letter to Phillip when I heard loud knocking as if someone was using the knob of an ashplant on the wicket gate. Kitty must have heard the noise too. As I stepped out through the back door of our house, she opened the front door of the cottage and the light behind her gave shape to Cornelia on her hip.

It was one of those November nights with a cloud-storm high in the moonlit sky and not a breeze stirring on the ground. It wasn't cold enough for a topcoat if you didn't mean to stay out too long. I love those nights with the moon charging into huge cliffs and black cloud-mountains and then, brighter than ever, blindingly emerging at the other side to send bursts of yellow across the calm world below and the storming clouds above. It was eight o'clock and the sound of knocking at the wicket gate at that hour could only be the sound of trouble.

As I headed along the noisy gravel path toward the gate, Kitty called softly from her open door. 'Matthias is in the Machine Shed, Sarah. I'm going to get him.'

I hesitated. Kitty whispered, 'I think you should wait till Matt comes before you open the gate.'

'All right, Kitty,' I whispered back, and wondered why we were whispering. 'You get Matthias and I'll call to see who's there.'

I was surprised when Kitty ran—sprinted—toward the shed,

Cornelia clutched to her side under her breast. Her quick foot-steps sent a shot of anxiety across my heart. Before I reached the wicket gate I heard her calling Matthias, and the tension in her voice made me hesitate several steps away from the wicket gate. I aimed my voice at the top of the wall. 'Who's there?' I called.

The moon charged out from behind a cloud and lit up the world with its mysterious light that gives shape to things rather than illuminating them. There were low voices on the other side of the wall, and then one clear voice broke loose. 'It's Johnjoe Lacy, Kitty. I'd like to talk to Matt.'

'This is Sarah Hodgkins, Mister Lacy. Is something wrong?' I knew Mister Lacy by sight and, from Kitty's gossip, I had gathered she didn't like the Lacy man, was even wary of him. 'I'll get Matthias to open the gate for you.'

'Miss Hodgkins,' Lacy said, and there were the sounds of scuffling feet on the other side of the wall. 'Miss Hodgkins, I have a mare in trouble, and I was hoping I could get Matt quick to take out her foal.'

My hand flew to my chest in fright because the shape of a man suddenly materialized on top of the wall directly above the wicket gate. And then, without hesitating, the shape jumped down and landed so close to me I could immediately smell animal dung and man sweat. I heard myself chirping like a startled robin. But I shrieked when he grabbed me by the wrist. He twisted my arm quickly, and I had no choice but to allow my body to save itself from broken bones by spinning around until my back was against his smelly body. With no hesitation he put his free hand around me, felt my breasts quickly, and then tried to force his hand between my thighs. I bent forward from the waist and cried out, struggled against his iron arms.

'Mattthias! Matthias!' I screamed. But the man behind me pulled me into himself and put a hand over my mouth. He pulled my head back onto his shoulder and with the other hand grasped at my breasts again. My feet were almost off the ground. From the far side of the wall came a shout. 'Do ya have her or what?'

'I have her all right,' the man holding me grunted. He had pushed his hand down inside my clothes and roughly groped his way around my chest. He jerked his pelvis into me from behind.

'Then open the fecken gate, will ya?'

'I'm trying to but she's fighting like a hure.' He dragged me over to the gate. He pulled his hand out of my blouse and pulled up my skirt, pushed his hand inside my drawers. The feel of his hand on my bare belly did something to my body. I kicked backwards at his shins, stomped on his toes with my heels, and when his hand came off my mouth, I screamed again, 'Matthias! Matthias!' The hand came out of my clothes.

Kicking and screaming, I was held as the man slid the flat iron bar out of the hole in the wall. The gate burst inward, and several men came staggering in as if they'd been pushing from the outside. And at the same instant the hands of the man holding me lost their grip and fell away.

It seemed I'd been panting since I'd been grabbed. I bent over to catch my breath, felt the pounding blood in my head bringing me to the edge of a blackout, and in the instant before my frozen muscles thawed, I saw the flaming girls staggering out of the flaming tent, falling down over each other, saw myself frozen like a wooden statue gaping at them. I stumbled backward and would have fallen if strong hands had not caught me and held me steady. I smelled Matthias and turned around, buried my head in his chest, tried to burrow my way out of the present, so I could escape whatever it was that had just been played out in the moonlight.

I felt the sound of Matthias's voice inside his chest. Then there was a hand on my shoulder gently pressuring me to go with it. It was Kitty. Still clutching Cornelia to her hip, she moved me away from Matthias. We only went a few steps.

I was very aware of Kitty's hand as it left my elbow and went protectively around my shoulders. The moon was gone and I couldn't see anyone, but my wits began to fall back into place. I adjusted my blouse, felt for the buttons, but only found one near the top. Then my fingers found that the hem of my skirt was stuck into the top of my drawers at the front. I spat on my sleeve and rubbed it obsessively around my lips and nose where the smelly hand had been.

The moon lit up the shapes of the world, and I slipped my arm around Kitty's waist.

Matthias, Kitty and myself, standing almost shoulder to shoulder, were facing the wicket gate. A cluster of men were standing with their backs to the opening in the wall. Shadows emerged out of shadows and, out of the cluster of intruders, five men took shape.

Everyone stood silently, as if all were waiting for the next thing to happen.

'There was no need to hit him so hard, Matthias,' Johnjoe Lacy said, and he knelt on one knee. The shape of a man lying on the ground emerged.

'What should I have done, Mister Lacy?' Matthias asked. 'Stand by while he raped Miss Hodgkins, and then say excuse me, sir, but that's not a nice thing to do?' I had not heard such hardness in Matthias's voice before, had not even suspected he was capable of such hardness.

'He wasn't the raping kind, Matthias,' Johnjoe Lacy said.

'No more than you're the burning kind, Mister Lacy,' Matthias said. 'He was raping her with his fingers, had his hands all over her.' The remark about the 'burning kind' went straight over my head.

'You could have killed him. What did you hit him with?'

Matthias was in no hurry to answer, spoke slowly as if letting the other man know he would not be rushed into speaking. 'I hit him with a hammer, Mister Lacy, and I still have it in my hand.'

There was another long silence. It was like everyone, except me, knew the lines of a play, and everyone was reluctant to move the action along by reciting their part.

Johnjoe Lacy stood up and said, 'He's dead, Matt. There was no need for anyone to get killed.' I pulled closer to Kitty.

The shapes of the four men behind Lacy did not stir. 'If you'd stayed at home, Mister Lacy, no one would have been killed,' Matthias said, and he did not turn to look at us as he gave his instructions. 'Kitty, bring Cornelia back to the cottage. Miss Hodgkins, you go with them.'

I put pressure on Kitty's arm to turn her, but Kitty's arm was as firm as the sword in the rock. When we did not move, Matthias said firmly, 'Kitty, Miss Hodgkins.'

Kitty said, 'I'm not leaving you, Matt.'

'Kitty,' Matthias said sternly.

'No, Matt.'

I finally found my voice. 'Matthias, what's going on?' I asked.

The silence following my question was so long I got the feeling everyone knew that the next spoken lines would add to the volatility of the situation.

'Mister Lacy, why don't you tell Miss Hodgkins what's going on?' Matthias said.

Johnjoe Lacy didn't say anything. The moon slid in and out through several wispy clouds, and the scene faded and brightened several times before Kitty said, 'Miss Hodgkins, Mister Lacy's not able to tell you why he's going around in the dark with his little gang of dwarfs. Mister Lacy is a day coward and a night hero, does to people in the dark what he's afraid to do to them in the light of day.'

'Listen here, Hatchel—' Johnjoe Lacy started, but Matthias stopped him in his tracks.

'Mister Lacy, you are talking to my wife.'

A cloud darkened the stage for a long minute, and before the moon reappeared, Kitty had begun to speak again. 'Miss Hodgkins, the men behind Johnjoe Lacy are Har Rogers, Mick Gorman, Bill Egan and Ralphie Blake.' The shapes behind Lacy shifted in the moonlight. 'You must remember the names, Miss Hodgkins: Johnjoe Lacy, Har Rogers, Mick Gorman, Bill Egan and Ralphie Blake. These are the men who burned down the Lamberts' house and killed the brothers. They're here to burn down Enderly. They want to be heroes. When the English are gone they'll be able to claim a piece of Enderly as the reward for their heroism. Isn't that right, Mister Lacy?'

The shape that was Johnjoe Lacy shifted from one foot to the other. The shapes behind him stirred, but still no one was willing to pull down the curtain or change the scenery for the next act. Only the moon was doing her part with the lighting but even she was working without a script.

Kitty turned toward me and pushed Cornelia on me. 'Take the baby into the cottage,' she said, with her lips to my ear. 'Wrap her up, wait a few minutes, and then slip out by the back. Go across the fields and bring her down to my mother. You must stay there till the morning.'

I had no choice but to take the baby. I whispered, 'I can't leave you, Kitty.'

Then Kitty's hand was a claw on my wrist. 'There's no use burning down Enderly if you're left alive, Sarah. You must leave. You must bring Cornelia. Matthias and I will try to persuade them—'

'No!' I whispered. Kitty squeezed my wrist, hurt me as she spoke in her normal voice.

'Matt, Miss Hodgkins is taking Cornelia in out of the cold.'

'You go in too, Kitty,' Matt said. 'I'll take care of this myself.'

'There's five of them,' Kitty said.

'I know there's five, Kitty. There were six a few minutes ago. An English army once beat a French army six times as big.'

And again the moon faded and flamed and someone couldn't remember their lines. Kitty squeezed my arm and twisted me around to the direction of the cottage. With the fingers of her other hand, she stroked Cornelia's face.

Ralphie Blake

The five of us stumbled through the wicket gate just in time to see and hear Matthias's weapon sinking into the top of Luke Boland's head. The bone-crunching sound was enough to make a man scutter and vomit at the same time. I made a bit of wet in my trousers myself. I had expected Matthias would be ready and tough. But the attack on Luke was so brutal that I felt icicles shooting up my arse.

To cover my betrayal of the IRA plan, I had come with John-joe and his lads. 'Don't tell Miss Hodgkins,' Matt had told me. 'Come with them. You won't get hurt.' I didn't want Matt to think I was an informer and I told him my made-up story about the old Missus Hodgkins helping my mother one time when things were bad. I even threw in a bit of religion: 'Our mother taught us to pray for Missus Hodgkins every morning and night for being so good to us. You'd be betraying your own mother and her family if you didn't help the Hodgkins family in return,' Matt told me.

And here we were, not three steps into the farmyard, and already one of us would be dead in a matter of minutes, would never walk, talk or go home again to his wife and children.

After informing on them, I made a huge big effort to avoid any suspicion by letting the lads know I was worried about them as well as myself. I told them that Matthias was a one-man army of two hundred. 'Just the fact alone that he survived the War for four years is enough to make him more than fierce in a fight, and we know nothing at all about what he did to survive. For all we know, he may have killed hundreds of Germans with his bayonet; rammed home the big knife and twisted it in the German bellies with a terrible screech coming out of him. We'll have to be very careful.' They told me I worried too much.

Of course if I wasn't a coward, I would have said that what we were planning had nothing to do with the English or the Irish, that we were just common criminals, common murderers, that we had let Johnjoe Lacy bully us into what we were doing, that we should all walk away and leave Johnjoe standing by himself. My cowardly way of doing it was to sneak in the dark to warn Matthias.

Even though Matthias had told me I wouldn't get hurt, I was shaking as I stood there watching Luke's foot twitching like the leg of a dying rabbit. It was very frightening the way Matt had dealt with Luke Boland. There had been no hesitation at all, no half-measures, no quarter given, as they say. There was total ferociousness the way Matthias had brought the weapon down. It was like the thinking of the man and the deathliness of the hammer became one thing, that the driving force behind the hammer was Matt knowing he was right. Luke had been doing something to Miss Hodgkins and there had been only one right answer to it. And it was this quickness to see what was the right thing to do and the instant ferociousness of doing it that convinced me that more men were going to die this night. The same force that dealt with Luke Boland was standing only six feet away from me, and that force was going to protect Enderly and Sarah Hodgkins to his last breath. There was no way out of this for anyone because Johnjoe Lacy was never going to back down.

As quick as a dried pig's bladder losing its shape on the thorn of a blackthorn bush, the little-boy bravery that had brought the lads this far fell out of them as we stood there watching Luke jerking himself into death. We had to watch his last shakes because we were too terrified to do anything else, every one of us afraid Matthias might pounce again. There wasn't safety in numbers anymore. And if Johnjoe Lacy was ever a leader, he wasn't a leader now. Matt was in charge here and there was no doubt about that.

When Luke Boland's foot hadn't moved for a while, Johnjoe stood up and made himself say something, complained to Matthias that he shouldn't have hit Luke so hard. Matthias didn't say he was sorry. Instead, he spoke like a teacher talking down to a small boy. He said Luke had been mauling Miss Hodgkins. And when Matthias moved the hand that held the killing hammer Johnjoe didn't say anything else.

It must have been the War that did this to Matthias, taught him to size up a situation while his eyes were still taking it in, and then to act without thinking about acting. Maybe this was what had brought him safe home from France and Belgium.

Johnjoe Lacy's plan had been as simple as he himself was stupid: the six of us would wrestle Matthias to the ground and tie him up; Bill Egan would 'take care' of Kitty if she started trouble; we'd set the house on fire; when Miss Hodgkins came running out, Johnjoe would 'take care' of her. Matthias would never be able to tell anyone who had committed the crime because he'd be afraid for the lives of his wife and baby and for his own life too. A different version of this plan had worked for the burning of the Lamberts, but the Lamberts were two men in their seventies and they did not have a Matthias to stand up for them.

Looking down at the dead Luke, I knew that even if Johnjoe and the lads were able to tie up Matthias, burn the house and kill Miss Hodgkins, they would never get away with it unless they killed Matthias too. Matthias would never be afraid that the IRA would kill his wife and child or himself because the minute he'd freed himself from the ropes, he'd be coming after the lads this very night before they even got home; before the sun came up he'd have sunk his hammer into more skulls with the same ferociousness he had used on Luke Boland. It was also clear to me that the only way out of the mess we were already in was to drag Luke Boland back out through the Enderly wicket gate, snake home in the dark, and make up some story about how Luke got the hammer buried in his skull.

Then Johnjoe Lacy said, 'Poor Luke shouldn't a got killed.'

'He should have stayed at home,' Matthias said, and his words were as hard and as cruel as splinters coming off a rock attacked by sledgehammers. Then Matthias told Miss Hodgkins and Kitty to go into the house with the child. I don't know where the hell Kitty had come from with the baby on her hip; a baby in the middle of all this! But Kitty was suddenly there as if she'd stepped out of a ray of moonlight like a leprechaun. And Kitty wouldn't do what Matthias told her to do. Then Miss Hodgkins spoke up and you'd think she had no notion about what the hell was happening in her own yard, like she never heard of what happened to the Lamberts and a whole lot of other Protestant farmers in the county. 'What's going on?' says she. And when nobody said a word, Kitty told her exactly what was going on. Kitty said everyone's name twice, even told Miss Hodgkins to remember the names. When Kitty said, 'Ralphie Blake,' I got very nervous; I suddenly didn't know for certain if Matthias had told Kitty I was harmless. Maybe she was just covering up for me by saying my name in front of the others.

The two groups stood facing each other in the yellow moonlight.

Eventually, the two women did some whispering, and soon afterward Miss Hodgkins went away with the baby. The five of us faced Matthias and Kitty across Luke Boland's corpse. It's hard to make out the details of faces in moonlight even at a few feet.

When we heard Miss Hodgkins closing the cottage door, Matthias said, 'If you want to end it right here, Mister Lacy, you can take Mister Boland home and it'll be the end of the matter.'

Oh, God. Thank you, God, I thought to myself, and I readied my throat to encourage Johnjoe to agree.

'There's five of us against one,' Lacy said.

'Kitty's here. Don't you remember how you couldn't frighten her that time outside Mister Ward the Harness Man's shop when there was no man around?'

I blushed with shame on the inside. Matt might as well have said, 'Why didn't you stand up for her, Ralphie Blake, you coward?'

Matt said, 'There were six of you a few minutes ago and now there's five. The other one is dead at your feet. Take him and go home, Mister Lacy. There's nothing else to talk about.' Matt's voice had no feeling; he might as well have been talking about a dead mouse.

There was a long, long silence. I don't know what the other lads were doing, but I was praying that Johnjoe would say the right thing, would say what I was afraid to say in case Johnjoe could accuse me of turning the tables against him by showing there was division in the ranks.

I knew Matthias Wrenn was not going to relax or change his position until he got an answer from Lacy. And God, I almost collapsed with relief when Johnjoe said, 'All right, Matt. We'll take Luke home to his wife. We'll make up a story.'

Neither Matthias nor Kitty spoke or moved.

The five of us stood there like we were waiting for Matthias's permission to move. Then Johnjoe said, 'We'll have to clean him up before we let the wife see him.'

These long silences were doing a job on my nerves. Why the hell wouldn't Johnjoe just count his blessings, drag Luke outside Enderly's wall, and get away from Matthias before he let himself loose again? But Johnjoe had to talk, had to ask for something, couldn't go away empty-handed.

'Can we bring Luke into the house to wash him?'

'No.'

Another terrible silence. 'Matt, as the Christian thing to do, let us wash him before his wife sees him.'

'Fuck the Christian thing; there's the horse trough at the church.'

I saw Kitty placing her hand on Matt's arm before he had finished, and then she leaned over and whispered. Matt did not turn his face away from us for a second. 'You can clean him in the Machine Shed where there's light, for the sake of Missus Boland and her children,' he said.

Still none of us moved to lift up Luke. 'You're a hard man, Matt,' Johnjoe said, and I clenched my eyes shut and prayed, Suffering Jesus, will you wither the man's tongue in his mouth?

'You're a stupid man yourself, Mister Lacy. When I say so, you will lift Mister Boland and carry him to the Machine Shed. When you get to the shed, you will put him on the floor near the water pump. Everyone, except Mister Gorman, will sit on the floor in the places I will show you. No one will talk. I will give Mister Gorman some rags and he will do the cleaning.' Then Matthias whispered in his wife's ear and she disappeared into a shaft of moon-darkness.

It was obvious from Matt's voice that every man was expected to do exactly what he was told to do. Without mentioning it, Matt made it very clear that he still had the hammer that had killed once tonight, that he was still in the frame of mind he'd been in when he buried it deep inside Luke Boland's skull.

Of course, Lacy still thought he was a leader and he followed empty-handed while the four of us carried poor Luke by his arms and legs toward the Machine Shed, Luke's head hanging down backward and his upside-down dead face pointing in the direction we were going.

When we reached the Machine Shed, the double doors were wide open and Kitty was inside lowering the glass globe on the lantern she had just lit. As we slowed in the doorway, we could hear the hissing of all three Tilley lamps hanging around the big shed.

'Walk straight across toward the far wall,' Matthias told us from behind. Then, when we nearly reached the water pump with its spout hanging over a wooden half-barrel, Matt told us to stop. 'Mister Lacy, you will take care of Mister Boland's head when the lads lower him,' he said from the door with Kitty at his side.

For the first time in his life, Johnjoe Lacy did what someone else told him to do without making a speech about it. He came to the front and put his two hands under Luke's head, held it out straight as we lowered the body. Johnjoe said under his breath, 'Grab Matt when I tell yiz.'

The stupidity of the man! Still wanting to get Matthias when everything said to get the hell out of there. I was so frightened I had a terrible urge to do my water, or worse. When Johnjoe gave the signal what was I supposed to do to hide whose side I was on?

When we straightened up after lowering Luke to the floor, Matthias told us to stay where we were until he called our names. 'Mister Rogers, you go over there and sit with your back to the turnip barrow.'

Matthias was standing at the right doorjamb, and for the first time I saw the hammer that had killed Luke; it was bigger than a carpenter's and smaller than a sledge, about the same size as the one a blacksmith uses to beat a piece of red iron into the shape of a horseshoe. It was hanging out of Matthias's right hand and there were bloody bits on it.

'Mister Egan, sit on the floor ten feet in front of Mister Rogers.'

Kitty was at the other jamb, eight feet from Matthias. She was dressed in a dark jumper, dark skirt halfway down her shins, leather boots to her ankles. There was a great glistening in her eyes. She was holding the long handle of a pitchfork in both hands. She wasn't holding it the way a person holds a fork to pitch hay. Her right hand was near the end of the handle, her left hand within a couple of feet of the two curved, vicious prongs of steel at the end. There was no doubt in my mind that Kitty was holding a weapon.

'Mister Blake, come over here and sit ten feet in front of me.'

Thank you, Jesus, I breathed inside myself. Matthias was moving me away from the others.

I don't know why he called us all Mister. Some of us had gone to school with him, and the rest of us were only a few years older than he was. Maybe it was because in the army he had to call everyone sir, or maybe he was making it very clear that he was far removed from us, that our past friendliness with him was not something to be counted on in a fight, that he was on one side and we were on the other.

'Mister Lacy, sit there in the middle.'

When Johnjoe moved, the only one left with the dead body was Mick Gorman, the one appointed by Matt to clean Luke. As Johnjoe walked over to the spot Matthias had pointed to, he suddenly turned to his left where all the hand-tools were attached to the wall.

'Now, lads,' he roared, just as he reached for the nearest tool, the one at eye level. It was a pickaxe, its two-foot-long spikes curving away from each other in opposite directions, one spike ending in a point, the other in a narrow blunt blade.

Kitty Wrenn: 1970

Why do I keep on coming here, people ask me, beating my way down through the high weeds and the bushes?

The children in the town call me Batty Bridgen, and most of them don't know my name isn't Bridgen, that in the beginning it was the Batty Bridge One. Batty Bridgen reminds me that the Aqueduct carrying the Canal across the Johnnies River came to be called the Dakeydocks, Ypres became Wipers, Ploegsteert became Plugstreet, the auntie became Dante.

'She never goes to Mass,' I've heard it whispered in shops.

'She got him with the first stab.'

'One prong came out each side of his spine.'

'She lives with Protestants.'

'She was a terrible one when she was young, always in fights and climbing trees.'

'Mad.'

The children cross the street when they see me coming. After all, it is true that I did kill a man and should have killed another before he killed my Matt. If I were a child and lived in a village with a man-killing woman, I'd avoid her too, maybe even have nightmares about her. The story of how Mick Gorman died has surely gathered moss over the years and my fearsomeness has grown with it. When Con and myself were small, Daddy used to frighten us with, 'Boney will get you.' It's Batty Bridgen the par-

273

ents probably use now: 'She'll get you with her pitchfork in the night if you're not good, in the front and out the back.'

Batty Bridgen!

'Redfingers Fitz' is what we called the woman who walked the Towpath every Monday morning to wash Missus Conway's clothes.

If you are different in a small community your difference is dressed up in kindliness and rendered acceptable, just like all that dreadful leftover pig-stuff gets dressed up in a skin and is called a sausage. Francis of Assisi was saintly because he was batty. I'm batty because I'm feisty. It's better to be saintly than batty, better to be a batty woman than a feisty one.

I'm as feisty as ever I was, not afraid to say my piece when I think it needs saying. I'm still nearly six feet tall at seventy-four. I keep my long grey hair tied up in a bun, and that gives me more stature. Height in a woman is a great threat to men, and I have used mine to shrivel many an uppity man simply by looking down on him. I'm as thin as a whip, and I limp from a fall off my bike a long time ago; Ralphie Blake's greyhound ran out of the ditch under the front wheel. Isn't it a small world?

Why do I keep coming here? they ask. And if I said it's because the familiar chisel marks in the smoothness of the coping stones gives me comfort, they'd ask why. Then I'd have to tell them a long story from years ago. So, I tell them I come down to the Bridge for a walk.

Coming to the Bridge brings me back to the place where there was happiness and I was a part of it. When I run my fingers across the dressed stone of the parapet, remembrances of Con and Matthias and myself in our childhood bubble into my memory.

The Bridge, too, was at the centre of my own love story almost sixty years ago, and I remember all the details, remember the ecstasy of Ali Baba's Cave, the agony of separation when Matthias and Con left to join the army, Matt's homecoming and his marriage proposal. Everyone should have a love story even if it ends as painful as ours did. I suppose we take a fearful risk when we love, leave ourselves open to the possibility of terrible loss. Millions of girls had a loss like mine during the War—were told about the death in an army letter and then were left to imagine for the rest of their lives how the lover had died.

Which was worse, I have wondered many times—not knowing and not being there or, like me and Matt, me having to watch his killing but being there, close enough for him to see my eyes and for me to see his and to be able to say with one gaze what it would take a poet a million words to say. That look between us as he hung impaled on the pine pole and I stood motionless, knowing I couldn't help him, knowing he was dying and knowing too that the only way I could tell him how much I loved him was to stand there and look into his eyes, and his dying eyes telling me how much he loved me and how happy he was about every second we had loved each other. Oh, Matthias. Oh, Matthias, how much I loved you, love you still.

Of the few minutes in the Machine Shed where everything happened it is only those last moments with Matt that I have kept sharp and bright in my memory. But I can still dimly see in the shadowy background the frantic movements of shapes as everyone tried to stay alive. And the background shadows flit by as if that part of the night happened in two seconds. One man, Mick Gorman, ended up with the prongs of my pitchfork sticking out through his back, one each side of his spine. Matt killed two men, one with his hammer. The other was trying to run out to start the fire that would burn Enderly, but Matt caught up with him and tripped him and smashed his head into the pine pole. When the man fell to the ground, he fell on Matt's feet. Matt was trapped for a few seconds, and when he freed himself and faced Johnjoe Lacy the pointed end of the pickaxe in Lacy's hands was already on its way. It went through the centre of Matt's chest with such force and weight that, when the point came out through his back, it kept going and pinned Matthias to the pole. There was a huge gasp: I can still hear it, like a sigh, like a deep breath blown out too quickly.

Johnjoe Lacy had been moving at such a rate that he stopped within a foot of Matt's face. And Matthias's hand came up clasping that long knife of his, the one he brought home from the War. Whether Matt directed his hand or whether his damaged nerves drove his arm, the point of the knife went into Lacy's throat behind his chin and came out through the top of his head. And whether or not Matt meant to do it, the knife came back down and Johnjoe fell at Matt's feet. And for a split second that lasted a century, we looked across a space of a few feet into each other's eyes and there passed between us something that doesn't have words, never could be dressed up in words.

Matt's eyes changed suddenly and he began losing control of his neck. He tried to keep his head up but it moved around like it was too heavy. In an instant, the life left his eyes, and his head fell onto his chest. His hair slid forward and hung down, almost covering his face. His right hand, still holding the long war knife, fell down by his side, and even when his knees buckled, he did not fall. And I ran to him like a whining bitch running to feed her pups, pushed the long hair aside, touched his face and kissed his eyes and whimpered his name and told him how much I loved him.

Is my love story more romantic because when Matt died our love was the love of young lovers? The love in our love story has remained young and unspoiled and unstrained by the sadness and pain that the average couple has dealt to them or creates for each other during a long lifetime. One way or the other, everyone should have a love story no matter how painful it might turn out in the end. Love is a sanctifying grace.

The Canal is full of warm sanctifying grace, Matthias said that day I washed him under this Bridge after he walked home from the War.

Today, the Canal is dried up; tall weeds are growing where

the water used to be. Rusting bed frames and bent bikes and old
tyres appear when the weeds shrivel up in wintertime. Of
course, the bream, the carp, the roach, the rudd, the pike, the
perch, the tench and the eels are all gone. The Towpath is over-
grown by a virulent bush whose leaves are sticky and whose
name no one knows. The gentler water-dependent wildflowers
have been evicted by the tougher dandelion, the ragwort, the
thistle, the dock and, of course, the nettle. The royal swans and
the red-legged, coal-black waterhens have flown away. The telephone wires are gone, and most of the poles have fallen, the rest
leaning at angles. Where the harbour was, there's a scrap-metal
yard, full of rusting hulks and noise, and old engine oil oozes
out into the nearby fields.

In many places, farmers have dug away the banks and built
roads across the bed of the Canal; fields that were divided in
1827 have been reconnected. On the wealthier farms, bulldozers
have levelled the banks for miles, and all traces of the Canal are
gone, as if it never was. The children of Ballyrannel could never
imagine the silent barges floating through the green fields, the
bargemen hupping the horse and slowly moving in and out of
the lives of the people who lived along the line, bringing news
and messages from Dublin. Mister Hayes told us about the
shooting in the General Post Office in 1916, told us about the
lads getting shot in Kilmainham.

The Canal bridges are still standing; leading to nowhere,
standing stark in the middle of fields, but someday soon a
builder is going to discover the beauty of the coping stones.

The Canal.

The Canal was ours. It would always be there. Each of us
knew that the other two dreamed about it when we were separated by the promise of India and then by the War. The Canal
was everything we did with each other until the two lads went
away; it was us knowing everything about each other; it was us
happy, and we believed, without knowing we believed, that it

would always be there. Before he went away, Con said that when he died he wanted to be pushed out into the Canal in a burning boat like the Vikings. 'A small rowing boat will do,' he said, 'or even a cardboard box.' But now, the Canal is fading out of the fields and out of memory.

The dead people who were once so important to us quickly become mere lines in a closed book when we who remember them pass from the scene. I still weep about the fire that killed Matt's family. I still weep for the two young men who set off to see the world in 1913 but ended up scraping other men's bodies off the floors of the abattoirs that were France and Belgium, as Missus Hodgkins would have said. Of course, the passing years have smoothed the jagged edges of the raw emotion of the times; no one can marinate in such agony for long.

When I die, gone forever will be the pain created by the loss of Lionel and Con and Matt, and now Sarah and her husband, Phillip. There will only be knowledge. History books cannot pass on the pain endured, the anguish, the terror of the times. I suppose it's good that they can't. Even a headstone in a cemetery, leaned on and wept at for years, becomes just one more piece of cold granite when the final rememberer dies.

The War and all the lads who died in it, who were crippled in it, will only be knowledge soon. There will be no one left to lean on the headstones to cry in sorrow. Twelve years ago, Cornelia and I found the cellar in Auchonvillers under a house calling itself The Laburnum English Tea Rooms. The owner charged us one franc each to visit the cellar where, she said, there was a carving on the wall for a man who'd been shot at dawn near the end of the War. At the bottom of the cellar steps I saw Matt's carving. I sank to my knees and bent my forehead to the floor and I cried for the innocent childhood of the three of us, cried for brave Con, for brave Matt. There I was in the same cellar in France, on the same floor where Con had slept that last night of his life and Matt had loved him enough to place Knifey in his heart. Oh Sacred Heart of Jesus, the things we do for each other, to each other.

And then in the small garden cemetery outside Ocean Villas, I rubbed my hands over Con's headstone, told him how much I loved him, and whispered to him the Canal Song.

And that's why I come here, to move my fingers around the smooth coping stones on top of the Bridge, to love again, to hear again the Canal Song in childish voices slipping along the polished surface of the water.

My side.

Come to my side where the yellow cowslips are speckled red, where the small daisies dance in the breezy grass. Come to my side.

Select Bibliography

1914–1918: Voices and Images of the Great War (London 1991)
by Lyn MacDonald
Back to the Front: An Accidental Historian Walks the Trenches of World War I
(New York 1998) by Stephen O'Shea
Birdsong (London 1997) by Sebastian Faulks
Chronicles of the Great War: The Western Front 1914-1918 (London 1997)
by Peter Simkins
The Collected Poems of Rupert Brooke (New York 1980)
The Collected Poems of Wilfred Owen (New York 1965)
The First Day on the Somme: 1 July 1916 (London 1984) by Martin Middlebrook
The First World War (New York 1999) by John Keegan
Forgotten Voices of the Great War: A New History of WWI in the Words of
the Men and Women Who Were There (London 2003) by Max Arthur
Good-bye to All That (New York 1957) by Robert Graves
Guillemont (London 1998) by Michael Stedman
The Guns of August (New York 1994) by Barbara W. Tuchman
Hill 60 (London 1998) by Nigel Cave
Ireland and the Great War (Cambridge 2000) by Keith Jeffery
Ireland and the Great War: 'A War to Unite Us All'? (Manchester 2002)
edited by Adrian Gregory and Senia Pašeta
Irish Voices from the Great War (Dublin 1995) by Myles Dungan
Johnny Got His Gun (London 1991) by Dalton Trumbo
Major and Mrs. Holt's Battlefield Guide to the Ypres Salient (London 1997)
by Tonie and Valmai Holt
Memoirs of an Infantry Officer (London 2000) by Siegfried Sassoon
Observe the Sons of Ulster Marching Towards the Somme (London 1986)
by Frank McGuinness
One Day on the Somme: 1st July 1916 (Peterborough 1998) by Barry Cuttell
Orange, Green and Khaki: The Story of the Irish Regiments in the Great War,
1914–18 (Dublin 1992) by Tom Johnstone
Passchendaele: The Untold Story (New Haven 1996) by Robin Prior and
Trevor Wilson
Patrick Pearse: The Triumph of Failure (Dublin 1990) by Ruth Dudley Edwards
The Regeneration Trilogy: Regeneration, The Eye in the Door, The Ghost Road
(London 1993, 1995, 1996) by Pat Barker
Testament of Youth (New York 1980) by Vera Brittain
They Called It Passchendaele (London 1993) by Lyn MacDonald
They Shall Grow Not Old: Irish Soldiers and the Great War (Dublin 1997)
by Myles Dungan
Walking the Somme (London 1997) by Paul Reed
The War Poems (London 1983) by Siegfried Sassoon